PORTHOLE

McSWEENEY'S
SAN FRANCISCO

Copyright © 2025 Joanna Howard

All rights reserved, including right of reproduction in whole or in part, in any form.

McSweeney's and colophon are registered trademarks of McSweeney's, an independent publisher based in San Francisco.

Jacket illustration by Sam Hadley

ISBN: 978-1-96327-028-0

10 9 8 7 6 5 4 3 2 1

www.mcsweeneys.net

Printed in the United States

PORTHOLE

JOANNA HOWARD

McSWEENEY'S
SAN FRANCISCO

·FOR FILM

"'Twas a story repleat with twists and turns. It took place near Nice, by the sea.... Alain Delon was involved, or a friend of Alain Delon. I had dinner at a restaurant whose owner knew my uncle.... Later, I wanted to go back there; I called but I ultimately didn't make a reservation.

I returned to Paris in a magnificent machine, ultra modern and very sci-fi. I remember panoramic portholes. Dizzying speed."

—GEORGES PEREC, "Seaside" from *La Boutique Obscure*

1
OVERTURE

I will not apologize, I told my driver. I am beyond apologies. They want me to work, they feel that I owe them work.

My driver remained mostly silent.

They think I will just pivot, but I won't pivot. If I could pivot, I would have done that years ago.

Who are "they"? the driver asked.

Everyone. The studio, my crew, the world.

That's what is called a consensus.

It was late in the summer, months after an accident on the set of my last film, and we were on our way to the asylum known as Jaquith House.

We curled on secondary roads through mountains covered in white pines along an enormous lake. Lupine bloomed on the roadside. We had been driving for several hours, the air growing steadily cooler and drier. I had not stopped talking for a second, or thinking audibly, as it seemed to me, and in fact there was little separation between my thoughts and my speech. I had become resigned to it, in the phase leading up to this exodus to Jaquith. I had come to expect phases. I was measuring my time not by film projects, as I once had, but by phases of breakdown. I knew it was happening.

I had known it was happening even in the midst of the accident, I told myself I was on top of myself, but that was a lie. All I could do was watch the phases arrive and eventually pass. There had been the period of disorientation following the accident, and then the phase of crystal-clear awareness, like the effects of a psychedelic drug, then eventually a merger of the two modes simultaneously. There had been the phase of absolute silence following the accident, then the phase of nonstop talking, then talking while silent. There had been the phase of nightmares, and then the phase of sleepwalking, and then the phase of insomnia, eventually the phase of sleeping while awake.

Mental health facility, the executives told me, a final shot at rehabilitating my film career, they said, and they would even pick up the tab: but what choice did they have? They were out on a note for one of my loose threads. They said it's about not attracting further bad press, but I had always been volatile, bad press was part of my draw. Yes, of late, there were other factors, I won't go into it. Keep me out of sight until I was back to myself, and then hold me to completing one last project. Then, of course, when that one final project is done, they can be done with me. That is what they think!

It's a wonder they want to help you at all.

It's for all the most superficial reasons, I assure you.

Money?

Cultural capital, awards. So-called acclaim—money is just the side effect.

An important side effect.

Or a harbinger of the death of art. Yes, I've made them money in the past, inadvertently—against my will—but I won't make that mistake again. They think they can pair me with an inside man, keep me on a short leash. Maybe I'd be more manageable. Collaboration, they say! Collaborationist, more like. That option! That ridiculous Spanish option. They are hemorrhaging. Anyone who knew anything about film has been put to pasture, replaced by venture capitalists. They have no idea what the future of film is, because there is no future for film.

At least you still have your...

My what? My health? My money? At least what?

Your looks?

Always one step behind. Beauty, they tell you when you are little, will get you everything. What a racket! And here I am again: not the lie, but where the lie has been. The great trauma of her life! I thought or said to the driver.

Whose life?

Mine!

If he had further thoughts, he did not dare voice them.

Well, I thought or said to the driver, a life of considerable confusion and lying!

Ms. Désir—try to close your eyes for now, he said. We'll arrive at Jaquith House in about an hour. "Restoration without demolition."

His voice was toneless, and when he spoke, I couldn't tell whether he was asking a question or answering it.

Are you talking about the building or the method of treatment? Do you report to the doctor or the studio?

It's in the brochure. I'm freelance. Nowadays it's all about the gig economy.

I had not yet met Dr. Duvaux of Jaquith House, who was to be newly in charge of whatever I had become in this aftermath of the accident. I have never coped well with rapid changes.

What's your name?

In times of distress, the doctor advocates simplicity.

For your safety or for mine?

Just for simplicity.

We're all in it together? Far be it from me to advocate complexity, I said.

Relax, and stop talking.

The drive was breathtaking. But I was inured to breathtaking. I couldn't roll my eyes enough over breathtaking. I watched a trembling mountain village scroll by, with a string of little false chalets. False chalet cafés and wineries, and little false chalets for ski waxing and repairs, and little false chalet strip malls of littler, even falser structures selling high-thread-count linens or artisanal mustards, or fountain pens or aprons silk-screened with exotic goats, or real estate. Every third false chalet offered real estate. But beyond the little Xmas village, there was a rising mountain, the lake, dark, and then this lake gave off to another lake, an even darker, glassier, and more expansive lake than the first, a type of lake district, for "district" seemed always to be the word attached to lake, while "region" is the word attached to coastal, and "country" the word attached to river. Or so it seemed to me. What did I know?

Stop talking. Just try to relax, he said.

Where are we? Have we crossed the border?

The doctor advocates remoteness. But we always stay close to the coastline.

Geographical fortification, I said. Against a coming plague.

Think of it as a retreat.

2

JAQUITH HOUSE

Jaquith House was more a compound than a house, although there was a house at the center of the grounds, a large white mansion in clapboarding. A farmhouse with a long front porch and two upper balconies. A gabled turret held sentry over the drive, with tall French windows and a small enclosed deck.

The driver let me out onto the gravel and went to seek my new keepers. He was right, at least I had my looks. My ever-mutable container, my compact symmetrical spirit vehicle, nothing wasted, nothing lacking, like a dressmaker's dummy. I had my features, which had not aged out, teetering on the cusp, but as of yet, still featured. And I had my costumes, my rich wealth of carapaces in several large valises, my wigs and accessories, my suits, my sock garters, corsets, cummerbunds, caftans, smoking jackets, leotards, cufflinks. My wardrobe had always been my passport. I thought of it constantly but spoke of it to no one. I believed that everything could be controlled with the proper attire. For arrival at the sanatorium, an ensemble of nouvelle vagaries: a square-necked cocktail dress, cut low, matronly sling-backs, my hair dark and shaped, Cleopatra liner. I don't know where I thought I was going; to my last year at

Marienbad, I suppose. The mind conjured only the settings of old films that no one watched anymore. I could no longer control the phases of my mind, but I retained an arsenal of imagery to impose composure on my general physique.

    I made for the large front porch of Jaquith House, hanging ferns and trailing geraniums, a basket of woolen lap rugs, and a line of wicker chairs, well-appointed on a glittering pond. The air was crisp for August. For a coast, it was lacking horizon. I was born on a coast, quite a different one, but one that nonetheless had taken. Me. Yes, I was a coastal tramp, but there was no coast in particular that claimed my heart above others, and the promise of coastal proximity had been the final piece in my resignation to try Jaquith on for size. I am a vagabond, and always have been—whatever I do, I do with location in mind. I had little interest in rehabilitation, I told myself, but even I could no longer tell when I was lying. I wanted to sleep again, or if not sleep, I wanted to enjoy the night hours, that much I knew. And I wanted to return to my strong silent type—this sound of a voice blithering on, alien to my ears, had also strained my vocal cords. My voice finally had the breathy basso notes I had been feigning for years, somewhere between Lauren Bacall and James Earl Jones. My voice had been made legitimate and, in this way, was all the more upsetting. Perhaps this was the true fear for my employers, I suspected, that my breakdown was not an aberration of self but a galvanization of self, an excess of self. An excess of Helena, which no one, least of all me, wanted.

    Assessment was required, a specialist to assess the actual damage and then weigh the financial pros and cons of my resurrection.

    Any coast in a storm, then, and onward to the sanatorium. But we were in the woods. I couldn't even smell the sea. A soft calypso recording floated in the air, and the front door seemed not only locked but permanently secured.

PORTHOLE

Beyond the western lawn was a garden plot and a fruit orchard in neat rows. Beyond that, the surrounding woods. A sudden grinding of an engine within the pond spit up a geyser, rattling the placid surface. This place is a fraud, like me. Wrongly placed in time. I was already working on my dialogue for the doctor. The studio will have had their say, now I would have mine. I had imagined a surgical strike: I confess wrongdoings, he absolves me of my crimes. I retire somewhere unobtrusive and go about the rest of my life in quiet daily repetitions: small tasks each morning, like carving a wooden spoon or embroidering a tea towel. No more screens or lenses. Screens and lenses would be forbidden. They were what got me into this mess. On this we could all agree. The specifics of my wrongdoings were still fuzzy. Out of focus. For me, it was a matter of subjectivity.

I set out around the house. A stone walkway through hydrangea and rhododendron and other threatening, tufted shrubs. The path itself was so overgrown and wove through the pendulous pink blossoms. In a turret room high above me, the French windows swung shut, and I heard the click of the latch. Marimbas and steel drums of a jaunty calypso soundtrack piped in at intervals.

It was a festive scene this little Jaquith House piazza. Several discreet patio tables in wrought iron scattered the court, flower-garden borders, tiny ponds, overhanging sun umbrellas in gay colors. Paper lanterns stretched between the house and an enormous barn. It was all trying a little too hard.

I saw the backdoor of Jaquith House and knew at once that it made its front its back and vice versa. The calypso music shouted now from an imitation rock in the herb garden.

Inside a lit paned-glass veranda, an older man in a dark sport coat with white piping and a knotted neck scarf tapped out his pipe on a saucer. He waved at me from behind the glass. I waved back. Hanging on the double doors was a cheerful sign in rope and plaster, which announced, in barely legible cursive, "You Are Most Welcome at Jaquith House."

And so it begins, I said.

Helena, I am so delighted to finally meet you! I have been a devoted fan.

Doubtful, doubtful, I said or thought, and with more enthusiasm, Dr. Duvaux, I presume!

He was the spitting image of Claude Rains, in his venerable years, an upsweeping quiff of gray hair, a round and solemn face, a practiced theatrical voice that belayed an underlying impediment. We were crossing the floorboards of the common room. A large, open fire pit failed to burn on its elevated slate platform. Above it a copper hood stretched rigid and gleaming for several stories.

Entirely at your service. As are our expansive facilities and our extraordinary staff. And yes, truly, Helena, I have seen all your films. I so look forward to working with you.

Yes, working. In your expansive facilities, with your expansive staff.

In situations of psychic exhaustion, Dr. Duvaux said, it is always the correct and best method to surround the sufferer only with individuals who are properly trained in therapeutic recuperation.

The room was cavernous and empty. The doctor gestured to a low bench near the smoldering hearth.

Sit with me, won't you, for a few minutes? Everyone at Jaquith house is a welcome guest, he said. But, also, everyone at Jaquith House is specifically trained. All our aides-de-camp are top in their respective psychiatric branches. Even our housekeeping staff is highly trained in the specifics of therapeutic recuperation.

I am a victim of psychic exhaustion? I asked.

You are a habitué. In the sense that you frequent that locale, but you do not yet inhabit that locale. Our job will be to stave off—

Let us get something straight, Doctor. Whatever the studio wants from me, I doubt they will get, ever again.

And what is it you think the studio wants from you, Helena?

To finish something I started, possibly. Something that may have incurred considerable expense. Or something they hope will recoup them financially. Then to let me drift. To cut me lose.

You can't mean the film—

No, not that one. An option. Oh, what a misleading term. This option has no option for me, that is certain, it was the beginning of the end: I can see that! Listen, Doctor: I am beyond rehabilitation.

I am inclined to think your studio thinks, well, that you have been a brilliant asset, and could be again. Do you want to tell me more about this option, as it were, Helena?

A collaborator, possibly locations. I don't know what they've dumped in already, maybe nothing, maybe something. I relinquished control, but they have something up their sleeves. But I had given up on it even before the... the accident... Listen, Doctor, I'm not going to talk about that.

The accident, Helena? Or the option?

Neither. I'm talking about other wrongdoings, of which there are many, I admit, but I won't apologize to the studio—

Oh, no, of course not. I think there's been some confusion. My understanding is that your studio just genuinely hopes to help you find some sort of balance, to pick up the pieces. And I hope that is true. I don't like to enter into these kinds of arrangements under false pretenses.

Ha! The studio is nothing but false pretenses.

We are not here for the studio, are we? We are here for you and whatever it is you are seeking. There was an accident on one of your sets, Helena, and I know you suffered a great loss.

It was part of a larger problem, obviously.

Yes, we don't have to go into it just yet.

I thought I would go back to work immediately after the accident. But there was no work to go back to, as it turned out, not on that film anyway. I had come almost straight on from the hospital in Rio—why they had flown me all the way to Rio, I have no idea. Perhaps they thought it was an excellent hospital. It was in fact an excellent hospital. They kept me for a few weeks after setting my bones and sewing up my hand—you see, I'm now missing the littlest finger. A minor sacrifice, I know.

Ah, trauma to the body! No, we won't discuss it yet, not yet.

I don't mind. Actually, not at all. It looks like a proper claw, like the talons of an eagle. Then they kept me in a deep sleep.

The studio?

The doctors in Rio. I could remember faces pacing through the room, the sounds of the pumps and the monitors. There was an endless stream of identical attendants, the language is like a blend of French and Spanish, both languages I know well, but still, to me, untranslatable. That period was glazed. After my release, they gave me prescriptions to help overcome the pain of the injuries from the accident, and these pills washed me in a pleasant calm and loosened my damaged limbs, truly, but made it possible to lose track of most of my mind. The studio had cleared the location of my film *Sanguine Season*, I was told, completely obliterated all traces of it. I was flown home. Home? Where was that? A sun-streaked megalopolis on the edge of a cold ocean? I hadn't been there for more than a few weeks at a time for years. My bungalow is rented. I got a hotel room that was very far from everything. With a little money, a couple of midcentury replicas, a cocktail cart, a little dog in a sweater: it's possible to live like you are stuck in a time flow, don't you think, Doctor?

   Selectively, I suppose. If you turn a blind eye to the difficulties, the drudgeries, the atrocities of the past. And, I would think, a blind eye to the speed of the now.

   Sanguine Season. My last film. Or my almost last film. They got me a driver, and I went into the studio. They call it a studio, but it's just a corporate building, a bunch of conference rooms full of silver-haired gents dressed like boys in T-shirts and sneakers, staring into their screens or forcing me to stare into screens, middle-aged men in crumpled-casual resortwear, in athleisure, phoning me from the golf course, from the tennis court, from inside a barometric chamber, middle-aged men, sometimes one woman, a woman but indistinguishable, phoning in to decide my fate. You see, they had to do something with me, while the insurance investigation went on.

   What did they say to you?

   They were ready to find a new balance, they said. They didn't even mention Corey—but what was the point after all?

   A tremendous loss, Helena, a brilliant actor cut short in his prime of life. You two were very close, I know. You did quite a few pictures together, didn't you? I think I have seen them all.

   They didn't even mention his name. They just got right into it: Helena, they said, we've seen the paperwork, they said, let us reassure you at once that we don't take much stock in documents. But you must know that it will not be possible for you to continue the film as... that film... in Guaporé. *Sanguine Season* is just not a candidate, do you see? On the other hand—*Madrid Plays* is. And it was your option, remember, your idea. And we love it! Once we sort out this insurance business, a little PR spin work, we'll get you back in the director's chair, and we think: really, Helena, we always thought, this next option is really the one. Or possibly the many—who knows, you might want to serialize! If you were to stick it out here in the studio, in the meantime, you would have time on your side. This town is a sandpit of disregard. Sure, there seems to be silver-screen nostalgia on every street corner, and the mansions and the aging celebrities, but the truth is this town swallows up everything for better or worse.

This town? There are no more towns. Everything is everywhere at once.

We think if you can just be agreeable about this, we can salvage you, get you back to working, it's a simple process, we get you some help, when you're ready you get back to filming—

The Doctor interrupted me: What did you say to that offer? he asked.

I said yes. Good. It wasn't Guaporé, I said. It was Iténez, but what difference did that make, the borders between countries, different languages, *Sanguine Season* was gone, obliterated, my entire production suspended. Fine, I said. Whatever you want, I said. They hadn't expected that! Compliance. I was dead set to be compliant. I comply, I said, and I flashed my bird claw. And they were relieved to hear it! To be perfectly honest, they said, we are incredibly relieved to hear this, Helena. Incredibly relieved. And you don't have to let this feel like a blow.

I was trying, Doctor. I told myself, I was a new Helena, a compliant Helena. I was no longer Helena the tyrannical, Helena the hysterical. Those hard-won years of control on the set, the manipulation, the violent rages, what use would they be to me now in an era where control is passé? Hierarchies, Doctor. Obliterated. You see, the details, can you hear me?

Perfectly. I hear you perfectly. And so that is how you find yourself here, Helena?

I suppose so.

Do you see this as the studio's way to phase you out or to bring you back to the fold?

I'm not sure. I'm not sure they are sure. I think they are buying time.

And what about you?

Me?

What about your future? Your future in film?

Future?

You gathered a very faraway look at that moment—as though you were in a distant garden, the doctor said.

And so I have been, I said, a kind of garden. But now I am here.

Oh, and I am so glad. We'll return to this conversation when you are feeling more settled. As I mentioned, everyone here at Jaquith House is especially trained. He suddenly produced a pamphlet with the floor plan.

There aren't any patients then, Dr. Duvaux?

Helena, I think you will find that even our sufferers are apt in their sensitivities, and that our aides-de-camp are investigating their own psychic crenellations via their practice. Yes, we are a very special collective, said the doctor.

Doctor, I'm not sure I will show the same aptitude for sensitivity that your other inmates seem to share. I am not a known sensitive.

I think it is evident that you will and that you do. It is evident in your artistic craftsmanship, Helena. Many of us are great fans of your films, he said.

I looked around me. There was only the doctor and myself. There was no one else. No one sitting anywhere in the colossal common room, with its gleaming pine floors and Persian rugs, there was no one around the open fire, no one in the table game area or the tea nook, no one seated anywhere, despite a number of plump, chintz possibilities. No one in the rattan fanback chairs or in the tartan-covered wing chairs, no one stretched out on the wooden benches, no one swaying in the highly symbolic rocking chair. It was an empty set.

Many of us, Doctor?

Helena, I thought it best for your first night to keep things very quiet. But I think you'll find a small but lively crowd gathered in the grand dining room just beyond those wooden doors. You must be exhausted. But they are there, if you are ready for them. Shall I take you through? he asked.

But suddenly, I could not fashion a reply.

3

ON THE BOAT

Water was always my weakness. I see that now. It is how it all began with my uncle: a temper tantrum on the shoreline, followed by the assuaging gift of a camera. Then the focal point, the horizon perspective receding, the play of light and shadow on the waves.

A pattern stuck.

I had parents, but not really in a way that anyone noticed. Mostly I floated, for the first few years, in the charge of different adjacent bohemians, on the extended edges of family. First in Greece, then Morocco, Scotland—I have no real memories of these times. I came with a small but convincing dowry, and artists, especially unsuccessful ones, are always looking for an audience. Children are not children to artists—who are themselves perpetual children—they are adoring fans. But I was a little tyrant even in those days, and what income I offered was not enough to offset my tantrums, or the material damage that followed in their wake, and before long even that ran out. So, I was settled finally on a derelict uncle who had not seen anyone in the family for thirty years. Why he took me, I have never known for sure—perhaps he lost a bet.

My uncle Yiorgos lived on a large boat outside Sausalito. He was a perfect enfant terrible, even at sixty. His life was a steady parade of the loveliest models and muses, and he "painted" nudes and seduced patrons whenever and wherever possible. His showings were few and far between, but he could always find someone willing to support his cause long enough to extract our living expenses for a few months or a year. What a spectacular staging he managed, moving bodies on and off the boat with such mechanized precision to ensure a moneyed guardian angel never crossed paths with one of his studio girls. He could pull up the anchor, if anyone got any ideas. For some reason, we stuck together, though no one stuck to either of us for long, God help them. They couldn't even if they wanted to—any third party was destined to fail, and for me, in my youth, watching the lovelies trying and failing to landlock my uncle was my true education. Commitment was fatal. I loved the old reprobate. He was such a charming bastard, and completely my own.

School was not even a consideration. The constants for us were the headlands and the tides. Any movements were labored, and "slow" was a great understatement—the boat, the *Anjodie*, she was called, was held together with rust and barnacles, a spurtling inboard engine neither of us could intuit or repair—movement felt even more stationary than mooring. Boredom was the only real danger between us. It brought on tantrums, and I was likely to make mischief—for my uncle or for one of his girls.

Hence, the gift of my camera, my little Spotmatic F, already ancient when I received it, is there any wonder I was arcane before I even began?

My attention successfully redirected, Uncle Yiorgos was left to his own games. I documented the tedium of the flows, the tedium of the models, coming and going in skiffs and water taxis, recumbent and lithe in their thin caftans, their bathing suits, their sandals cast off immediately, closer to my age than my uncles'—they were creatures wholly apart from me in every way, photographic items only, specimens for study. I came away with the sense of the shape of femininity, but only as sheer overlay. I had the eye, that much was certain, but ultimately it was too much stillness. My ancient Spotmatic was swapped for an even older Braun Nizo, and suddenly motion was in my hand.

When we hit shore, I took myself to the cinema. Then took this erudition back to the shore. I adjusted the focus, and let the lens do its work. I don't want to be sentimental, but my camera made movement meaningful. So, in those years that followed, first behind the lens, a transparent eyeball, then adjacent but finally pulling the strings, whenever I got stuck, I went looking for water.

Oh, poor old Yiorgos. He was not destined for duration. If he had been, I might be with him still, on that boat in Sausalito. A bleeding ulcer, we thought. That was the rough estimate of some decommissioned quack he played cards with, and that was that. My uncle began to put his affairs in order and sent me packing to a school for juvenile delinquents in Switzerland. There I picked up several skills—legitimate and illegitimate—and made friends of the most disreputable kind, most of whom had family money to pull them out of any significant scrapes. My formal education was short-lived, as it turned out, with no one actually paying the tuition. Seventeen years old, and I was once again the vagabond. I thought I would make my way back to Sausalito, but time was not on my side. Within the year, Uncle Yiorgos sank the *Anjodie*. All that remained of my youth was his racoon coat, a French basket, and my Braun Nizo.

I floated among the families of rich delinquents, where with concentration, it wasn't hard to act the part of the better brat. I had an eye-catching portfolio, all those years of sunbathing beauties. All I needed really was to hunt for the right entrée into the art I thought I so rightly deserved to possess. And I had learned the tricks of my uncle's trade: select carefully, seduce completely, harvest what you can, and move on.

But was I speaking? Ah, yes. *Anjodie.* That was the first boat. And now onward to my last boat.

The film was to be called *Sanguine Season,* a romance. The plot was as follows: a confidence man called Flynn, played by the actor Corey, comes onto a riverboat with the intent of killing the lover of his estranged wife. The river would be its own character.

It took only one day. One day with the boat to bring me forward to this place. The weather was foul already at dawn, that first slight allay after several days of storms, and the Guaporé River had risen nearly three meters, but I went ahead on schedule. I was militant about schedules. The crew had warned me against the dangers of the river, I don't remember what I said—I raged, several members of the crew walked off, the others begrudgingly began the preparation for filming. Corey never hesitated. He was the first on the boat. We had been filming for only three hours when the moorings broke and released us onto the river.

I wasn't scared, it seemed impossible that the boat, a large spindle-wheeled affair, could break up. I felt sure we would stabilize. But the sounds were horrible: the sound of the water and solid things within the water, the sound of the boards reshaping.

The boat was poorly built: a hodgepodge of balsam, tin, shingles, striped canvas, and veneer scrollwork. It was all surface and no substance. I picked it for its interiors—grand staircases, carpeted lounges, and luxurious passenger cabins. In a matter of moments, water was moving through the air, and curling onto the deck, like something from a film.

I saw something, someone, threading through the currents. Corey was a good swimmer, very athletic. Good enough? I didn't know. Yes, we were close to him. I was closest to him, yes. But Corey was not a big talker, and I was not a big talker, and I had strict rules about the personal lives of my cast and crew—they simply did not exist, could not exist, when we were filming. There were no hangers-on allowed on my sets, no love interests, no children.

I did not know, in such a moment, if his body would carry him through, but I thought it might.

We were Corey's crew, his director, his community: we had pieced his backstory together. Lies, no doubt. The press lies, and everyone lies to the press. Corey's biography changed constantly, if it was entirely invented, that wouldn't be strange for an actor. Another director told me once Corey had been discovered on a beach in a borrowed suit, discharged from the Merchant Marines.

So, there were pieces of a biography, but none that lined up exactly. He was a notorious playboy, by report, but also had been married several times. Another story was that he had to marry for immigration purposes, but from which country to which other country we had no idea. A wife in a photograph would turn out to be a sister, then a sister would turn up in a magazine looking nothing like him. There were reports of scandals with the wives or girlfriends of other people—this I had no doubt about. Gossip in tabloids that he'd killed a rival lover, and more sensational narratives, probably started by our camp for publicity—for instance, that Corey and his elegant entourage were somehow connected to the shadow of the criminal underworld. A policeman might turn up, milling around a set, eating our sandwiches, but everyone ignored this. In interviews Corey said he couldn't be bothered by anyone: he preferred to be alone, with his whiskey. Except he never drank whiskey, he was too vain about his figure. Whatever the story, I didn't care—you can't let low-grade celebrity gossip delay a day's filming. The rumors were impossible to sort through. Alternate and conflicting versions, Corey seemed to have lived every life possible by the age of thirty.

It's hardly worth mentioning. What is an actor's biography if not simply the thing that gets in the way of his performance, the thing that blocks us from the character? If there was one thing I had been shouting down for years, it was the threat of a personhood emerging in that lovely blank body where a performance was supposed to take root. I wanted no part of those difficult things that remind us there is something beyond the frame of the film, the world the film so carefully builds. Eventually, locations name-checked by Corey in interviews could be placed, Paris or Cairo or La Paz, it didn't matter. When Corey spoke of himself, which was rarely, the stories fell out flat and stripped of the interest of their context, delivered with that faint hint of his unplaceable accent. He had come from and belonged to everywhere, interchangeably. And he was unimpressed by all of it. Corey's personal biography was the last point of interest for me, even though consideration of Corey is something that takes up my mind most of the time. Took up. Takes up.

Was I speaking?

On the boat that fated day, we began with stills. Every look was perfect: a sort of lone animal, an animal whose fear of water bespoke wisdom, a man on a boat. Of course, we were playing up a type. I wanted to make that sort of film, and Corey wanted this as well, he claimed. To return to the old cinema, the old new cinema or the old old cinema, a world of beautiful doomed men. Expendable men—men in my films rarely escaped unscathed. And I cared very little for dialogue—talking, I hated it so! Oh, to be cursed with this constant voice running, running. With Corey there was little need for dialogue.

The idea that he might end up working with someone else was a constant threat. I spied, yes, I kept tabs, I had little birds watching his every move, not because of jealousy, whatever the tabloids might say, our fights, the public scenes, why would I care who he fucked, where or how? This charge of jealousy—as if I were a desperate ingenue, clinging to the fantasy of monogamous devotion from an actor? Any possible angle to diminish authority, to reduce me to base parts.

And who am I? At the moment in the recounting of this tale, in the semi-historical present, I am little more than a blur awash against a waxed deck, unsteady on foot, my damaged hand grappling and grasping, in search of Corey. Not the lie, but where the lie has been. Under other circumstances, I am Helena Désir, the film director. A working name, of course, a pen name or a codename: a nom de guerre.

4

THE HOUSE AND THE BARN

I held the floor map in my hand. I was suddenly very afraid of Jaquith House.

Helena? The dining room? Dr. Duvaux was asking. The evening is getting away from us and dinner service closes promptly at nine-thirty.

Was I speaking, Doctor? Was I speaking about the boat again? I could hear the buzz of dining hall voices beyond the oak doors near us. They were heavy, and closed. I couldn't imagine these doors any other way.

We have been speaking now this last half hour, you must be truly exhausted.

I think it might be best to just send me to my room.

Yes, we've already done tremendous work, Helena, tremendous, he said, and took the corner of my elbow and propelled me gently along the stones of the patio.

I know the place is a bit overwhelming, he said. But you'll soon see it has very simple operations. A well-oiled machine. So much happens invisibly.

The house seemed to end and then begin again. There was a second wing, set on a rise, like another attached house. It had its own back stairs and cedar deck. Growing up through it was an enormous red tree.

Is that a redwood growing through the house, Doctor? I asked.

It is a sequoia varietal, yes, he said.

It survives the winter?

We harbor it, Helena. As we harbor all those whose constitutions may not be exactly suited for the conditions into which they have been cast. It is something we have inherited, that came before us, and it was harbored even by the ghosts of Jaquith House. Do you see the little apartment whose balcony curves around the trunk? We call it the Syllabary. It's my favorite accommodation.

Then it must be the best. I like the best. Charge it to the studio.

It is occupied, I'm afraid.

Well, there's no shortage of views.

In any case, I felt it best if you were not in the main house. One of the other cottages, I think.

You must have a very large population.

Oh, yes, Jaquith House is not just a house. It is an organism: the grounds, the lakes and streams, the orchards and the hills, even parts of the forest. And myself and my aides-de-camp and the guests are all Jaquith House. So the options are abundant: Lagoon, the pool house, Cascades is upstream and has a little waterfall, very isolated, best reached in an electric cart. Queen's Club adjoins the tennis courts. And there are the Baths—not a lodging, but where you'll find the therapeutic niceties: massage, mineral soaks, various mind-body disciplines.

A sort of spa?

Very contemporary, I'm afraid. I don't agree wholeheartedly, but many of our guests find these little luxuries restorative, and I make a point not to voice my disapproval within their hearing. Jaquith House strives to embrace a kind of eclecticism of space and mood in order to accommodate our diverse population.

You sound like a pamphlet.

The old with the new, the arcane alongside the ultramodern. But tasteful, Helena, we are nothing if not that, but I suppose I find it a bit—

Schizophrenic?

Well, discordant. Our little secret. But, Helena, we have decided to put you in Barbarêche. I hope you will be comfortable. You can see it off to the left of the courtyard.

That large barn?

It was a grange for threshing, pressing, and storing apples in the nineteenth century, modernly insulated and with lovely woodstoves, and the feeling—forgive my assumptions here—the feeling of a kind of nostalgic space, a space with very old and very simple origins. Very functional but very simple. Simplicity, Helena! That is what we seek at Jaquith House.

Is that calypso music piped through the rocks 24-7?

We do like to keep the sound of music in the air, but the flavor changes regularly. Nothing too jarring, I assure you.

I value silence, I said.

The stables side of Barbarêche serves as a garage for our few vehicles—some of the guests find it useful to keep a car on the grounds. We find that music, gently filling that otherwise industrial space, gives a rounded edge to the modern convenience, a convenience you requested, I believe? You can come and go to your car in the garage via your own private passage, so you'll have a sense of autonomy.

The barn above the garage it is, Doctor.

Barbarêche. Adjacent to the motor pool. I thought it would suit you.

We'll soon find out. I tend to speak freely.

Barbarêche is spacious. There's room to prowl. You like to prowl, Helena.

Did I say that?

Quite audibly. The yellow door will take you into the front entry, the bedroom is on the right, and the bath is up a short flight of stairs, ensuite. The courtyard stream runs right under your bedroom window. You'll find two staircases to the second floor, one public and one private. On the second floor there's a studio, however you'd like to make use of it—the windows overlook the orchards. It gets superb sunlight throughout the day.

Jaquith House is full of superlatives.

And the grounds, of course, are completely at your disposal. Make yourself at home in the main house, as well. And explore! The grounds have so much to offer us! However, I must warn you, there are some barriers between us and the woods beyond, and some of those barriers are electrified, so it's best to always come and go through the gates, even if the gates are out of your way. The deer can be so destructive. It's a pity to deter the wildlife. But I'm afraid they will always do as they are expected to do.

And what exactly is expected of me, Dr. Duvaux?

That you rest, that you take some exercise, that you participate to the best of your capabilities in our little community and that you meet with me each day.

Each day?

Each and every day that you are at Jaquith House we will have a little chat.

How will I find you?

I'll find you. The grounds are large, but not so large as that. Also, Helena, regarding the outside world: there is some wireless connectivity, but given our remote location it is very intermittent. Really, a passing cloud, a bit of wind, anything can put us off the network, so if you have a pressing digital need, I think it best to visit one of our stationary models in the Venetian Room, or leave a note on a docket, and one of us then can aid you with your request should connectivity be restored. Although even this, I am afraid, has no guarantee of success, but then I do not love the speed of our current age or our visibility within it. And, Helena, in that regard, I do ask that you surrender your phone to us, for at least the first few weeks. I hate to ask this—it is so invasive—but useful in ensuring that interfering personalities, should any exist, do not immediately disrupt the tranquility we hope to offer you.

I have no device, Doctor. Screens should be larger than the palm of the hand. And I am free of interfering personalities other than my own.

You are a refreshing throwback, Helena. How do you manage?

Someone somewhere must be handling my details, or you wouldn't be getting paid.

And I want to reassure you, though I may be paid by your studio, I want you to trust that my only real commitment is to you.

Trust, Doctor, is of the essence, I'm told.

In any case, I assure you our time together, our modus vivendi if you will, is ours alone.

My barn, please.

A final thing, Helena. Regarding Barbarêche: there is a recreational room on the upper floor. Our guests often utilize this in the evenings, but the night hours will be yours entirely. Make use of the billiard tables. We ask only that you leave the door unlatched from three p.m. until eight p.m., at which point you may flip the "after hours" sign. I hope we are going to be good friends!

If so, it will be a first for me.

Which is exactly as I would wish it! Good night, and count the beams before you fall asleep.

I always do, I said, and bid the man farewell.

I hated meeting people, I told myself. I loathed social conversation. I thought: I'm a misanthropic personality. But how could this be true? It is nearly impossible to be alone when filming. I could remember nights on location where everyone gathered until dawn, despite my demands for starting very early, because I loved shooting in the first natural light. In hotels, it wasn't enough to pass between one or two rooms, inevitably some single small space was selected as a common room, and in fact, in situations where I wanted to be alone with one of my actors, it would be difficult to pull him away from the card table or the cocktail lounge, or the gym—even Corey, who was a recluse. A recluse but with an entourage. Alone, but completely surrounded.

As for me, scripting was a lonely process. My love was the camera—that anything be written in advance seemed impossible. But scripting was the only way to gather a budget, so I adapted. I came to love it, this being alone, and scripting. But even that, over time, became collective.

I learned from the great film masters: with distance, with reconnaissance, secrets were eventually revealed for my generation—in the golden days, location was an illusion, a careful construct—everything held in the actor's voice, the actor's delivery, against backdrops and stages. That was the old cinema. The new cinema was natural location, nonsynchronous shooting, fast film stock, small crews, and superb cinematographers. The new cinema in the sense of that which was once new but is now arcane. I'm extremely nostalgic for the new cinema. I'm a throwback to the new cinema.

Now, the new new cinema is a virtual construct, filmed nowhere, free of materiality, free of content. Green spaces gave way to green screens.

All this mattered very little under my current circumstances, because I didn't see a way back in. Though I intended to play that close to the vest.

My luggage had been offloaded for me on the steps of the barn, and with some fumbling in the locks, because I'd forgotten the door was already open, I finally pushed through into a very long dark hallway.

In the dark passage, I could make out the rough-hewn stair rising up to the pool hall above.

As per Duvaux's descriptions, a heavy oak door led me into a large sunken bedroom. On the far side of the room, another short flight of stairs and an un-railed gallery, a half floor, which followed the windows on two walls. The half floor had a small writing desk and long window seat below the plate-glass window looking out on the stream, the foothills, the covered bridge, the distant woods in shadows. A transom had been left open to the night air, and a moist breeze drifted in. There was a large bathroom with a small stove on slate tiles, a vanity with mismatched antique mirrors, and separate cabins for toilet and shower, two wooden sink basins thickly greased like baker's paper. The bathroom smelled cool, and woody, with walls of stone in plaster, and glass bricks in a small window casement.

I stood in front of the window of bricks, which with the night behind it was like a mirror of bottle glass. It seemed to hold my likeness somewhere in its depths, but only as a watery silhouette. I tried to adjust my position in its patterns, but no clear reflection was to be had. I forwent the vanity and darkened the room. I still had my features, even if they were swimming a bit. What I looked like suddenly seemed immaterial.

The curtains behind the bed were open and I could see the colorful lanterns of the courtyard and obliquely, through the atrium windows, the brightly lit interior of the main house. A small group of people were pouring out onto the stones and saying their good nights. Two men shook hands and shot off in different directions: in shadows scarcely discernible—one, bald, pale and blue veined, swathed in a voluminous scarf like a French chanteur; the other of a strapping physique, with a flash of copper in his curls—they quickly disappeared into a hedge immediately at the back of Jaquith House. They reminded me, in their silhouettes, of some of my own ghosts, living ghosts, but ghosts nonetheless. Trailing behind them, an attractive young girl, compact build, maybe twenty or so, in a baggy sweater, searching for something tangled in her capacious handbag. Then the lanterns snapped off without warning, and the courtyard plunged into darkness.

The bed was large and modestly dressed. The bedroom glowed with the dim light of a modern chandelier.

I was tired, but once again, Sleep, we meet on the field of battle!

Since the accident, I had been not sleeping. Or I had always been sleeping. At times, when I thought I was not sleeping, I was sleeping. Other times, there was a stinging lucidity as I passed through dream states. Patterns or shapes, or movements of my hands across the day became passages through other types of meaning, as if I had solved a little puzzle in a newspaper, and through that passage found myself in sleep, or near sleep, stuck in similar types of rearrangement, and the numbers in a game of simple encryption became a code for breaking other kinds of thought, other kinds of problems. In the moment of these wanderings, games and their patterns seemed the only way to resolve rather grandiose things in my mind, as if my love or my anger, whatever or wherever those emotions might be placed, was a matter of bringing three similar numbers into a kind of logical alignment, or three similar shapes, et cetera. Time would pass, while I solved these puzzles nervously in my mind, and morning would dawn, and I would know that I was no longer as I had been, which is to say, I was awake, and whatever the subject matter, the specific subjects of the night before had been solved, solved incontrovertibly by matrices or by word games, and were now absent. That I had solved them, I knew. What they were, specifically, that I had solved, I couldn't remember.

In my sleep, I felt that I was not sleeping. When I slept, I would awake in phases as if from a kind of deep coma, aware of the impossible effort required to surface into the world again, and I had in mind the notion that one sleeper must replace another, so that for someone to be waking, I must be sleeping, and that for me to be asleep, someone else must be fighting through the dark weight in those moments where the body had lost all its resources. Why would someone, anyone, unknown to me, make such an effort to come into consciousness simply so that I could, for a brief time, fall out of it? I did wonder.

And then the talking, which both calmed and panicked me, and passed through me even in sleep, so that to sleep was not restful. It had occurred to me that this might be how some people live, as time goes on, the greater part of the day spent in sleeping, and not only while lying in bed. There was no way to be particular or discerning about sleep, or confident in any assumption about where it might finally seize one. There was no way to be sure what secrets would come pouring out of my mouth. At any place or time, I must be ready for it, this sleep-to-come, my head propped against the windowsill, in the studio commissary, walking across a sound stage, looking into a film set in disuse, even behind the lens of the camera. The continuity of the day loosened so much that it ceased to matter. Sleep instead had become for me a kind of terrain that I wandered through, for irregular stretches of time, for days or for weeks, wandering through blank landscapes with no discernible horizon, in a kind of desperate or broken respiration, chattering, chattering. And in these moments, these moments of either sleep or the refusal of sleep, I could not be sure of things I had seen, things I had said, or things I had heard.

So when it seemed to me that I had glimpsed living ghosts escape into the shrubbery, or when it seemed to me that the sound of the stream outside the barn's window simply stopped, and that all I could hear was the clicking of billiard balls, I was not inclined to trust this.

No matter, now I was awake.

I made my way up the stairs to the second floor. It opened up like a hayloft. The barnness of the space gave me a pleasant little shock. If the first floor of Barbarêche obscured her origins, the second floor flaunted them. The enormous high peaks of the barn and its beams ran for twenty or thirty yards. Several sofas, armchairs, and rugs surrounded a large woodstove, which had clearly been in use in recent days, and there was ash in the cauldron and on the tongs. There was a makeshift bar, with mirrors and bottles of whiskey, likely decorative. The room ended in a raised stage with a very large writing desk, under dormer windows. There were two large billiard tables. A pendulum light hanging over one of them was swinging a little, as if it had been bumped before I arrived. But there was no one there.

I poured myself a whiskey in a cloudy glass and was shocked to find it authentic. I drank it in one gulp standing up. I had gotten used to the look of my talons on a whiskey glass. I had the feeling of being in a western, but a television western. It felt shoddy and staged. Unattended.

I checked my watch. It was well after midnight, but my watch had long ago given up. I kept it turned into my wrist, an affectation picked up from Corey. It made the gesture of looking at the time far more theatrical. No one wore a watch anymore, no one except sports figures trying to sell watches.

5

BODY IN DISGUISE

In *Sanguine Season*, Corey played the part of the confidence man Flynn quietly, without affect, his hair shellacked, a black mustache, a slicker. Meanwhile, he was circled by other men who might also be the confidence man Flynn, at times also played by Corey, who appeared on screen in masquerade, unidentifiable as himself. It was part of the film's charm, this disguising of Corey from scene to scene. It took some effort, and editing. His eyes were always distinguishable, his jaw, his cheekbones—and he was not the kind of actor whose talents allowed total transformation. He was always recognizable. One thing all my actors have had in common is remarkable physicality, in varying forms. I hold to the old ways—an actor on the screen should be beautiful. We are looking at him, after all.

Corey could run effortlessly through takes, fit and driven, his life off the set was spent in training. He could work his body to exhaustion, and then move his body beyond exhaustion. He should have been able to survive me.

Sanguine Season begins as Corey passes through a brightly burning field of green barley. In the distance, a beech grove. The season is spring and the light is gold, and he is dressed as the confidence man Flynn, in cream trousers, a shirt open at the collar. He may have been completely outside of time, or he may have been on another planet.

This is really the only footage that I have from that film. And only this because I filmed it myself—having fired two cameramen already, I was working with my handheld to gain perspective.

It was the gangplank sequence. Corey, again as Flynn in cream linen, at the waterside. He pauses before a placard affixed to the pier pylon: a flyer announcing a reward for the capture of a mysterious impostor. Extras cluster about the flyer, noting the reward sum, showing camaraderie. Corey, as Flynn, continues forward onto the boat, taking no notice. The long arm of a stevedore blocks Corey's passage as he reads out the WANTED placard, his cheeks are sunburned, and one eye is twisted into a scar which runs the length of his face.

A youth addresses the stevedore: What says you, whiskerando?

The stevedore, aloud, to no one in particular: In the old countries, they hunt such charlatans and kill them without much question, like wolves in the hills.

The camera finds Corey, who finally speaks: There are those who say that where the wolves are killed off, the foxes increase.

The stevedore turns his blind eye to Corey: Aye, some do say it.

The two regard each other. The stevedore lifts his arm for Corey, who mounts the gangplank and moves steadily onto the boat.

From this moment forward there is only Flynn aboard the boat, in pursuit of his rival, in pursuit of revenge.

All that was left was to move onto the boat. A skeleton crew, myself, my actor.

But shortly, the boat was untethered. It growled under the pressure of the current. Beyond the bank of windows, the landscape moved of its own accord.

I could not look down the lens to this moment, this boat. We had barely begun filming.

I sheltered in the ballroom, which a thin salty stream swiftly penetrated. It slipped along the glassy surface of the dance floor in meandering rivulets. The water, which in the depths of the river appeared dark and mottled, glided across the surfaces of the boat in clean, sparkling lines. The boat began to know water's intimacy.

Next, the lurch, and what followed. I fell. My hand caught in a bit of loose paneling, and the weight of my body crushed it badly. The smallest finger appeared quite disfigured, the curving shape of the bone shown white through the skin. The claw-to-come. And it seemed I had cut open my head.

For a brief instance I glanced a slice of my face in the moving mirror of my lens. I was blanched, and my eyes were only slips, and even in my own reflection, the light refracted in blinding flashes, as when a watch face, picking up only a slight bit of sun, projects a spotlight into the eyes of another person. Instinctively, I turned my watch face into the inside of my wrist. The fingers on that hand jutted askew, alien to my eyes.

There was another great crash, and the boat lodged. It was the last thing I remembered before I awoke briefly, on a stretcher, in our base camp, surrounded by paramedics. Corey had fallen almost instantly and split his head open on a rock. My boat had ended him. And I was to do without him now for good.

Had I been speaking?

No matter. There was no one to hear.

I shut off the lights in the billiard room, and went downstairs. I locked the front door. Never in my life had I paid attention to locking doors, but somehow, at Jaquith House, I felt a new need for protective measures.

I returned to my bed and thought no more of the sounds above.

Go on, they said. Go on, we're listening.

In my head, I counted in patterns of three, and grouped shapes accordingly to these patterns, shapes that in the long run would solve some aspect of my desire. Then at some point in the night this stopped. I could not possibly say when, and that moment was not distinguishable to me from the moment of the rising sun.

I awoke in Barbarêche, the light rising behind my bed, shining on the bookshelves, the sideboard, and the cabinetry. It was indeed comforting in its rustic simplicity, and as the doctor said, it spoke of its own discernible history. The stream burbled softly outside the window and there was the sound of birds, though agitated in their song, as though bracing against the coming of the fall.

6

A PICTURE STORY

The pamphlet was tucked into the drawer of my bedside table, like a Bible in a cheap hotel.

The images moved from daguerreotype to tintype to photogravure—1891, the staff were mostly men, all mustachioed, suited, and attended by only two seated nurses in floor-length capes and lace caplets. A 1908 laboratory—overseen by a gentleman gambler, or perhaps a member of a barbershop quartet. By 1910 doctors performed rounds on horseback. The 1918 nurse's softball team in their long full skirts and sailor-suit chemises suggested that at least by the turn of the century women were sturdy enough to stand up in a photo. I immediately recognized the 1951 inaugural snack bar, with its chrome stools and wood-paneled bar and countertop, because it was my own recreational room in Barbarêche. It still had the original cash register.

There was a portrait of the very young Otto Duvaux, upon his arrival in 1968, looking rakish in a turtleneck and conventional lab coat, smoking his pipe. His hair was swept up in a wave over his forehead, and he had his arm around an adolescent mental patient trying to launch a model sailboat on the edge of a pond. The young sufferer was lanky and gaunt, dressed in a kind of somber uniform of dark starched cotton shirt and short trousers. He looked fraught and hunted, but his face was directed imploringly toward the camera. A man and a woman flanked: Doctors Jorgen Flochs-Vy and Mehitabel Lenday, the caption noted. Both were lab-coated, stern, and dour. In an adjacent photo from 1975, Duvaux christened a new Jaquith House sign with a champagne bottle: all the stern lab-coaters were gone, and instead in the background there were quite a few suave-looking Trappist monks in checked flared trousers, a female jug band, and a tall bearded Black man—Dr. Theodore Samba, of New Orleans, tuberculosis pioneer and specialist in veteran trauma. Only the tall Black man wore a lab coat; he was stern and dour, another product of the changing political times. All others looked lit, if not wasted.

The pamphlet touted the unconventional methods of Dr. Duvaux. No lobotomies or electric currents pumped through the gray matter. Totally open and voluntary, simple, tranquil remove.

Decorous and compassionate treatment for a highly selective cast by a highly skilled production crew. To be within a walled compound was either heartening or the final, ultimate blow. Asylum, however. Now, that was what a girl was looking for!

There were almost no pictures of the sufferers, prior to the youth in dark starched cotton, with his model sailboat, so I didn't know how I fit or didn't within this fine tradition of nervous disorders, breakdowns, and psychic exhaustion. One thing was for sure, that since the original inception of the asylum, the archival approach was to present more as a vacation house or a country club than as a home for the mentally disturbed. There were no photographs of fraught paranoids slinking through the Venetian room in their filthy bathrobes, no hysterics tearing at their hair in the music salon, no psychotics hurling their own feces in the grande allée.

I tidied myself and lay out my own uniform: indigo silk on indigo linen. I aligned my upswept loose coiffure with my claw. A face of sharp turns, and mutable, sunken amber eyes, bloodshot and darting. A square chin with slight cleft. One flirtatious, slightly jutting tooth. Everything else kempt and even, smooth, a poker face. I checked myself in both the mirror and the glass bricks, looking for incongruities, disparities between the two reflections. But they were rough corroborations. I looked like something tasteful and authentic, but disoriented, displaced. I was very Jaquith House.

The barn was truly transformed by morning light from a high skylight overhead. A kind of material beauty that I found suspicious. The stairwell scaffolding rose up, and even in the weight of its materials, was sprightly and vaporous as it ascended to the loft, and the entire space held an air of frivolity. But my hallway, in the morning sun, revealed its one dark embellishment: it dead-ended in an enormous tapestry.

This tapestry, woven in an embarrassment of silk, linen, and velvet, seemed to tell a story.

7

THE TROUBLE WITH ACTORS

There has always been the trouble with actors. In the very early stages, I thought I would be the voice of women, and I had inherited my uncle's eye for beauty. But, though I was a woman, or thought I was, I did not have the voice of women. I kept my mind in a silent, criminal, brutal encasement. I was a locked box, and I had a past that might catch up with me.

What has come to pass leaves this largely inaccurate, even while it proves its point. You can see my concern.

But if the problem of actresses is how to dress them, how to suit them to my films without suiting them out of their potential careers, rendering them leaden and plodding, and therefore unmonetizable, if the trouble was only how to avoid personal entanglements that end up imbalanced, it was ultimately no different from my actors: the puzzle of how to dress them, how to get them not to speak, or to speak volumes with no words, convincing them not to destroy my film or themselves. All actors, as it turns out, are also actresses.

And in the end I was a product of my training, and Uncle Yiorgos was a master. He could seduce women and men in five languages! I had seen everything and more on the *Anjodie*, and I was blasé in the face of it, but the trade in sex was Yiorgos's only currency, and I picked it up quickly, carrying as I did the family features, and learning early to keep them in good repair.

My romantic entanglements with actors were blown out of proportion by the trade journals, and shoddily reported. But they weren't entirely wrong. There was some truth to it. Actors are so empty, so vain, so incredibly shallow. I was uniformly condemned for my liaisons. I just let things sort themselves out. This strategy, I admit, was rarely in anyone's best interests, even my own.

I have had three lead actors to date: the acrobatic waif Emile Laval, my first, the dapper thespian David Trevor, my second, and Corey, the all-sorts.

When I parted ways with an actor, as I inevitably would, we were all exhausted by the process. But those days were so tiring in many ways. With my early pictures, I was still feeling my way. I was young; we all were very young, safety was a luxury beyond my budget. Good behavior, unheard of.

With the arrival of Corey, the trajectory changed. My first two actors were given a boost, it wasn't without some result, and they were both glad to be done with me, even if they claim otherwise. Once I found Corey, there was no going back, I hoped. If anyone could, or would, follow Corey—but this is a problem now covered in water.

There is no understanding Corey without first understanding David Trevor. And no understanding either of them without first understanding Emile.

What was I saying? Again! The order...

Emile, my first:

I did *Mechanism*, my first film, with no stars. Emile Laval wasn't an actor when we began, he was a Québécois circus performer. He spoke an odd patois of nasal French and English. Later, of course, his name was widely known for his dance and acrobatics, and he became a cult idol.

But when I began to work with him, Emile was practically a vagrant. His circle was a disparate group of threatening and wounded souls. Tattooed, soiled, plagued with madness, addicts of one kind or another, grifters, carnival people. Emile breathed fire and swallowed swords and appeared clad in filthy loincloths or tattered cut-off denim. As a street performer, he did somersaults and jumped from great heights. He hated to be in clothing, and felt skittish if he was wearing it, like a dog on a leash. Out of his clothes he was able to talk to anyone. He was only twenty when I lured him out, and he wasn't pretty. He hunched, his face was pocked, his teeth gray and broken, his legs short and uneven from a birth defect, he said, his left leg had been broken during a stage stunt, and not properly set. He walked with a lurching gait. I know now that these things were lies; he was older than we thought, and his deformities were performed deformities. Now he is older still, and his body is agile and fluid, and he is an incomparable dancer, as if age is slowly perfecting him. I chose him for the authenticity of his face and his body. It was my first project that was completely my own, and naively, I still believed in authenticity. So much so, I fell immediately for his masquerade.

I found him by chance—performing on a street in Marseille, and I lay in wait. I wasn't yet *with* the studio, I was only a potential consideration of the studio, and my budget was a shoestring. I had wormed my way in as a cameraman and served my masters well enough to venture out. My eye behind the lens led me, and I let no one edit my eye. But I had also quickly gotten a reputation as a script doctor: a script surgeon, to be exact. I could cut away a cancer with laser-like precision. I never slept, even then, but that was on my own terms. And because I had cut my teeth on action films and had shown myself unafraid to research in the field, it appeared that I might pass for a man in this industry, as I had for so long in my own mind.

To begin *Mechanism*, I had been given a short leash, but I was frugal and cynical, and I knew how to stretch to the end of my chain.

I ambushed Emile Laval on the fire escape of a patisserie called Clafoutis with a sugared cake. It was the beginning of many more outdoor scenes between us, public and demoralizing scenes; on that fire escape, we spent several hours discussing his past. He was abandoned as a child, he said. He never knew either a father or a mother. So, I thought, we have these orphaned beginnings in common!

He told me about the cost for the antibiotics he took for his lungs, a disease from living with rodents. He told me about a bacterial infection attacking his eyes, too much contact with live chickens. I lied that his medications were covered by my budget. He told me he had committed some crimes that might catch up with him. I said no one's past is free of skeletons. He whispered me some of the crimes. I whispered a few of my own. All of this whispered on the fire escape of Clafoutis, because, he thought, someone was following him. (Someone was following him. I had been following him for days.)

Emile Laval played the role of the drifter Kestrel in *Mechanism*, my first real film, the film that allowed me to finally be *with* the studio, a reasonable financial triumph, but something that I now look back on as a descent into hell. But a descent from hell into hell. Emile lent the part something tough and inscrutable, but I had been left entirely out of control in my own picture. I know now he terrified me: not as a threat to my person but as a threat to himself, or worse, a threat to my autonomy. I had gotten involved with him, and I had become carried away, something my uncle Yiorgos would never have done. But I could never let on about this, about whatever terror I had about the imminent ruin of the boy Emile Laval, because I had to believe that he was the tough drifter Kestrel. And he had to believe it as well.

I also terrified him, though that was not yet evident to me. It was evident to those around us. To the crew, our relationship was the dance of two tyrannical infants. We attacked without warning, we slapped each other, we broke things, we clawed at each other, we called each other the foulest imaginable names in several languages. I burned him with a cigarillo, he put a pen knife in my thigh, and at one point a pistol had to be wrenched from both our hands—a prop, but the effect was the important piece. I was starting to cut my teeth.

He had added some wounds as the drifter Kestrel, some new wounds to his already damaged body—but what could be done about this? Did he expect me to apologize? I would not apologize. The drifter Kestrel was looking to be wounded—he found violence even where it shouldn't lurk, and I was after authenticity. I had no love of brutality for its own sake, but I did love resilience in the face of trauma. And I knew, or thought I knew, that Emile had been witness to trauma, and I knew, or thought I knew, that if I pushed him enough I would return him to just the point of trauma he felt most, and there we would discover his resilience. And I believed that, like the drifter Kestrel, he would push me to the limit of my cruelty in order to be delivered to this moment. And I had few limits.

And yet, Emile seemed to be attaching himself to me. At night, things were different between us. I always booked adjoining hotel rooms (if it had been possible to get him to sleep in a hotel and not in some cruddy little tent in a parking lot). If I could get him into a room, a room that adjoined my own, at night, he would come to the threshold between the adjoining doors and knock lightly on the door on his side. I came to my door and knocked lightly to let him know I was listening.

So, when he knocked on the adjoining door, I did not dare say to him, I am so sorry. Hush, little one, everything is going to be fine. If I had done that, he would have torn the place apart. I said nothing to him through the door. Instead, I listened to him, as he told me the stories of Kestrel the drifter, as he imagined them. Horrific stories:

abuses, indignities, and violations. Every gory detail, until I would whisper, Stop inventing! I wrote this! I made the drifter Kestrel!

He would go on more with this gore, the filth of the upbringing of the drifter Kestrel, and I would finally yield and as loud as I could, Enough, I'd say. Have it your own way. Then I would open my door to better hear his voice, and I would start to transcribe the stories of the drifter Kestrel, in shorthand. None of these stories ever became part of *Mechanism*, not in the sense of the actual dialogue or scenes in the film, but they were, I suppose, essential to the result of *Mechanism*.

So, yes, I opened up the door on my side between the adjoining rooms, so we were separated by only one door, knowing that the door on his side remained closed. And some nights he did the same. We could survive this way, I thought, if only there was still a door between us.

But sometimes, both doors opened. Such an occasion would mean that he had not heard that my door was open, and I had not heard that his door was open, because really neither of us would have wanted it confirmed that he or she had been the first to unlock and open their door, no matter how many times it had happened already. Such vulnerability could only happen by accident.

But it happened, and when it did, he liked to lie across my bed, his head on my knee, alert, watching the patterns of the ceiling, without talking. His naked body uncurled, the legs suddenly level, even and equal, the scars of his skin softened in the light, the dark eyes resting below his thick lashes, and growing slowly erect in his own hand, he watched his member ascend beyond his fist, as it curved up and back toward his body, toward that slope in a man's body that curves up from the groin, up into the hip, into the shelf of the ribs, into his belly, which clung to his skeleton almost too tightly but swelled outward from the sway of his back. Like this he was in his most perfect element, the curvature of his limbs looping out and in, up to the sky and back in to the torso, the curvature of his spine, curling over his back, over his belly, down into his torso, his groin, back up though his cock, back up into the center of his breathing. God, how I longed for my Braun Nizo then.

I mean here to say—surely, it is clear!—nothing I did was without love?

At this point, the stories of Kestrel the drifter softened and became inaudible. His voice, it seemed, could operate only under those particular constraints of the double door. Sometimes from here we slipped into a different position, a different collision of bodies, and I found his curved body in my fingers, and his curved limbs around my own limbs, but I was hesitant about what parts of him I was willing to let in to the parts of me they were seeking, but of course, this kind of resistance cannot go on for long. I was hesitant, but I didn't know how to resist such a creature in such a moment, in those days. I had not yet learned, as I quickly would, the problem with actors. I didn't trust where he'd been, where he was, or where he would soon be, so I could also not have abandoned myself completely in such a moment: bodies, yes, but anything beyond this, anything that would allow him to attach himself to my project, no. These were not embraces, then, in that sense. We were neither of us sentimental, I believed. However, they culminated, they had to end ultimately with a great bodily wrenching, and each of us restored to our rooms on either side of the double door.

Nothing I thought I understood was accurate. He was only twenty. I was only a little older, though I felt a great deal older. I always feel older than I am, which these days, is to feel old indeed, as I look down the road to my Jack Benny year, swiftly approaching, and then, hovering, forever thirty-nine.

Emile was a great success with audiences, and perhaps there was something of me in *Mechanism*, though I doubt it. I knew that I could not work with him for the second film. My eye behind the lens, my eye behind the door. I kept this card close to my chest. My intimate crew was losing tolerance already with my whims. And they grew attached to Emile, even in so short a stretch of time—*Mechanism* from start to finish took eighteen months.

When it finished, when I knew what had to be done, I was already trying to find a way to talk myself into or out of whatever the next step might be. It was then that I met David Trevor.

David, my second.

I recall it so well, the evening of the (lightly attended) premiere of *Mechanism*: we had gotten Emile into a silk shirt, a pair of formal loafers, and he couldn't help but stare at his own reflection in their high shine. We had gotten him into a very elegant hotel room adjoining my own, where it seemed, finally, he no longer felt the ceilings too low or too high. I left him in the room, in front of an angled mirror, being brushed down by one of my new assistants. A blue racquetball was moving between his thumb and fingers in a fluid figure eight while they dressed him. He watched me in the mirror, but said nothing.

In the cocktail lounge of the hotel a group from my crew were already gathered, as well as several last-minute producers, producers after the fact, and their starlets, and these producers had conjured a gaggle of young celebrity meat to raise the sex appeal of the red carpet entrance for the press. The meat was diverse and appealing; youngish, constructed bohemians with artfully disheveled hair for the ladies and prohibition pomade for the men. Among them was David Trevor, who was sitting at the bar and finishing up something cold and clear in a round glass and asking for another. Even though at that point we had never met, I recognized him easily. I had seen him in *Robespierre's Wishes* onstage in the West End the previous spring. It was a ridiculous swashbuckler of a talky nature, with Trevor for the most part seated, in stockings and a gold waistcoat, enunciating violently in his poshest accent. Strictly a stage phenomenon: historical fatalism and beheadings recounted from a chair; I was charmed by the sets, which were spare, bleak, and torch-lit, with the silhouette of a guillotine looming across the backdrop.

However, this David Trevor was looking surprisingly contemporary in a pale gray suit with a thread of blue neon running at the level of his knees along the base of the bar. He was talking with my stuntman, who made a hasty retreat at my arrival. I sat next to Trevor.

That little man struck me in the abdomen, Trevor said to me before I could open my mouth. He thumbed toward my stuntman and added, He was going on and on about his core, and then he began going on and on about my core.

My stuntmen are fanatical. They're very fit.

You own stuntmen? Am I in LA? I thought I got off the train at Twenty-Third Street; but it *was* a long walk. He offered me his hand, I'm David Trevor.

I saw you in *Robespierre* in London. You were very period, very convincing.

Thank you. "Undeniably attractive," the reviewers said. I think it was mostly the hair extensions.

Did the studio buy you for tonight?

They did, but it works for me also. I have six days under a bridge in Brooklyn where—

You saw the film then?

I did! Your Frenchman is unbelievably good. Like a bird of prey. Where did you get him? How did you get him? He's not one of us, is he? Stage, I mean.

I can't tell you, you wouldn't believe me. And he's not French, not exactly.

What? Go on. There's always a story. Did you bail him out of jail? Rescue him from a cult? Or I guess you just ordered him from a website. How very American.

No, it's worse.

Is he an orphan?

Practically.

Your people did the scarring on his face?

Not most of it. Emile came to us pre-scarred. Some though—side effects of the set.

Then you don't need stuntmen.

They are nice to have all the same. Emile has very sweet eyes. Deceptive. He's no innocent, trust me.

I trust you; you look like you know. Anyway, if you don't want to tell me, I can't fight you. I'm an underling, tonight. Come to London in August, and I'll treat you as an underling. I'm in a Kleist piece. Very serious. Condemned warrior nobleman. Anyway, I'm just making polite conversation.

I can tell you the story if you have time.

There is time, said Trevor, as he waved over the bartender. He was solidly drunk.

All right, I said. Imagine this: he had a recurring dream of a woman in a white silk dress, off the shoulders, tailored to her figure perfectly.

Like the one you're wearing now?

A version, certainly. Her hair was short and dark, cut around her face.

A little like yours tonight?

A little. In the dream, he saw her only for a brief moment, and she was running around a corner.

Quick on her feet, Trevor sputtered to his glass.

Well, that's all. Any of this can be easily re-created: for her to appear as flashes when he comes out of a door, to dash haphazardly around a corner, to be seen only in catches and glances, distressed, in flight, under the flickering street lamps. It's a cliché, I could have shot it a hundred times over. It's just a quick trip to the costumers.

You put yourself in the dress.

At first, I did, yes. At other times, another girl. That's a lot of running around corners! He came to us, no questions.

Ridiculous. How could you know something like that?

One of his circus told my casting woman.

You're trying to be serious! I'm dismayed: I thought you were just flirting. You literally lured him? Poor exploited bastard.

Mechanism is very good, I said (with very little conviction).

It certainly is.

It functions. I pulled Emile into a new world. Everyone should be so lucky.

They should. I definitely should.

It's not your sort of thing. What I'm hoping to do—I don't think anyone like you—well, no heroes or romantic leads.

You know, I hate that. Just because I talk a certain way? It's very prejudiced. I could stand a new world. But for me, promise the bait will be almost anything but a vamp in a cocktail dress. I'm romantic, yes, but cynical.

Are you looking to leave the stage?

Oh, no. The stage values me. I'm lucky with that. I was born into it. You have to be. It's like royalty. Or a wolf pack. But it doesn't hurt to do the odd film.

Trevor, you talk like someone who's had his lines written for him.

Both my parents were actors, and I was on the stage at age seven. I have an enormous arsenal of memorized lines. I never have to think of anything original to say again. I never have to listen to anything anyone is saying either. It frees up my mind for so much more.

What a grand show of confidence and bravura David Trevor mustered that first night. Indeed, he was lovely. I was absorbed by and completely convinced by him. I did know, or quickly gathered from gossip among the crew, that he had a reputation as a fantastic flirt, high on charm, better after a few drinks, unstoppable after many. He was at his very best in a first impression. He had a reputation for being good in bed, and he had been in so many beds, and on so many couches. It was disgusting to me to be susceptible to this sort of thing. No one could beat me at my own game. But I had other motives. The spark of the hustler Calloway had already been present in my mind, and the hustler Calloway would need some of that bravura and some of that charm. I had decided that I wanted to be the one to draw David Trevor up out of the breeches and waistcoats and drop him into a suit of clothes befitting a more modern man. It was one of those mistaken moments of power where the original object is lost.

It was later that same night, after David had returned to his hotel room, that I heard Emile scratching at the adjoining door.

Why, he asked me, do the women I fall in love with never love me?

They do, Emile. Just not in the way you imagine.

I left the door locked. From beyond it, the sound of glass being smashed, fabric torn, the howls of a feral cat.

I was with David, having coffee in my room that following morning, when my assistant found us.

Where is Emile? He's not in the room.

David, go for a walk, I said.

Your wish, et cetera, already, et cetera, he said, and bowed.

Where is he?

How should I know? He's not my child.

Isn't he?

The film is out. Officially launched, and so is Emile. He's fulfilled his contract to me, and now he can go where he likes.

Where he likes? He doesn't like anywhere. He lives with you, wherever you decide to stick him. A year ago he didn't even wear shoes.

And now he does—if you believe in progress.

He's never even been in the city, Helena, he doesn't have a phone. He barely speaks English!

He'll manage, I think I said—that or, He's his own man. Some careless clichés dropping out. I said, He could be anywhere, and it's out of my hands. Or I said, I think you are overstepping your station...

She was beside herself, we were supposed to be promoting the film, a junket had been arranged.

What did I say, I wonder? The fact is some conversations escape me like mist, whereas others arrive in my mind with the clarity of the light in my lens, like rewatching a scene I've written.

What did I say to my assistant, whose heart was certainly on her young sleeve, and who rushed in to speak logic to what she imagined to be my madness or my cruelty even though it would surely cost her a job? (And in fact it did.)

I think I said, I need to be somewhere else, somewhere alone.

Helena, I might have said, to myself, there are a lot of us that are counting on you to follow this through. And Helena, I might have answered, I am following through, but with whatever is next. David

Trevor is next. Though I should perhaps have said, Helena, if you want to fuck a stage actor, take a few days, fuck the stage actor, and then mend things.

But there was no mending, I knew. And Emile knew before even I knew. Helena, this is not reasonable. Not realistic, the assistant said that day.

I have never been one for realism. The thing that I am, doesn't exist, as you well know.

What if the film fails? Then, the film fails. Emile fails. Helena fails. What difference does it make? I'll reinvent myself.

(I told these kinds of lies, from time to time. And I believed them from time to time, if I delivered them with conviction. This was a trick I had learned from actors.)

But *Mechanism* didn't fail. It wasn't a huge success, but it held its own. It announced itself. And, yes, Emile Laval dropped off the map for a short time, and I didn't try to find him. What would have been the point? Did I owe him something? His life before me had been a series of indignities. His life ahead would take a steady, powerful rise. I wouldn't pretend that I could work with him again. I was on to something else—someone else.

I saw Emile recently, no more than a year ago, shortly before Corey and I began filming *Sanguine*. That summer was a parade of ghosts from the past, it seemed. Someone had made a documentary of Emile's method of dance training, and it was being shown at a festival where I was supposed to give a talk. I didn't give the talk, of course. I often agree to give a talk, but in the long run, I never give a talk, I go only to see the films. The film was long and odd, consisting mostly of scenes of Emile stretching at the ballet barre in the gutted Parisian department store he purchased a few years ago—partly his home, partly his studio, and partly a boot camp for his groupies and novices. He speaks only French now. And his body lurches no longer—but his face is still beautifully pocked. That much was authentic. He's collected a whole commune of avant-garde musicians, some quite famous, living in his gutted department store, composing at all hours of the day and night for his ballets for no audience, pounding on hubcaps and sides of beef, a crooner warbling chansons amid the horrible cacophony. In the documentary, Emile clung to the rafters, and released himself on gymnast rings; in a stocking cap and canvas slippers he crossed a tight rope over what would have been the furs section of this grand old building, had so many of the floors not collapsed in the fire. Everything was scorched black and even the film audience could smell the place. Surely, this film had been made by someone who loved him completely.

His method of instruction was understated-mystical. For one very long sequence he limbered his ankles. In another, he taught his followers how to juggle a ball in such a way that it appeared never to touch the fingers—I knew that trick, I'd captured it in *Mechanism*. In this documentary, he was unbearably sexy, and I was now old enough to see it, or perhaps I had just forgotten what I had once seen and was now being forced to reckon with its full, blunt force.

After the festival screening, when the film credits were running, the audience gave him an ovation. Emile appeared on the stage before the screen, barefoot in blue silk trousers and jacket open along his bare and polished chest. He was aging slightly, perhaps, and his hair was much thinner, but he was still the petite sinew from *Mechanism*. Now the body, lean and straight, had corrected its hunch, its limp, its misaligned limbs, and its stagger, and he was instead fluid and satiny, as if molded in some space-age polymer. He bowed to the waiting audience, whispered something inaudible in his strange French, and indicated that he was going to dance. An atonal musical concoction was running along with the credits, the banging of hubcaps, the slapping of beef. And he did dance: a dance that at times looked more like a man walking, hands in pockets, or neurotically adjusting a sleeve, cracking an elbow. Very understated this style of dance, very deadpan, and he trained for it like a triathlete. Even I was taken in. The woman beside me was moved to tears.

Do you know him? I asked.

I saw him in a film once.

Me too, I said.

Afterward, I crashed his reception. He moved through his own party as he moved onstage, his blue silk suit, with its high tunic collar, floating around him. His waxed chest gleamed out in a little V from his jacket, below the bunch of his fringed scarf. I felt instantly proprietary of that little triangle of flesh. I could smell him as he once had been, in our hotel rooms. He held a glass of champagne. I caught his eye, and I saw him turn toward me.

Stupidly, I had gone in thinking he would never recognize me. It had been so long, and also, I change as much of myself as I can as often as I can manage, and I thought I was significantly incognito in a tailored suit of charcoal silk, not dissimilar in cut to the one he was wearing, and I also kept the plunging neckline bare to my waist, much as he had done, and I was littler—shorter, perhaps—in my flat espadrilles. My hair was hidden under a small panama hat of an identical dove color, tipped low over my eyes. I could barely see. But I could tell he recognized me. He stopped what he was doing and watched me for a long time, and I tipped back my panama and held his eyes. Then, he began toward me with an uncharacteristic lilt in his step.

He's recognized me, and he's coming toward me, I thought for a moment. Then I thought: I'm forgiven, he's forgiven me, after all this time.

How can he be so easy? How can I?

But as he approached me through the throng, gliding in that silk suit, the picture of sophistication, androgynous comfort, and as I, for that one moment, was gliding toward him, a similar visual monstrosity, I suddenly remembered his once young, dark eyes under their heavy lashes, the scar that broke up his left brow, which I had given him on the set of *Mechanism*, and then there was his jaw that has always been clenched slightly, in distrust.

Of course, he had taken it straight to the bank! And no doubt he'd learned it from me.

J'en suis tombé, tombé sur le cul, he sang, approaching me, his hands outstretched, but I was already on the run.

To have ended him, to have ended any chance of a career, to have sent him into despair, on the streets, that would be one thing. To have driven him to suicide, or madness. To have crudely seduced him, and then allowed myself to be more crudely seduced away by David Trevor, for this I could repent and move on. But I couldn't stand to be forgiven for such a creation as the one before me, this perfect brand, and I couldn't forgive him for whatever part he played in the creature that stood before him. We had been in it together, after all. I lurched left and dashed into the crowd. I slipped out behind the caterer's bus bin.

8

SCOUTING LOCATION, THE DINING HALL

The grand dining room of Jaquith House was completely empty when I arrived, the tables laid with gingham napkins and white porcelain coffee cups, which gleamed in the light of the tall glass doors on the eastern wall, the sun rising over the patio flagstones where more tables were laid and waiting. All empty. Perhaps I was too early?

My watch was clouded over with permanent precipitation. Water damage.

I heard the clatter of a pot, the opening and closing of a cupboard, water running, the sound of a working kitchen. The sound filled the cavernous dining hall.

I popped my head through the swinging doors. There was no immediate kitchen. There was only a long stone hallway, which I followed, and took two turnings at least before I found a chef slumped against one wall in his crisply laundered whites, checked trousers, and rubber clogs. He seemed to be sleeping despite the din, and his legs were outstretched across the tunnel. I tiptoed over him. I saw in the distance another set of swinging doors.

Finally, I was in the great kitchen, bright and gleaming with stainless steel. There was hardly a surface that was not metal. A chef in impeccably crisp garb was running about, not cooking. Not precisely not cooking. He seemed instead to be readying himself to cook. I was either much too early or much too late. The chef seemed unconcerned about my arrival.

Over here! a voice shouted at me. I turned. At the back of the kitchen, near a walk-in freezer, a plump man of late middle age sat on a bar stool. His pasty jowls sloughed from his cheekbones into the shirt collar of his crumpled casuals. His face seemed to be slowly dripping its weight down his throat like a lump of taffy on a pull. But two small bright eyes beamed out from the expanse of white, above his high ruddy cheeks. He was hunching over the work surface, eating an oatmeal mélange. Sticking out of his oatmeal was one crinkled sausage, nearly but not entirely erect, curving hopefully toward the pots hanging overhead. He popped up to wave me over and clanged his forehead on a saucepan, which crashed to the ground.

Oh, God, he said.

I restored the pot to its hook. He looked as though he felt I should be sorry. He rubbed his translucent pate.

Do you need some of this? He gestured toward his semi-phallic repast.

Did I miss breakfast?

Miss it?

Or are we both too early? I also have no idea what time it is.

It's half seven, he said.

Does that mean it's halfway after seven or halfway toward seven? I can never remember.

He shrugged at me, affably, and thrust out a hand. George Prawn, sufferer, he said.

I'm Helena.

I know. We were briefed on your fame. He settled back onto his stool.

How flattering.

No one eats in the dining room for breakfast. It isn't the custom. They all go to the café at the spa.

Ah. And so why aren't you at the spa?

I don't go there. All that massage going on around me makes me tense. I eat with Chef Anatole. He gestured toward the chef, who, in hearing his name, turned and nodded.

I didn't know the spa had a café.

You haven't read any of your brochures, I see. Of course, there's a café. A small one, but you know, there aren't that many of us at the moment.

Aren't there? The doctor led me to believe the whole of the house was booked up with trained sensitive personalities. He's got me in the barn.

I suppose the house is full, but there aren't that many of *us*. He lowered his voice. The guest sufferers, he whispered. There are so many of *them*! He gestured toward Chef Anatole, who scowled back over his shoulder.

Chefs? I asked. Yes, I think I saw another one sleeping in the corridor.

Chefs, domestics, nurses—the staff sufferers.

The staff are also suffering?

Everyone is suffering, he said with a jolly lilt.

I guess that shouldn't surprise me.

You're taking up valuable work surface, Prawn, said Chef Anatole. Do you want to eat something? Is that why you're here? he asked me.

If you can manage, I said. Or I can also just go to the spa, I suppose. I rarely eat, it's an afterthought.

That's very unfair on Anatole! said Prawn. And to me! he added, munching his sausage. You don't want the doctor to get the idea that our chef isn't necessary, he'll have to pack his bags. Wouldn't that be a shame? Back to the real world. The working world!

I have a contract, Chef Anatole shrugged.

That contract won't hold water, Prawn said.

OK, Prawn, time's up, said Anatole. He came closer to me, almost shoulder to shoulder, and lowered his dark lashes, and peered down my neckline. His hair was thick and dark, and pulled back from his face in a loose chignon, and he had the build of one of Corey's entourage, the one called Grisha. He had his fragrance as well, Bave Cèdres, that expensive men's eau de cologne, the fragrance of a forest floor. They all wore it, and Corey dripped in it. If they had been in a room within an hour, it was easy to tell. Where did they go after the accident? I wondered. Without him, did they evaporate? Or switch themselves off? It is hard to smell Bave Cèdres without smelling all of those others.

All of who? Anatole asked.

No one, I said. I must have been thinking aloud.

I had not seen any of Corey's set since the accident and had been afraid to ask too many questions about who was paying their tailors' bills now that Corey was gone. This chef must be an impostor, or a ghost—but a ghost of someone who was presumably still alive. Such a ghost, theoretically, would be dead only by association.

You're familiar, I accused him.

I'm overly familiar, Chef Anatole said softly to my cheekbone. I am going to make you a little hamper.

Have we met before?

He lifted his dark eyes: If we had met, I'm sure you would remember me. I'm memorable.

Be seeing you! shouted Prawn amiably, as Anatole hustled him out the swinging doors with his oatmeal bowl.

Do you like Bavarian breakfast? I was trained in Bavaria, Chef Anatole confided. For you, I've got a hot pretzel, he continued. And walking over to one of the doubled ovens, he pulled out a sheet of enormous bread plaits: long, swollen, and burnished. He gave one of them a brush of something waxen from a little pot so that it shone in the light, and then blasted it with a palm of salt, and wrapped it in parchment paper.

Nice, right? Perfect size, he said. But you need a little senf, he said, and drew out a small crockery with a wooden plunger. I make this myself. Taste! he said, and thrust the little wooden plunger toward my lips. I stuck out my tongue and received it. It was some kind of sweet mustard.

Right? he said. That's where it's at. Course but sweet? A little smokiness. A little woodiness from the hickory. Do you like a little wood in your mustard?

I had no response, stoppered as I was with the senf wand.

Or maybe you prefer some weisswurst? He wagged a pale sausage at me.

Fat and white. And soft, just like your friend Prawn?

Just the hamper, please, I said as I spit out the mustard depressor. You've been too kind.

Suit yourself, Anatole said, his shoulders slackened. He looked a little relieved. But take some honey. I keep the bees myself.

I'd like that, I said.

I have a lot of things you'd like, I bet.

I bet you do.

And don't go to that shit café. I am here for you, Anatole whispered.

I hate spas, I said, but I beat a hasty retreat into the tunnel. Another time, I thought. I made off with my hamper. I turned once in the stone tunnel, twice, but instead of coming out in the dining room, I hit a little door of pink glass, which popped open, and there stood the doctor, a tartan lap rug slung over his arm!

Your timing is impeccable, he said. Is that the smell of a piping hot Bavarian pretzel? I hope that is a hamper for two!

Doctor! I think I took a wrong turn in the tunnel.

No, you took the right turn in the kitchen. You came out by a different tunnel. He took my hamper and offered me his arm. Beyond the pink glass door, we were in the hallway immediately adjacent to the piano salon. I could hear someone butchering "Begin the Beguine." The doctor pulled the salon door shut with a crash.

Impossible, he said. To be making that racket at half seven! He led me through the library and snapped apart the brocade curtains. The French doors were already standing open.

I think the western lawn is what we are after, the doctor said, leading me out of the thick garden along a pebbled path. He spread out his lap rug on the grass. He kicked off his loafers and flopped. I settled in beside him.

Let me see, he said, flipping back the top of my hamper. Oh, perfect. Chef Anatole has taken excellent care of us. He pulled out the enormous pretzel, the mustard, and the honey pot.

Does Chef Anatole have a last name? He reminds me of someone.

I find surnames barbaric in that upstairs-downstairs context, Helena. It's feudal. Everyone at Jaquith House is on equal terms.

Should I call you by your first name, Doctor?

Well, that's an excellent question. But you began by calling me Dr. Duvaux, and so, I feel you set this precedent.

But I didn't know your first name when I met you, Doctor. Or may I say, Otto?

Didn't you, Helena? Did you really learn nothing about myself and my practice and the methods of Jaquith House?

I don't like to over-prepare.

Given our proposed time frame, the glistening surface is quite enough for us to start with. But I do hope we can speak about your films. After the accident, it must have been very hard to return to the studio with all those memories.

I always film on location, so the studio means very little to me.

No, I don't mean your own memories—of course you will also have your memories, your other films, your liaisons. These are immaterial to locations. We carry these memories with us at all times. Yes, we might avoid certain places of pain and seek out safe havens, new and unblemished, to escape our memories for short periods—our carefully constructed domestic lives, our travels to other locales, these are merely distractions from the terrain of the mind.

You make it sound like the world is entirely made up.

For some more than others, I fear. Perhaps the studio is similar: so many different worlds coming together in one location, so many quiet escapes.

No, it's very boring. It just absorbs.

Do you resent being constrained to the studio?

I never imagined, given the way I've built my career, that I would end up in the studio, and if that is all that is left—serial plots, green screens, digital flourish. I want no part of that.

You are a woman of great strength of will. If you demand things, you'll be able to find your own way of proceeding.

What, work with actors again? That ship has sailed.

I do think we might think about *the way* you worked with actors.

Tabloid exaggerations and base innuendo!

I mean the methods, the controlling methods.

I have often wondered how it can even be said of a woman that she is a tyrant—it can, it has been, along with so many other things that are more frequently said about a woman, a hysterical bitch, a true cunt, she fucked her way into power, or she was born rich and had it all given to her, or she was an Eve Harrington clawing through her rivals, amoral, immoral, a vicious cunt, but a lucky cunt. It has all been said, of course, all that could be said has been said, but I stopped hearing it; I simply put down any receiver to the opinions of the world. My tyranny came hand in hand with a blissful silence. Dead air, static, the radio tuned to a distant shore. And it was through this, Helena Désir was forged. Yes, there have been problems with actors. Problems with actors are perpetual: their neediness, or their fragile egos. If I thought about their troubles too much I would never finish anything. You can't let this sort of thing undermine your vision.

It is a wonder you worked with men at all.

It is a wonder. But then something happens, and you see them in a certain slant of light, and the fire is rekindled, and you are back on the set, camera in hand, trying to bring them under rein. Their solid bodies and delightfully empty heads.

They were just objects?

Doctor, the camera objectifies. I'm just the messenger.

Power is so rarely at its zenith if it is visible. Perhaps you brought out something special in your actors?

I doubt they would agree.

Then perhaps they brought out something special in you?

I doubt I would agree.

You see yourself as an island. But I wonder if this is ever how art such as yours works. There are so many movable parts.

Yes. My crew, my actors, my technicians, my movable parts.

And your last actor, was he a movable part?

Corey always returned to me, so we had that.

It was a love affair—surely, that was a factor?

Not in our field. You see, Doctor, you work in close quarters for long periods where you are also isolated and where emotions run high. There is also something about the way every aspect of the real world empties out. These are not romantic entanglements, they are part of the terrain, like the catering buffet or a drafty trailer.

Did you ever worry you would cross a line?

You can't show fear to a dog!

And did he show fear to you?

Everyone showed fear—it was in the contract. Doctor, I came up through the ranks, and I have connections. But that, too, is play-acting. I am not maternal. When asked what I think, I give my unvarnished opinion.

Only that? I am just trying to find my way into Corey's shoes for a moment, to see you through his eyes. I am trying to decide if you are quite the tyrant you imagine yourself to be. At the heart of tyranny is fear.

Delightful platitude, Doctor. No one in my industry is sure of anything. Filmmaking is a nest of insecurity and paranoia.

I'm sure you offered all your actors excellent counsel.

I counseled Corey from a place of unblinking honesty. If anyone wanted him, what did they want him for? For his looks! Which were in fact excessive, precisely *excessive*. In a typical sort of film, he risked coming off unnatural, a manikin. In my kind of film, his looks worked on behalf of brutality; they were their own cruel weapon, and they had their own fluidity, their own androgyny. They made him *l'homme fatal*. He was *l'homme / la femme fatale*. I felt I owned his face, but we do grow tired of the things we own.

You planned to part ways?

I planned to let him go at the end of every film. And then there would be another film, another seduction. But now we've come to the end of it, and I think that is evidence enough. It had been quite a career, Doctor, until the boat.

A career is not the same as a vocation, Helena, it is not even the same as an occupation. We can shape, create even, vocations. But a career has a life of its own. The more you try to direct it, the less it is likely to comply.

I'm not stupid, Doctor. I know you can't build an artistic career like you build a house.

What an interesting notion. How does one build a house? Do you know that we've had to rework the balconies of the Syllabary twice since I began at Jaquith House? Rather pricey and difficult renovations. Not to do with any compromise in their structures, mind you, but to allow for the expansion of the tree they surround. So, I'm not even sure one builds a house in the way one builds a house, Helena. Not a distinct house. Not a house like Jaquith House.

What would be the point in trying to return me to film? There is no longer a place there. I don't mean for me, I mean for film—no place for it. I was always a niche market—my time was limited. But the death of film—that's more final. I don't want to make things people watch on a treadmill or a screen the size of a filet mignon. Film used to be the place, and it was unimpeachable. A dark room, completely silent, no access to the outside world, completely inside the fantasy. People don't even watch in the dark anymore! Even without the accident, I wonder if I would have done another film. Yes, I might have done something with a camera and an actor, but it wouldn't have been film.

What about the option you mentioned? You clearly had that in mind for the future before the accident.

I was buying time, and making a compromise. The studio's hope for a commercial return of the auteur. Suffice to say, it would never have worked. Will never have worked.

Are you struggling with time orientation, Helena?

Always, and never, Doctor. If you can get me sleeping again, or not sleeping again, that will be enough. Sleeping when I am supposed to sleep and not sleeping when I am not supposed to sleep, within reason. And the talking, Doctor. It has to stop.

The strong silent type, Helena?

Just a little peace, for myself, even if for no one else.

Goals! Marvelous! Not impediments, Helena, goals. My day-to-day is filled almost completely with patterns of resistance. You are already my favorite pupil! I should give you an apple. No, it's you who gives me an apple. The favorite student gives the teacher an apple. He bit into his plait. I offered him the honey pot. I received into my claw.

I really shouldn't, he said, patting his midsection. I'm reducing.

You're the picture of health, Doctor.

Am I? Oh, perhaps. But our bodies are sometimes in our minds, and not the other way around. But as regards your sleeping, how do you find your rooms?

All the things you said.

Yes, yes, but did you sleep in them?

I really couldn't say.

Oh, my. Well, I really couldn't say either. So, we are at an impasse on that front. What could you say, do you think, about the passage of the night?

All the sounds seem to change.

Change?

Change positions. Sounds coming from one place are suddenly coming from a different place. Sounds that are there are suddenly not, and then other sounds appear. I don't know. Do you want me to keep some sort of notebook, Doctor?

There's no need to pander.

I'm not on the set anymore. But I still have little rituals. Quotidian practices, like notebooks.

We'll talk about your films. It's really just selfish on my part. I'm quite a fan. Yes, I'm quite starstruck in your presence. But I won't forget myself, Helena. Ah, but what's this? he said, and turned the hamper up to show me its interior: nestled inside was a crystal decanter filled with liquid of the palest pink, stoppered with faceted ruby glass. Kirsch! he exclaimed. Oh, I can see you are going to be one of Chef Anatole's favorites.

He's a friendly type, I said.

Yes. He suffers in that regard. We have to try not to overindulge him, if you catch my meaning.

I catch it.

His ethical nonmonogamy is both a blessing and a curse to our community.

As far as I am concerned, I'm on the wagon. I think. Curiously, do you treat all your staff?

My ego is starting to suffer a certain blow, Helena. I don't think you really appreciate the situation you are in. We really never need staff at Jaquith House. There are more than enough individuals who are desirous—ecstatic, really—to participate in this community, so much so that they put their skills and their enormous talents on offer.

And the guests? The guest sufferers?

Obviously, some pay, Helena. Some situations, such as yours, call for simplicity in that relationship. But some of our community is involved in a healing practice that includes sharing their talents with others.

I think I'd better pay. I'm not really in a position to share my talents, whatever is left of them.

Well, of course, Helena, from each within his means, you know, and I know your means are considerable, so I certainly intend to hold you to it. But don't worry.

Simplicity, Doctor?

You see? Everything is coming together, he said, and poured me a small goblet of kirsch. Oh, heavens. I've got to go.

But I didn't have a chance to ask about the tapestry.

Tapestry?

I'll save it for later. And, Doctor, was that our little chat for the day?

It was a little chat, yes, but Helena, do you think I have punctuated your thinking? If so, you should try to meditate on that punctuation.

Thank you, then, Doctor.

For what?

For the picnic.

A pleasure, he said, and kicked himself back into his loafers and loped off across the grass as I sipped my kirsch with the sun steadily creeping up behind me.

9

THE TROUBLE WITH ACTORS, REPRISE

The first time I filmed on a boat was for a short escape scene in *The Tightening Knot*, my second film, in which the hustler Calloway, played by David Trevor, is pursued by two detectives. Calloway boards a small fishing boat as it sets out to sea. The harbor is rough, the sky overcast, the chop of the sea tosses the little fishing boat. Throwing off his coat, the hustler Calloway makes a quick change into a soiled fisherman's sweater and a woven cap. He settles himself on a coil of rope. The other fishermen on the boat, who are Greek, do not fully understand him, but they are intuitively aware of a sinister code that ties him to them, and so say nothing when the detectives pull alongside in a launch and board the fishing boat. Calloway takes a pipe from the mouth of one of the sailors and begins to smoke it—however, he holds it upside-down, to prevent the spray from entering the bowl. The detectives examine each man closely. Calloway leans into the knee of another fisherman, leans into this other man's body. Pausing in front of Calloway in his disguise, the detectives examine him intently as he releases a puff of smoke from the inverted bowl, which curls back over his right shoulder. His ability to simply melt into this other form, the form of the fisherman, makes the ruse a success.

In that case, the boat was in a protected harbor, with some mechanical tinkering to generate the sea spray. I was, by that time, *with* the studio, but the studio had given me basically nothing to work with, and had little confidence in me, despite the success of *Mechanism*. If I had stuck with Emile, my haggard little acrobat, perhaps they would have had more confidence. Instead, here I was with David Trevor, a British stage actor who was utterly unknown to filmgoers and who had been in two films only, and worse still, European films. I was out on a short leash with *The Tightening Knot*.

It came off all right, ultimately, it looked good enough in the editing booth, concentrated on Trevor's face, giving off a breezy elegance, with the slight indication of dimples, which we had to work very hard with, lighting-wise.

At the time, I was enamored with the effect of Trevor's face clouded in the smoke from the bowl of the inverted pipe. We had not yet begun to fight in the ways that would characterize our future together: vicious quips, insults, double entendre. Leave it to David to bring the lexicon of Noël Coward into a tawdry farce. Once such a performance begins, it is hard to ever leave it behind. Alone, we were often something else, but that, too, is hard to explain. There was never a question of my control, or lack thereof, over my story, as there had been with Emile. David was hopelessly, cloyingly, in need of direction. But once given direction, was never convinced. He was without trust. All that confidence, that bravura I'd seen in the bar that first night, went straight out the window the minute he was cast in *The Tightening Knot*. He could be confident of his sex appeal and totally unselfconscious, but only in bed. Out of bed, he was a neurotic mess.

Watching the rushes together for his boat scene as Calloway:

Did you really need to hire the most handsome Greeks? The extras upstage me.

They don't.

You've only got my bad side. And what have you done with it?

His dimples had been obscured, his eyes dulled. What I saw was mean, moody, and brooding. I was hopeful.

David said, It looks like steam is coming out of my ear.

That's what you see? That's not what I see. It's a solid delivery, I said.

It's not the delivery I'm thinking about, it's the head. It doesn't even look like my head. Can we fix the hairline?

I don't know what to tell you. It is your head. Stop thinking about your head. Think about your delivery.

I am thinking about my delivery. I'm always thinking about my delivery. I'm classically trained, classically indoctrinated. I can't order a coffee without thinking about my delivery. You're not going to say "Trust me, David," I hope. You say "Trust me, David," and I want to go out and fuck a whore, instantly.

Look at this, I said. It's as if there's a bruise on your cheekbone growing out of the shadows of your eye. We've finally got your mouth lines in order. They're masked on the left side very well.

Like Bell's palsy at work. On my last film they filled me in with some sort of rubbery plaster to prevent my mouth lines. They said my mouth lines age me tremendously. And I was still in my twenties then! They asked me to get plastic surgery. On my own dime! They also said not to move my mouth *at all*, or they'd have me in the role of the pedophile uncle. Then they taped down one of my ears because it comes up too much.

Your ear? Your ear is perfect.

I had it fixed. It's better than perfect. Luckily, I was going on at Clifton Terrace as Marat, so I had to have my head in bandages anyway. I know you hate this.

I do hate this, David.

Just talk me through it, again, Helena. Are we even working with a plot here?

"Talk me through it, Helena." It was a constant litany on the set, in the car, in the hotel in Athens, even on the beach in Cyprus, where I had fled under a canvas umbrella, to think about the hustler Calloway. I had to clear my mind completely to conjure up Calloway and try to resolve whatever fiasco was going on with him. All those stories that Emile had offered me night after night when we were working on *Mechanism*—I was now conditioned to seek out the even darker narratives lurking in the past for my already dark characters. I was mining for trauma. My head was deep into storyboards, the rewrites, the correction of the stills, but I had only to raise my eyes, and David jogged out of the water to demand sympathy. Dripping and glistening in snug black trunks, freckled across his molded shoulders, the auburn hair on his thighs lit like the threads in a crystal chandelier: this was the body I had requisitioned in his original contract, the specifications of which my production had paid for to give Calloway his shape. David, who had naturally the slender build of a tennis player, wasn't allowed a scrap of food that wasn't chemically ensured to maintain his new physique—I had to employ someone to follow him at the set buffet. Also, he wore a wristwatch that alerted me if he missed even a minute of his prescribed workouts. And I had not done all this just so that his body could be photographed by giggling tourists while he jostled and pitched in the sand, demanding sympathy: Helena, can you talk me through this bit where Calloway awakens from a nightmare? Helena, walk me through, just once more, this thing about his memory of the gas lamp? Helena, a recap on this part where the buttons are torn from his shoulder exposing his scars...

The bickering that followed, the cat fights on the set, the vicious things we so gleefully said to each other. I admit it: parts of it were fun. And by now, it was second nature. But such diversions are ultimately undermining. I had no doubt the project would succeed—David was charm itself on screen. But was he the hustler Calloway, in a silent and brutal passage across a nihilist hellscape?

In short, would it be my film?

When the reviews did come through for *The Tightening Knot* they were in unanimous alignment: "David Trevor cuts a dash in heroic theater roles, but he is in more splendid form here as Calloway, the idealist who is passionately in love with life, but haunted with guilt about his own bloody part in this criminal revenge tragedy..." and "Trevor swaggers round the screen with panache, but also discovers quieter moments of tenderness and fear, that convey a touching, flawed humanity..." and finally, "Under Désir's famously *intimate* tutelage, David Trevor bursts forth. He fills Calloway with his own charisma and brings out the character's central contradiction: he both seeks to defy death and surrender to it."

And so there it was: back to the drawing board.

Therefore, Corey.

Corey, my third. My last actor.

I was on a great lull after David Trevor, after we finished our second film, *Slipcase*, in which he played the gambler Doryan. David was threatening to sue me, to sue the studio if he wasn't given the lead in this new film. He claimed he had been instrumental in the development of the concept. Our fights had spilled over into my hiatus, and even when we parted ways, it seemed we never completely parted. David was impossible this way: no matter how angry he was, he was always ready to hop into bed, even if he emerged swearing and threatening me, as if he had never drawn breath. But I had struggled so completely with the gambler Doryan and struggled so completely with David Trevor, that at times I wondered if I shouldn't retire from the profession that I had barely begun. I had come into the writing of *Walkway* under duress from the studio, who actually was thrilled with the results of *The Tightening Knot* and even more thrilled with the results of *Slipcase*. They pushed me directly into *Walkway* before the script was even beginning to crystalize in my mind.

As I worked as quickly as possible on *Walkway*, I felt each moment was the same as the last: an unbearable fragility was piercing the surface of the gangster Talbot. I feared that whatever had happened with Trevor had conditioned me toward the temptation to create something human from something otherwise less than human. That less-than-human thing was somehow more desirable to me: it was toughness and exactitude. The script for *Walkway* demanded toughness in the way a film like *Mechanism* demanded toughness, but where would that element reside? The studio wanted the kind of cool elegant toughness that sold Rolexes and men's perfume. The minute he begins to speak, it is compromised. I knew both my types had missed the mark. I knew with each film I was going backward, moving further away from the place where toughness and exactitude were quartered. I was perhaps less manly than I imagined, and I would not stand for that.

But things clipped along with the script, and before I knew it we had moved into casting, which was going spectacularly bad. The first day of auditions was hopeless, and we were well into the second day when I started to think it was best to halt the process. The scene was, in retrospect, too difficult for a casting test: it required sharpening a small knife on a whetting stone, and then cutting a piece of overripe pear. I didn't mention the pear's ripeness; I wondered if an actor could recognize a very ripe pear and recognize the effect of slicing a very ripe pear. My actor could not recoil from a pear in a way that suggested unfamiliarity with pears (though he could perhaps recoil from it *on principal* against its ripeness), and I wasn't interested in working with an actor who I would have to teach about pears, because pears would just be the beginning, and I had been there before, with David Trevor.

In the scene, Talbot retches, or nearly retches, and speaks a story from his childhood about a paper bag of pears that his father had gathered from the ground of a neighbor's yard. The pears were infested with worms, but the boy's father insisted that he eat them, in any case, and this is my character's memory, stuffing his face with the wormy pears, the feel of the worms in his mouth, retching and being forced to swallow, et cetera. In the audition, Talbot would wear a driving jacket, a brimmed cap, and dark glasses.

The script was rough, and the character needed to be found in the actor. How little could be said? Could the scene be managed without the word "pear"? Without the word "worm"? What about the word "bag"? I felt it was necessary to obscure these clichés so the true trauma might shine through. Otherwise, it risked sentimentality, and I would collapse the project.

After the first few actor auditions, I knew that the lines had been written without much instinct. I was lacking a muse.

I would finish out the day of auditions, of course, and avoid the conflict of confessing myself to the gathered staff.

It came time to see Corey, and I anticipated the worst event yet, another Trevor, or something even more blithe than Trevor. I had been briefed on his first few films: smaller roles for rakish playboys in varsity colors, a derelict nephew, a disgraced fraternity brother, the perpetual graduate. His only lines had been whistles or catcalls. I didn't have to see them, I knew all the tropes. He stumbled in mid-scene, sweating and wearing tennis whites, or toweling off and dripping in swim trunks, and then he draped himself over a sofa as if he was part of the scenery, and glanced knowingly at all the women under fifty, who then glanced knowingly at each other, as over a shared secret, or nervously, at each other, as if finally figuring something out, or territorially at each other, et cetera. Coming in through a window in snow-sprit evening clothes, before uttering a one-liner, something like, "Pardon me, darling, but the Jag is on fire."

"Pardon me, darling" was just the sort of lightness the studio imagined could be forcibly infused throughout *Walkway* to commercial effect, in the same way that the studio thought David Trevor's dimples gave a certain charm to the hustler Calloway, that softened his character and made him relatable, in the same way they thought Emile Laval's heavy lashes lent his face a certain vulnerability. If the studio got their way, I imagined, Corey as the gangster Talbot would walk on in the second scene carrying a polo stick saying "Hello, girls."

But then he arrived. And what was immediately clear was that he was none of the things I imagined he would be.

What he was, however, was no less constructed, no less spectacle. He was an entirely invented creature.

He was escorted by that small and somber entourage of young men I came to know so well, in their tight-fitted trousers, dress sneakers, and striped sport coats in smoky tones, the type described in *Gentlemen's Quarterly* as aubergine or kohl. With them came a cloud of that potent herbal cologne, the smell of a forest floor, Bave Cèdres. They wore their shirts open at the collar, with no jewelry, some were bearded and wore long hair twisted into a knot on the top of their heads, as was the trend of that era, or had heads shaved only half way up to a luxurious dark line, and they were all sleek and sculpted and deadly silent as they poured in around him and filled up the waiting area, making the otherwise sterile office space suddenly look like a nightclub in Corsica or a Croatian soccer team. Corey himself wore an expensive suit in a similar fashion, a silk scarf, and dark glasses, which he quickly corrected with the driving jacket and brimmed cap of the gangster Talbot. As he introduced himself to me, he paused over my hand, almost as though he were about to bring it forward to his trembling lips. Would he click his heels, I wondered? I stepped back from him and crossed my arms and leaned into my midsection, the fearsome, hunched posture I'd learned from working with Emile, and dressed as I was, a little like Clark Gable at the bookies' in my starched black shirt and tie, cufflinks and tie bar, and pleated high trousers, I was braced for a fight, and I looked at him over half glasses. It communicated that I wasn't to be trifled with. He seemed not to notice.

Corey had the pages—those nascent, ill-imagined, ill-wrought verbal stumblings that constituted my early skeleton of the gangster Talbot—already curled in his manicured fist. I had never been so convinced of the complete failure of a project before it was begun as I was in those moments before Corey began the pear scene from *Walkway*.

And then what happened, happened, even as I look back at it from this staggering distance and through all this water, he did what I couldn't imagine—which is to say, very little indeed. He handled the pocketknife convincingly, but not exaggeratedly. As he cut into the fruit, he showed no reaction to the pear's ripeness, and when he retched, he retched blankly, only to eat the pear in any case. He used the lines I had written but drew them out between downward glances and silent pauses. The scene emerged flat and humdrum. Already, he had improved it noticeably.

As I watched, I considered his stealth. He feigned insensitivity with such ease, and he seemed nearly hollow, and it was as though the surface of the gangster Talbot was a murky one, something impossible to penetrate, but once penetrated, offered up nothing further than misunderstanding and confusion. But he, Corey, knew a bit more of the surface perhaps than I yet did, and the depths plunged revealed it all the more shallow, vapid, seemingly inconsequential. When we had finished, he looked at me, his chin over his left shoulder, his sunglasses slightly lowered, his eyes square at my chest.

Wouldn't you like to adjust me? he asked.

No, I said. No, you are fine as you are. Do you like the scene?

The pear is very good, the lines were very short and enigmatic. Should I run them again?

I inquired, Do you like the lines?

Yes. I like Talbot, the gangster, the assassin.

What is it you see in this character Talbot? I asked.

I see something of myself.

Sure. How would you describe that thing that is like yourself?

I can't articulate it. It is just that I understand this character, although much is enigmatic about him.

It is enigmatic because I haven't written it. I haven't figured it out.

Oh. Perhaps this is why it is so good.

Maybe. But it will have to be written, won't it? Eventually? I said.

You must forgive me, but I don't bother too much about this type of thing. There are so many events that construct themselves absolutely before the eyes without our questioning their origins. Like atmospheric barriers. Like the fog completely consuming the body of the Tian Tan Buddha, and only his hand or his finger is visible, even though he is over a hundred feet tall, seated.

Is that some kind of spiritual metaphor?

Not at all. I am talking about walking down the mountain and I am thinking about the smaller monasteries, of course, Po Lam and Lo Han.

I don't follow.

The smaller ones down the slope of the mountain, not, of course, that huge amusement park at the top of the mountain. The smaller monasteries where if the monks want to walk to an urban location it is an hour either up the mountain or down the mountain. You can't bring a car up those paths. They are often washed out. There are enormous carvings there, the heart sutras. Have you heard of them?

Vaguely.

There is mist as you go down toward the bottom of the mountain. Always partly hidden and then suddenly so——. That calligraphy is—I can't speak of it. The walk takes about four hours. I did it recently with my friends: Bhutor, Chaz, Valasquez, Grisha. He motioned behind him to the members of his entourage, who nodded in agreement.

Are we speaking about the gangster Talbot? I asked.

Aren't we?

I am asking how you will play the part.

I would play the part as you would.

As I would?

As you would have me play it.

The moment was vital. I kept him in the office for several hours and rewrote the pear-bag scene as it stands currently in *Walkway*.

I had given up David Trevor, and I was set to discover something now with Corey. But I'm no fool. I entered with trepidation, suspicion.

That night was one of many to come together, even as his entourage hovered in the hotel bar.

You want the part very badly, I said.

I want it more than anything.

Tell me why?

It is what I am. The world will finally see me.

If we are going to do this, I will need your complete agreement, I said.

And for me, what is exchanged?

If you can agree to this, you will have the full power of my artistic vision, the strength of my name in the industry, and I will make you into something unique.

A star?

Stars are meaningless. I will make you iconic. Singular. But it will require your submission.

Surely, you already know you will have it.

I have had some trouble with actors in the past. Arguments, debates. Personal lives. Career aspirations. My films are particular. Brutal, violent, unblinking. I won't have them airbrushed by a playboy. And I need to know that I will have your absolute focus. There is no past. You have no past before this moment. Whatever else you might imagine matters in this world, you will leave it at the door when you enter my project.

I am without ego.

I must be sure that you will consent to anything I ask. Will you consent to anything?

There will be no question.

Everything, every detail will be in my hands. Your clothes, your hair, the circumference of your waist, the tilt of your head. And you will remain in character.

I am a method actor.

The realization of my vision is all that matters.

You will have my complete obedience.

Never forget, I said.

And so began our journey.

10

SCOUTING LOCATION, LAGOON

She was huddled there in a reclining chair—the young girl in the oversized sweatshirt from the previous evening—now free from her sweatshirt. There was a line of lounges turned toward the pool. She was small but curved and neatly formed in her black bandeau and her tiny shorts. But there was something about her face. It was as if a large but very faint birthmark crossed half of it at an angle. It was hard to say which half of her face was the normative half and which the aberrant. In all other regards it was a very pretty face. If all of her face had been either one thing or the other, it would have looked perfectly on trend. As it stood, the two faces side by side did each other no favors. Dark hair hung over her shoulder, and she tugged at it nervously with one hand, while staring into a novel in her lap. I lay down in a neighboring chaise longue with intention. She slunk a bit more into her book. This was all new to me: this taking in people who were not in my lens or on my screen, or who would not soon be in my lens or on my screen.

The sun was suddenly very strong and pleasant overhead. The bossa nova played on a little old-fashioned radio in the tiki bar that opened up from the pool house. Its awning jutted out with thatched fronds. Behind the bar a tall, burnished gent of about forty in tennis whites was making an espresso in a gleaming red machine. He gave a wave to me and showed me a cup. His head was festooned with dark curls, which dropped over his darker bedroom eyes and their thick lashes. It was going to be hard to stay on the wagon at Jaquith House.

From the patio of the pool house one could overlook the grounds, the little flower gardens and coiling pathways, and the long drive, all the way to the vegetable gardens, the large pond, the small pond, and the electric gate in the distance. Anyone coming and going from Jaquith House could be easily spotted from this panopticon. I could also see the edge of the trees, the fine line of the electrified fence, and the apple orchards in the distance.

I'm Helena, I announced. Helena! A part of me suddenly felt compelled to shout my name until someone acknowledged me.

She looked up. I'm Tina. Oh, it's very nice to meet you, she said, but put her head down again, shielded in her hair. Did the doctor send you up here to find me?

No, I—no. I'm new, I just arrived.

I thought I was the only one left, she said. I used to be in a group, but now there's no group. I hate to upset the doctor, though. I'm nearly twenty-six, and I know my own mind very well. I live in the Mod.

The Mod?

I can't stand the way the common room comes to a point. It makes me very nervous. It isn't very well designed.

Comes to a point?

Built into a circle with a central courtyard. Each room is like a slice of pie.

Is it a dormitory?

It's like a halfway house. It's more for outpatients. But there aren't any these days.

A language unto itself, I said.

She gestured toward her face: It isn't always totally like this. I mean it wasn't always like this. I went to school for a while, but now I'm on leave. I feel like I can't express myself like this. I think it is very important to be yourself and express yourself the way you do naturally. Don't you think so?

Naturally.

I was staying with my mother, but she finds me difficult. It was her space. In many ways a nice space, but still not mine. It made me difficult to live with. This—she gestured again to her face—is just the latest aspect. Now I'm difficult to look at as well. I used to take pills, which did nothing. But the doctor, maybe you know this, prefers for us not to take pills. To take pills would be a breach of his trust. Do you take pills?

I have taken a lot of pills in my life—but not out of distrust.

Dominick had a problem with opiates. That's why he's here, I think. She gestured to dark head behind the espresso machine.

I thought he was the tennis pro.

He is.

He shares his talents like the chef.

Yes, but he's also really rich. He grew up in Monaco.

Do you share your talents, Tina?

All I ever really wanted was to be the absolute best at one thing, just like virtuosic at one thing. I *can* be popular. But I am just *not* popular. I really want to be surrounded by interesting, dedicated people and not airheads. That's the problem.

I used to work with actors, I said.

High expectations. I've always had them. I just can't wait any longer, because I'm getting older, and this—she gestured toward her face—is making it impossible to just do the thing I need to do.

Did you want to be in pictures?

I really tried, but where do you start?

Oh my God, that was just a wild guess. I didn't really think you wanted to be an actress.

Actor. Or model. But I have this impostor syndrome thing. I would need to come out at the top of my game.

Virtuoso.

I tried photography for a bit, but—

Too technical?

I don't think my camera is very good. Plus, it feels wrong to take pictures of everyone. Do you like to talk about cameras?

I like cameras. I don't like to talk about them.

I definitely need a better lens. Don't you think it is absolutely essential that our art expresses our goals toward global betterment?

I don't.

You don't think politics matter?

I've heard it said that, at best, art might hold up a mirror to something, that it might expose something to view that was otherwise just out of reach, and that might be toward progress.

Did a man say that?

Almost certainly.

But expression is important, don't you agree?

No. I don't care for these trends. All this need to express. It leads to sentiment, and a skewed account.

Who says?

Documentarians, I think.

Do you know many documentarians?

A few too many.

Since I've been here I haven't really done much to express myself. I write, of course. I've always been writing.

Now there's an excellent field. You don't need any special equipment. It's very cheap.

Are you trying to hurt my feelings deliberately, or are you just super insensitive?

The latter, I've been told. But probably the former, as well. Let me be clear: I think I've been being positive. You see, you don't have to have any sort of special face to be a writer. I write things. My face never comes into it. Sometimes I wish it did. My face was always on my side.

It probably does, and you aren't aware of it. I think maybe that was why the doctor sent you up here.

The doctor didn't send me up here. If anything, the doctor told me to stay away from up here.

I studied art, but it was too much. Film is the same. It just put me off.

It's off-putting. I wouldn't recommend it, I said.

Were you subject to the casting couch?

I own the casting couch.

How did you manage in the beginning? You're a woman, obviously.

Am I, obviously? I was just there with my camera.

But you somehow got famous.

What an accusation!

I think professional women find other women threatening.

I think that is the sort of thing that gets said. Maybe by a mother? I never had one, so I was blessedly free to get on in the world.

Do you think faces matter?

I think faces do matter. Bodies matter as well—an even less popular notion.

Don't you think that's sort of awful, like, as an industry?

We go to the pictures to look. Sometimes at a desert or at an explosion. More often at faces. I didn't make up the rules.

But don't you think I would make a good actor, if not for the face?

I don't know. I've never understood anything about actors.

But you make films? I saw one in school: about the war prisoners.

The war picture? Someone showed you the war picture? On purpose?

It was good, but I wish I understood about the ending.

You and me both. If you like dancers, you should see my first picture. It was called *Mechanism*. There is a very good dancer in that picture, and a good actor, quite an unusual face. Virtuosic.

I'm sorry to be so aggressive, but it's just my personality.

Forget it, I said.

What will you do now, then? If you are giving up film?

Did I say that? Out loud?

I thought so.

Nothing, probably. For as long as I can afford to do nothing.

Don't you think that's sad?

Not in the least. Anyway, Tina, it's been a pleasure, but I must be on my way.

I think you are supposed to stay with me, and be my group.

Unlikely, Tina.

No, I can tell you are my group. I'll stay with you.

I'm not your group, I said, I am no one's group!

And I left my coffee untouched and strode with purpose down the hillside.

11

WALKWAY

When I remember those early days on the set of *Walkway,* I am pleased, and I am calmed. It was little more than sixty days together, filmed in Buenos Aires. The weather was extremely mild, even if the driving conditions were dismal. Corey was so affable. His manner was winning across the board, and those who had been loyal to David immediately yielded. Emile was already a distant memory, that is how easily allegiances shift in our profession. We were all getting along well, for the first time in my career, and we were growing in numbers, so there were more personalities to sustain, but more people sustaining them, and more people handling the tedium of the operation. The studio was with us rather than against us, I thought wrongly, but I thought it and believed it, and so a rose hue imbued all of those sixty days in Buenos Aires, this lull in the storm of Helena Désir.

But I knew that I was having trouble articulating what I wanted, and I was being somewhat indecisive, which caught me off guard. I fatigued Corey on these first days dressing him up like a doll and posing him for test shots. I was a new me, I thought, a new Helena, determined to lavish attentions on my latest pet. (It bespoke a kind of feminine vanity that I'd be charged with later in the tabloids.) At that time, it was a problem I blamed on the fact of having only just finished the editing on *Slipcase*, the story of Doryan, the gambler, a safe-cracker and a soldier returning from the war in Europe, shell-shocked, with a wooden leg, adrift in the metropolis. It was a terrible film. The problem with *Slipcase* was a problem with David Trevor.

Helena, where are you going with all this?

Why do I keep returning to David Trevor, when, of course, this is the story of those blissful sixty days in Buenos Aires with Corey? Is this once again the problem with actors, that they flow together and blend so effortlessly that you cannot think of the story of one without the story of another? Another face, another body, an other, on the opposite side of the lens.

Especially in consideration of the editing of those two films I did with David, I came to know his face so well, to think of it often, to deal with it in all its difficulties. This is the true intimacy of the transparent eyeball, no longer behind the lens, but in the editing booth. There you have only a face or a body to consider, rendered flatly on the screen. Whatever words are flying out of the mouth and head of the vapid actor as he jostles and demands sympathy, all of that is cleared away as you follow his face: what the lens allows, and what the editor eliminates. What the lens ignores, and the illusions the editor creates. When the editing of one film falls swiftly upon the filming of another, sometime this afterimage, this trace, this ghost is not yet ready for exorcism.

And to be fair, David off the set, when he could get out of his head, was fun. He was up for anything, anywhere, anytime. But I was a professional, and so off the set meant very little to me.

When I looked at Corey in his overcoat and dark glasses in those first few days in Buenos Aires, his mustache darkened, his skin tanned from the beaches at Mar Azul, it wasn't his face that I was seeing. There was the ghost, the afterimage of another face. The flecked and lined face of David Trevor, threatening at any moment to dimple—cool and polished in profile, structured and gaunt without mustache, Victorian with mustache—his mouth parenthetically creased, his lips in a signature purse, somewhere between smirk and pout: in short, all things that had to be got around, or managed. Certainly, they couldn't entirely be got around, or I had not yet taught myself the necessity of getting around them, instead I let myself indulge Trevor's face too much, and for this reason *The Tightening Knot* and *Slipcase* were little more than David Trevor's face. David Trevor's face above the high, cabled neck of a fisherman's damp sweater, smoked with coal from the boat's stack, against a steely sky, removing a scrap of tobacco from the tip of his tongue. Trevor's face in war flashbacks, green-gray eyes under auburn brows, emerging from below a snugly fit officer's cap, chin resting confidently on the fleece collar of his flight jacket, fringed in the white silk of an aviator's scarf. Or, later, as the ruined gambler Doryan, unshaven, in the midst of the heist, flask in trembling gloved hands, held to lips pressed thin and bloodless, brow furrowed into deep brackets slipping down into sunken, debauched eyes, pupils shrunken to needle points, darting peripherally, wordless, mouth reduced to uttering little more than sharp intakes of breath, which are truncated, as though about to speak, he stops himself, stops even his breath. Or as best I can remember. This was the face of David Trevor, the face I had given up in favor of Corey.

When I began my story in pictures, there by the sea, as a tough little thing, an eyeball in becoming, with my little camera and that steady line of muses in the background of my uncle's boat, I already had a clear understanding of the parade of exchangeable bodies on display for art's sake. If I felt something like lust it was for the water beyond my lens. Projection! This is how the confusion began.

David, of course, when he found out I had cast Corey in *Walkway*, left me in an infantile rage, saying anything he could think to say, as vulgarly as he could think to say it in the press. He went forward with his lawsuit. The quiet static of my off-shore radio signal was temporarily shattered with David's airing of the dirtiest imaginable laundry. Even my buffers in the crew couldn't curtail the influx of publicity. Which, of course, delighted the studio. The innuendos of my involvement with David ceased to be snide hints or subtle suggestions, and my new renown was born. There was no lying low from this. I had to take this tide with me into *Walkway*.

And so I found myself, in Buenos Aires, with this next face, a new set of problems. Only it became quickly clear these problems did not exist. The ease that was Corey was dizzying.

In the few brief hours before midnight, when filming for the day was done, and I had finally let the crew, looking worn and battered, retire to their tourist cabanas or their fruit-laden cocktails, and after I had put in those few minutes with everyone together, those essential minutes of equilibrium in which all of us were on the same plane on the same mission, radically equal, the new Helena, those few exhausting minutes of laughing, talking, pretending to enjoy each other's company when we were all so tired and so fixated on our own concerns.

After this was done, when I wanted nothing more in the world than to be alone in my small cabana with a historical novel and a flask of whiskey, it was then that Corey shed his entourage and took me out driving. And while I could barely keep my eyes open—in those days of the ease of sleep—I knew we were only a few hours away from resuming filming, I rode along with him in his ridiculous rented sports car, along the Avenida de Mayo, where the glaring neon script over the café awnings spoke volumes to both of us about the tawdry grace of the world of the displaced gangster Talbot. Here forever in my mind is the image of Corey, in his driving gloves and loose slung cap, meandering the streets of Buenos Aires, the darkened Plaza de Mayo onward into the nearly rococo ornateness of the government buildings of Monserrat, with their delicate wrought balconettes and corbeled stonework and toothed cornices. Imagine the destitute gangster Talbot, meandering these impossible baroque locales at midnight! Corey, who was always nearly silent, nearly speechless on the set with the crew, spoke as he drove, in the voice of the gangster Talbot, so that I might retreat into my own silence, my own watching. As the buildings passed before us, so Talbot emerged from Corey's lips quietly, sparely, and I wonder sometimes if I was even there. I mean to say, that even in my own memories, I am not there, but instead I am watching a film of Corey driving the streets of Buenos Aires, or perhaps more correctly, I am editing a film of the gangster Talbot driving the streets of Buenos Aires. And while those evenings almost certainly were the thing that led to immediate exaggerated reports in the trade journals about our involvement, picking up and rehashing the slurs and accusations of David Trevor, and cementing my reputation as a reckless libertine, without these few hours of artistic magic—the essence of *Walkway—Walkway* as it currently stands would almost certainly have remained buried, under my own leaden script.

I know that actors find it impossible to be alone. An actor at his core wants to be looked at all the time. The fear of being alone and unobserved is too overwhelming. But the problem of being always with other actors is the awareness that everyone around them is always acting, and no one is really watching, because they are far too busy acting. The problem of being with non-actors was that they, too, were always acting: everyone was always acting, but non-actors just did it poorly, because they were untrained, undisciplined, or untalented. Had I learned this from David Trevor? Or was I learning it then from Corey?

What I could do, in those days, was fall into a kind of deep and silent observation. I was a wonderful watcher, and as I became that eyeball, whatever material strictures existed of the creature Helena Désir dissolved. Whatever happened between us in those days, in Corey's ridiculous sports car, was in part possible because I was a captive audience, an ideal and captive audience, but also because I had become liquid. And Corey had always been liquid. This giving of his body, the absolute grace with which he offered it up as an extension of his voice, captured my attention completely—but even this I see from a great distance, again, as a scene in a film, rather than a memory of proximity.

He had come on my set free of resistance.

Corey possessed none of Emile's defensiveness, and none of his volatility, even if no one could approach Emile's animality. Corey possessed none of David's easy charm or sense of humor: he seemed incapable of a joke, or even recognizing if one was taking place— Corey was deadly serious. Corey also had none of Trevor's desire for interpretation. And moreover, I felt something for Corey that I hadn't felt for the others. I had begun to dote. It was a crutch. I couldn't work with anyone else as well, had not to date, and my films had begun to reveal a pattern of writing that suited us both: a single protagonist, a grim figure, a stolid blank, numb isolation, and a roughly masculine projection from a bygone era. But I'm getting ahead of myself, moving too swiftly toward the water.

In those blissful sixty days in Buenos Aires, I kept in my mind this image of Corey in his sports car on the Avenida de Mayo, and I drew in that color, the color of the midnight sky, and his face illuminated in the glow of the blue neon. Audiences, having seen *Walkway*, often went away from it with the impression that it was shot in black-and-white filmstock. It wasn't, of course; it was shot in color, and there are two moments of bright yellow and red, which the careful eye will recall. The trick, once I fell upon it, was simple—the filmstock is filtered blue. An amazing thing. It yielded something like a black-and-white film in terms of shadow and light, but ultimately it gave us more visual options. All of the problems of how to approach Corey's face were instantly resolved. On the Avenida de Mayo I came to see his eyes as everyone would see his eyes, against the night sky, in the incandescence of the signage. Suddenly there was blue in my film. It was a world of blue possibilities.

Corey would never have what those others had—that much I knew. Emile Laval was an actor entirely in and of the body. This is not to say that Emile didn't find brilliance deep within himself through his own memories, his own experiences. And this is not to say that David Trevor was not very attractive, very present in his body, very memorable out of his clothes as well as in them. But Emile led his acting with his body. David led his body with his interpretation. Corey's mind and body had shallower depths, but they were inseparable.

Will it come as a surprise that five years later, and a handful of films between us, when I began with the character Flynn for *Sanguine Season*, knowing that I had nearly lost him that day in the Blue Lily and that I had regained him on the strength of the promise of an option I didn't intend to keep, and the invented title of a boat. The threat of a return to water. I also knew somehow that the boat was our inevitable and final pathway together?

But again, I'm getting ahead of myself.

12

SCOUTING LOCATION, THE BATHS

I was greeted by a tall, thin Finn called Osku and given a series of items in waffle weave—a towel, a dressing gown, a pair of slippers—by Lotta, his twin sister, and directed into a changing cabin. These specialists were so slender and lithesome that they were somewhat indeterminate in their sex apart from their voices, complicated further by a rising tonal lilt in Osku's accent, and a cultivated low sultriness in Lotta's. Their long blond hair was piled high and haphazardly on their heads, and they were outfitted in identical white coveralls. Even obscured by their coveralls, it was easy to see that their bodies were the definition of perfection. They padded on the raffia floors in bare feet. Osku, upon seeing me, proposed a course of deep relaxation, the goal of which was the most appalling systemic exhaustion. I was ordered onto the massage table.

Do you drink?

No.

Smoke?

Never.

Any other bad habits?

None come to mind.

This is going to be so healthful for you, Osku said to me, before the lights dimmed. Your body resists healing from a recent trauma, I can see. We must create a work of art together that will purge all trace pollutants.

Through my massage table peephole, I could watch only his bare feet as they padded back and forth below his wheeled stool, upon his toes like a dancer. A pan flute warbled gently. He pumped a mechanism on his tool belt, and then lathered his hands with the discharge. I felt a stinging substance between my shoulder blades, and the air was thick with camphor.

But you must yield more, said Lotta.

While Osku pulled my calf muscles down and off at my ankles, Lotta shoved the skin on my shoulder blades up and over my head. I wedged my temples deeper into the padded cylinder and tried to yield. Yielding took the most extraordinary effort. Since Rio, I had been under the sweet protected lingering haze of an opiate, but these twin masseurs of Jaquith House were keen to steam, soak, and knead it out of my system.

A pointy joint from Lotta inserted into my sacrum, working its way toward my skull one vertebra at a time, as Osku continued to tug at my extremities. Even my thumbs and toes were dislocated and realigned. Surely, I was becoming taller, and perhaps this was the real reason for the willowy physiques of the twin Finns—they had literally been pulled like taffy into a narrower form.

My buttocks were flogged with heavy fronds, and my hair was skillfully scraped back from any line of origin. My hands were plunged into something that felt like warm, wet gravel, then they were extracted and toweled off and smeared with a cooling liquid. The siblings handled me alternately and simultaneously thus for the better part of an hour. Then, Lotta stripped me of my slippers, towel, and dressing gown and offered me an athletic one-piece.

Quite sterile, she assured me.

She showed me along another raffia corridor, padding along sweetly in her coveralls and pedicure, and then let me into a much larger cedar cabin. There I was plunged into the hottest "spring." It was scalding, and my skin turned a lurid red. She placed a carafe of water beside me. Perfect little disks of cucumber floated on the icy surface.

For integration! she said, and spritzed me with a fragrant oil.

You look OK, but inside is not great, Lotta said. Don't get fooled by outside looking OK. Is like not always accurate. No more morphine; that shit makes people kind of crazy. Plus no whiskey, because you got a weird liver. And no sugar and no flour. You got poison making you like a slug.

You can tell all this from the massage?

I can tell this from you're standing in front of me! When you go to the café, request "Norwegian sport," but for you no egg. Juice of beet and juice of greens and nice rich fish, sliced tomato. This is like best imaginable restorative.

On her way out, Lotta flipped a switch and the paneled ceiling slid apart in the middle until I was completely exposed to the open air. Sheets of steam began to rise up off the surface of the pool toward the open roof. This pool was less a hot spring and more an elegant concrete trough with a submerged bench that faced a wall of sliding Plexiglas. Beyond the Plexiglas was the mountain, glowing and sunlit. The mountain looked very close, but the forest formed a dense barrier at its base. I knew better than to believe the accessible look of it. It was just that sort of trust that would have cost me days during filming. Hard-headed, uncompromising days.

A slug indeed! I had always prided myself on my proportionality. I was holding on to my features tooth and claw! My compact form was a useful mechanism for quick disguise, given the ease with which I could slide into or out of a pair of trousers. But the perfections of the twin Finns could give anyone pause. And I thought for a moment of the potential distractions of a disciplined regime. But what, after all, did I hope to do with my compact package? Hadn't my philandering always been a means to an end, an end that, it seemed, had been finally reached? To swear off film was, for me, to swear off dalliance.

I sat demurely in the hot pool and considered the mountain hike that had been recommended. The last time I had walked along on a mountain was when I was filming the fiasco war picture. It was in Grenoble, and I thought, I am walking up the mountain in the way a D. H. Lawrence character walks up a mountain. Irrevocably. Even then the likelihood of being followed by someone in need, some actor, was very high, and so the risk, therefore, that I would lead that actor into terminus was equally high.

Some days I didn't care. I would have happily taken all the sheep over the cliff with my barking.

Above my head, tinsel flags with some manner of Buddhist motif fluttered on streamers across the divide of the retracted roof. I had been provided with the complete works of Proust in compact, laminated, waterproof editions, but I couldn't really be bothered to lift even the slimmest volume. I suddenly felt so exhausted. Here I was at the Baths. A complete surrender of values, I felt an immediate guilt toward Chef Anatole. But at least I wasn't in the café. Yet.

And so, something happened, something like sleep but not. And when I emerged, I found myself dripping, in my one-piece, on the tiny pebbles of the courtyard outside my barn.

I let myself into the cool, dark interior of Barbarêche, and I was grateful.

On the bed were my clothes and a note from Lotta encouraging me to return my athletic one-piece for sterilizing. Another little hamper: a cucumber, a whole tomato, and a tin of sardines, alongside a bottle of thick green liquid, almost certainly the juice Lotta hoped would go to work on my liver.

And even though it was only late afternoon, I thought I had done enough to merit a meditative respite from my meditative respite, at least until the supper hour, so I flipped the "after hours" sign on the barn door and settled under my chandelier with a historical novel. Prehistoric: the only real protagonists were glaciers.

13

THE BLUE LILY

Sanguine Season was supposed to be our salvage, Corey and I. Our salvage from the damage of the fiasco war picture. Five years we had been together, a professional monogamy if nothing else, but then the fiasco war picture and our difficult conversation in Norway at a brothel called the Blue Lily. It was at the Blue Lily that I came to see that Corey was not so different from the others, that his eye wandered. But with him, I was different, and this was where I had allowed things to go wrong—but no, not now, Helena.

So, I was in my worst desperation that year after the war picture, thinking as I did that I might have to begin again, without him. I don't dare think of it even now, not now, Helena, not two things at once, not the fiasco war picture and its fallout, and the day at the Blue Lily, however inextricably they were linked.

The war picture was in postproduction. The studio was attempting triage, they were optimistic it could still be salvaged, but I was not. Nothing had gone my way on that set, and a rift opened up with Corey in the last weeks of filming in Grenoble. We had simply stopped speaking when not on set. And I believe we were hiding from each other. I was certainly hiding from him. I was almost resigned to the fact that I was going to have to shed him, and I was postponing—indefinitely—the moment this would have to come out. But at exactly the same time, I thought perhaps he was trying to shed *me*, and I didn't want to give him the satisfaction. So, I fled. I ran for the sea to the South of France to a hotel in a small seaside town near Marseille. It was winter, and there were no tourists, just a small community of shop owners and restauranteurs who remained in the offseason in a perpetual bad temper. I was also in a bad temper, wandering aimlessly on the narrow roads and the sea cliffs, moving between meals and coffees, in my overcoat. I would not apologize for taking the necessary steps to survive the war picture, I was after all the person left holding the bag when things went wrong, and things had gone very wrong.

And then, in a moment in Grenoble, the sky had opened up and delivered a lifeline, and I had taken it, and it had gotten us through. What if that lifeline came in the form a devil? So be it, I was already a sort of devil myself. I suspected it could cost me Corey, it was a gamble I took. I regret nothing, I told myself, as I walked through the freezing winds in that village in the South of France where I had fled from Corey.

The mistral was terrible that year, and it affected all communication lines. But I was always incommunicado. I kept no phone, personally, even then. This is the privilege of the eccentric artist, I told myself.

But I was not without informants. Corey had gone to Oslo after we wrapped. But he had begun calling the hotel where I was staying, and either they weren't giving me the messages or I wasn't asking for them. If someone wants me, they'll find me, I said to the concierge. And soon they did. Corey sent a pair of his entourage to arrange a meeting between us.

A meeting? A business meeting? I asked.

He just wants to see you, they said.

Is something wrong? I said, as if nothing were wrong.

He'd like to let you know how he feels.

Then why didn't he come himself? To see me.

He prefers you go to him.

Does he now? He wants me to go to Oslo in January to have a little chat. It's beautiful here, I said, snuggling deeper into my overcoat. Let him come here.

They looked into their glowing black devices for guidance: He feels like he only just left France, one of them said.

He doesn't want to come back, said another.

Are you speaking to him now?

We can be. Do you want to speak to him?

I do not. A meeting of the minds seems impossible, I said, and I ordered his seconds out of the drafty maps room of my stone hotel. They paused in the entryway tapping away on their devices.

It was a beautiful old hotel. I was told Winston Churchill used to rent the whole thing in the summer. From my window, on the third floor, I could watch the harbor, the little string of sailboats children took out in all weather, learning to sail. I was truly in a foul mood and thinking often of Uncle Yiorgos. It was that way with me: I fought like the devil to be alone, and then when I was alone, I longed for my dear Papa. You are too soft, Élena, he would say. Too soft! Pull up anchor, I heard him say, move along, find another port, another mooring. Do what you want—never what they want!

A more complicated arrangement when who "they" were and who "I" was had blurred: Uncle Yiorgos had a simple rule, make love for money or make love for love but never combine the two.

I knew that whatever was ahead of me, it was sure to be a painful negotiation. I could simply cut my ties, call it a day with this actor, and find someone new. Who would care, honestly? To the studio, one attractive body was relatively the same as the next. But I would end up training a new dog, once again. If I went to Oslo, perhaps I would find that things were better than I assumed, and a negotiation would take place that could allow us to swiftly move on to the next thing. But the next thing did not yet exist in my mind, and I sensed this piece would be key. I also couldn't shake the feeling that if I negotiated with Corey, I was going to lose some piece that I wouldn't get back, much as I had lost something with Emile and then again with David. Why was I prepared to accept anything else from an actor?

But, no, Helena, I thought, no, you can't blame Corey for what went on with the others who have taken so much from you, or tried to. Corey had only ever been compliant, and yet I had not handled things well on the war film. I had left without warning, I could tell he was upset, he was exhausted. In the past, we had never ended a film without a clear plan—a plan for the next thing, the next stage, whether it was approbation or fallout.

He had pledged total obedience and had for the most part delivered to me in our five years together. He was my vessel: what I did with him, and to him, was integral to the process of our art together, and he had, it seemed, not only complied but relished our collaborations.

Again, I heard my uncle's voice: You are too soft, Élena! You can't let a gigolo call the shots!

It was impossible for me to conduct the voices in my head with the winds howling through me.

That day, in the South of France, I could see Corey's two thugs strolling away from me in suits of bamboo or soybean fabrics that were probably woven by robots in Yokohama only hours before they were shipped to them. Their lurid dress sneakers, their headphones worn around their neck like accessories. Every time I saw them they seemed more futuristic, and less human. And Corey was with them perpetually, like they were familiars. A tide was turning on me and on my methods, and the signs were all around me. The time window for my type of film was rapidly closing. I knew that much, and Corey was the only person who had even tried to entertain my vision. Why not just go to the meeting?

I slumped down to the marble slabs, and rocked on my haunches, because thinking for me seemed somehow connected to a nervous oscillation of the body. How had things managed to go so wrong?

But of course, I knew how. It was that fiasco war picture!

A patron of the hotel was completing their checkout. The concierge's reception area was a glassed in marble chamber, cordoned off to create a small technology nook, climate-controlled, and where the whole of the modern world could be carefully redirected and managed, leaving the rest of the building historically intact, for the romantics who wanted to stay in something like a marble sarcophagus. I have never been so cold, before or since, with all that stone! I crouched, shivering, transfixed by the modern reception area. I thought it was an eyesore upon arrival, and here I was, forced into a full confrontation of it, as it smugly witnessed my crisis, my scene with Corey's entourage. I was faintly reflected in the glass, faintly staring my own self down. And having seen myself, I found it harder to look through myself and see into that space of whirring contemporaneity. A practical space, an unaestheticized space. It made me afraid.

I chased down Corey's suits outside the hotel on the road, which was slick with black ice, and so, as I caught up to them, I fell on my ass on the cobblestones. They had clearly been waiting for me. One of them offered me a gloved hand, the most beautiful one, the one called Grisha. I consented to meet Corey wherever he liked.

It's better for everyone if you two work this out, he said.

Work what out? I said, I don't even know what the problem is.

He shrugged, Keep telling yourself that. See how that goes.

In nine hours, I was on a plane. Then five hours later, in that brief window of a Norwegian winter day, I was in a brothel called the Blue Lily, which, of course, was a place that I had been before, so I suspected a tip had come to Corey from a source, from someone in the know. An implausible notion, a diabolical notion, but one that increasingly threatened most of what I believed to be the resilience of my partitions between my actors. Because if they began to conspire against me, that, I thought, would be the end of everything.

Corey looked amazing. He always looked amazing. Even feigning despair, anxiety, depression, whatever he thought was required.

He barely let me out of my coat before he began his performance. And I had been drafting my own script in transit, but I was still working out the fine details.

You look amazing, I said.

Thank you. The Scandinavian diet agrees with me.

Well, I said. You've got me here.

Old friend, he began. I'm at the end of my rope.

He held his head in his hands and looked at me through his fingers, over the garnet ring on his smallest finger, the one that I had given him. It cost me an absolute fortune. It was not Richard Burton's ring, as the tabloids loved to suggest, like we were playing out *Who's Afraid of Virginia Woolf?* In fact, it had belonged to Laurence Olivier, who, it seemed, Corey intended to play even in this grim neon.

Ah. Are we playing this scene, then?

Don't be cynical. I thought you wouldn't come.

Why wouldn't I come? You sent your sergeants, and now I am here, and we parlay.

You look thin, Helena.

PORTHOLE

As ever. Soon only a sliver of me will remain, like a sheath or a shrug.

I'm serious. I'm here to have a serious conversation. I care for you genuinely.

Oh, now it's to be that scene. All right, I said. I took his wrist. It's nothing, I said, It's just a headache. It's coming out suddenly into the daylight like this. When it's foggy, it upsets the eyes. There's so little sun. It's you who looks—exhausted, Corey. I'll order you a marc. No, I'll order you aquavit. Let me play wife.

I waved for a server, without letting go of his wrist. Oh, in the days to have five full fingers to lock onto someone! My grip tightened until I could see the veins of his hand pop forward in a web. He pulled himself free.

Stop it, he said, and dropped his head into his hands.

My wave was to an empty room, the blue and gold depths of the open dome, the backlit cutout stars of the carved screens, the mirrored floor and ceiling, the curving empty bench opposite us. They'd done away with all the brocade and tassels and fringed antimacassars when they'd banned smoking, but it seemed now they'd done away with the girls in their heels and shifts and all the customers and probably all the sex as well, that was the flavor of our current age, antidepressants and celibacy. Perhaps they'd done away with the service staff, and now the brothel was simply a giant self-serve tearoom or a front for oligarchs. Some auntie's sitting room that Corey had commandeered.

How did you even find this place, Corey? It's not really your style.

I had a tip. From someone I trust. That you wouldn't refuse me if I asked you to meet in the Blue Lily.

Someone you trust?

Implicitly.

In the gallery above, one lone dark-haired beauty in yoga clothes leaned over the balcony drinking a green shake. She blew me a kiss. Corey sighed into his cupped hands.

I was surprised that you summoned me, Corey. To be honest, I thought we were done with scenes when we left Grenoble.

You literally disappeared! And I know you were not alone. There's no reason to deliberately misunderstand me, he said. This isn't a personal matter. I'm not possessive, not in that way. We should all be free to do as we please in love.

I'm grateful for that—but then, I never pegged you for a jealous schoolboy.

I know I can choose to involve myself in whatever things I like, with whomever I like personally. But for art, I must commit myself through action. I have always been this sort of personality. How could you not know that? I can't hide and sulk in the shadows and wait to see what you have in store for me and maintain this blind loyalty. If you want to work with other actors, this is natural, and for me, perhaps to look for other projects, this is also natural.

I confess I was caught off guard by his sudden direct approach: Corey's speaking manner was always toward obtuse affectation when possible, his pastiche of Euro-Zen sport-drink affirmations, arcane masculinisms, and fey affect. I had trained myself to feed it back to him and felt inclined to do that even now, when it seemed suspiciously absent.

Granted, I don't deny that there have been limits imposed by our situation, between us—

Limits. That's how you see it.

And don't you?

My total compliance and obedience? My time, my publicity engagements. The erasure of any past that came before us. Helena, I don't eat or drink, I can't even put on pajamas, without asking if I have your permission.

As we agreed in the beginning.

But then you left me without a word. Have you no feelings for me at all?

PORTHOLE

When the film fails, you can't expect me to continue to playact a love affair with you, Corey.

The film isn't even finished—it hasn't failed. And if it does, you can't blame me for that. And I am not asking you to playact anything. I am asking for consideration. I've kept to my part of the bargain, I've let you keep me as a pet, and now, I am here in Oslo alone. You are throwing me away, and I have done nothing!

You became sullen. You were acting out at the end. Everyone saw it.

You told me daily the film would fail, we would all fail. How could I be other than sullen?

In the end, it took a toll.

The studio doesn't think the film will fail.

No, the studio is delighted. They are thrilled, it's just the kind of schlock they were hoping for, they will probably be able to recoup some of the money they poured into it. But that doesn't matter: the film will fail if it is not what I wanted, what I intended. And that is all that matters to me.

But you cannot blame me for this. You pushed me aside, you collapsed my role. You never trusted my thoughts, my ideas. And I never complained.

I didn't hire you for your ideas, Corey.

And so, like that you think you can throw me away? Like you did all the others?

Like that, Corey, I have barely had time to gather my bearings. I need time to even know what might come next.

I don't believe you, Helena. You always know what is next—you have your eye on the next thing, the next film, the next body, before the last one has expired. No part of me wants to leave you—and yet you would leave me here, alone without direction, and for how long? It has been months already. Will it become years? I must think of myself, of my own career. And if you don't understand that, why are you here?

I don't know why, Corey. Because, I want to understand. I believe you, that... that these limits in our relationship—our professional relationship—could be addressed. But what is it that you want?

I want to get around all this childishness. And I want some freedom.

Ah. You want to work with someone else?

I want to have the knowledge that I could, between your projects only, Helena, if a situation should arise, such as this, where I have been cast into the weeds. I want to have options.

Options! You want to put my projects on the backburner while you whore your way into... into... what? A superhero role? A rom-com?

No.

My film should sit by the phone while you film a video game tie-in?

What film?

My hypothetical next film.

You told me you would kill yourself if the war picture failed.

Metaphorical suicide, Corey! But I won't be underestimated. Helena will always rise from the ashes!

This is exactly why I couldn't speak to you before. You leave no space for anything other than your own extremes. Is there a next film or isn't there?

There is the hope of another film!

I have to work, Helena. I won't look like this forever, I have to work while I can.

Corey, I am not in the habit of addressing anything beyond the focus of my own lens. You have to understand that.

I thought we worked well together. But this war picture, it has me confused. Is it art? Is it artistic compromise? I trust your vision completely, but your vision is so well guarded. I am a professional. I have a career that is worth more than this.

If I have a project on the horizon, Corey, obviously I will tell you. I am not going to audition for you while I sleep in your bed.

What are you doing right this minute, if not that?

I am giving you a chance to offer me something.

What would that be?

Something that will work for both of us, something that breathes new life into these genres of yours. Different voices. I need recovery.

I told myself in that moment, I should just start fresh, as I had done before. This would be my uncle's advice. And yet the thought was terrifying and unimaginable, another actor, another actor, endless actors, dropping like flies over time until I could no longer tell them or myself with them apart, each one eroding the thin scrim of Helena.

I saw in front of me a possible conveyance, like a row of railway carriages, or a slow ferry with a canvas awning, something I might board, something moving somewhere soft and restful. I heard my uncle's voice, a new harbor, a new name, a new family. It would require me letting him off that easily, and it would leave me entirely on my own, once again, beginning from scratch. But if I could figure out a way to give Corey what he wanted?

I'm capable of more, he said. And you have known that from the very beginning. I wouldn't take anything that you didn't approve, obviously, and I even think you might help to ensure that I made excellent choices.

You have something in mind already?

There is something, Helena, and I know you will agree: set in Madrid and adapted by you. And you already own the option.

No past, Corey. We agreed!

You have always known it would be an amazing film: there is crime and intrigue, and it's incredibly sexy. It's all of your favorite things. It would be perfect for me, Helena, and we could make it into something extraordinary, and it could be very fun for us. You have always thought so.

I am not good at adaptations, Corey.

Perhaps I could adapt it myself? Or you could work with him yourself. I don't want to take anything away from you, Helena. I have always trusted you, even before I knew you, I trusted you completely. Even in Grenoble when things were so clearly going to shit, I trusted you.

Yes, I said. But, Corey, I don't want to collaborate with anyone.

What is the point of any of this? he said, and again, he returned his elegantly disheveled head into his hands, his garnet ring gone purple in the blue glow.

Corey, you said you trust me. When you look at my next project, you'll see that it is all the things you're searching for. Intrigue, crime, sexiness, ideals. So why don't we begin there, and if you like, we can revisit your Spanish option and see what's possible for the future.

He looked up. You *have* already started something new? he asked.

Corey, it's all the things you are describing. I'm not against the idea of this Spanish option—if the studio agrees. (I thought, An option, after all, is merely an option, and nothing more.)

You've written a new script? he asked again.

What did you think I was doing in Marseille? And, Corey, it's as if you wrote it yourself, really. The "more." The "more" that you are capable of doing, the "more" that we have been working toward, I said, and I began to talk at a fevered pace about the confidence man Flynn, and the riverboat, an idea that had come to me out of thin air, at the pace that my lips were speaking.

I teased it out, this rough sketch, this desperate return to the water, but even before I'd finished speaking, I thought the look in Corey's eyes was that he was not listening. He was looking at me, and he had let me move closer, and let me put my hand on his hair and to stroke him lightly, but he was not listening. He seemed to be searching for something behind me that had been lost, or something he had forgotten, a watch or a handbag dropped in the azure velvet carpet, or perhaps something ticking deep inside the light wall, behind the gold screen cut out with stars, or the deep interior of the brothel.

He continued to look for the lost thing behind me.

It is the sort of thing that only stings in the aftermath, in the reflection of a rest cure.

I stopped my pitch.

What is the boat called? Corey asked.

I looked into the depths of the brothel: empty, cold, dark. It's called the *Anjodie*.

She is called the *Anjodie*.

She is, I thought, and she is mine, and mine alone.

It sounds wonderful. But, Helena, you agree, I must protect myself, I must have my own path forward, should you... should you become displeased with me. An insurance policy. I am asking for so little.

I'll look into it.

Soon?

I said I would look into it, Corey. But this must be the end of this conversation—if we are going to move forward with Flynn the confidence man, surely you understand I need your total focus, your total compliance.

His eyes were in front of me again, and my presence cast a chill on his well-made frame, on his hollow face, and his sharp jaw. There was going to be no way for him to learn, no way other than more bitter experience, which, apparently, I was prepared to give him.

You have too much freedom, Corey had said to me, that day at the Blue Lily.

You have too much strength of character, I had said, in return, and then I paid the ladies myself.

14

A NOCTURNAL VISITATION

I lay in my rough-hewn bed beneath the very modern flanged and faceted chandelier of steel and birch. When had I gotten into my negligee? I couldn't remember. An exquisitely diffuse light drifted down on me from my mobile fixture, and I considered the way in which every muscle in my body seemed to have gone numb.

Once, I had always loved the night hours, because I was always working. I loved the splendid feeling of being engulfed in darkness, as one is in a cinema, utterly alone in the dark, locked in an intimate gaze with a single face, a single pair of eyes. I loved closed shutters, stormy skies, deep forests—I loved all the obscurities of the night; I feared the moment the sunrise broke into the room. The Helena behind the camera—that is, a former Helena.

In my barn there was the sound of the night, and the sound of certain creatures of the night, but there was no sound of the stream. I got out of bed and climbed straight onto the half floor. Outside the window the terrain was well lit—pink and milky—by the blood moon. The stream was dry except for a thin trickle, and a few curious pools amid the rocks. A long bit of black tubing was well exposed, the telltale reveal of some distant mechanism driving it. So, the stream was a fake after all!

I knew I had missed dinner, but I didn't know by how much, and I suspected now that I was done sleeping. I wondered if it would be possible to rouse Chef Anatole?

It was then that I heard the clicking of the balls upstairs. And something else, a scuttling or a scratching, a light tapping against the floorboards, like fingernails.

There seemed to be a surprising coolness in the air along the stairs, I could tell the recreation lounge was brightly lit, and I smelled the smoke in the air from the woodstove. When I reached the top of the stairs, I saw someone making use of the billiard table.

I saw immediately before me a medium-sized dog, all in white with rose-colored freckles, and darkly lined eyes. She was silent but stood looking at me.

The man at the table was tall and thin, and very well made, in the manner of a bygone era. There was something of a déjà vu about his somber uniform of dark starched cotton, a picture that seemed carved already in my mind, like an afterimage. He wore a patchy beard, and his dark hair rested on his collar. It looked hacked at from all directions, as though he'd cut it himself, and he had small dark eyes under dark lashes and brows. He finished his run of the table and stood to face me. He waved. His smile barely notched his face.

I put my hand down at once for the dog, who approached. I had forgotten myself or my intentions: it seemed to me an unfair advantage to have a dog on hand, when trespassing.

I thought I heard someone and... I began.

You thought you heard someone and?

I thought I heard someone and... well, I did, I said. Obviously.

Not her—she's very quiet, he said of the dog.

There was a fire burning in the stove, and the moonlight had made its way to us through the dormers in great stretching patches, it flowed from above our heads. The pendulum lamps over the tables glowed pleasantly.

I don't mean to be blunt, I said. No, I mean to be blunt. I thought I had locked the door and flipped the sign.

That may very well be true, he said. His voice was soft and measured.

Is it after nine-thirty?

I would say so.

You would, would you?

I said so.

This isn't a saloon. It's where I live. At the moment.

But it looks like a saloon. How do you account for that?

That's immaterial. Curfew, or well, you know what I mean, closing hours.

I don't follow Dr. Duvaux's rules, he said, and returned to his game.

Don't you? The pamphlet promises consideration.

If it is your rule for your own well-being, I will consider it. Not immediately, but over time. But not for Dr. Duvaux's general rules. They don't apply to me. I was here before Dr. Duvaux.

Only if you were in short pants! He's been here since time immemorial, practically. I read the pamphlets.

I certainly wouldn't trust any pamphlets if I were you.

Why are you here? I asked. At Jaquith?

I live here. Why are you here?

Why? Because there was an accident.

Accidents are rarely accidents. They are often subconscious, intentional acts. Do you want to ask why I am in your saloon?

All right.

At night, I come here because I'm not working, and because my cabin is small and stuffy, and because I like playing games. What kind of accident was it?

A tragic one. A poetically tragic one, the kind filmmakers invent, rather than live through, as it happens.

A car accident?

A boat.

You were out of your depths.

Unexpectedly. You see, I grew up on a boat.

You are the filmmaker.

You didn't know that? Everyone else seems to know that. I don't know why.

And will you still be the filmmaker?

I think that might be the question at hand. If I comply with the studio's wishes.

You don't seem like a compliant person.

It was a coercion situation. The motivation is still murky to me, but the doctor would know. I think there is some hope that I will finish what I've started.

Have you undergone an epiphantic shift in your time at the asylum? he asked.

No, I have not undergone any such shift. I've only been here a day. Maybe a day and a half. Two? I'm not actually sure, to be honest.

Oh, I see, he said.

I don't see how you could possibly see. I'm not able to sort out time very well. I don't sleep!

He laid his cue on the felt of the table and put up both his hands and began to pet the air as if to soothe me from afar, and as he did so, the dog slid down into her splayed posture at his feet and laid her head against his ankle. But in allowing my anger to rise in the night hours, I was finding myself again and remembering myself, or seeing myself from a distant remove. It felt that I was almost *working*. I shook noticeably.

You should sit, he said.

I flopped on the sofa, and the cushions oozed out below me. What kind of dog is that? I asked.

Herder. Cattle-dog. A working dog.

What is her name?

Ruby, he said.

But she isn't red.

No, she isn't.

She's white. Shouldn't she be called something like Angel or Snowy?

She's called Ruby. She was thrown down a well as a pup. When she came out, she had a wound on her elbow—here, he said, and raised the cuff of his sleeve to show me his elbow. He also had scars, long scars that twisted up and across and around his forearm like the braid of a rope.

Are those scars on your arm the marks of a sufferer, I asked?

An accident.

An accident on both wrists? With scars that cross upwards toward the elbow? Try again.

I can see you think you've been around.

I've been around that sort of thing.

As I was saying, she had a scar. Here, he continued pointing to his elbow. A small wound that was shaped like a diamond, but which bled for some time. And she was called Ruby, he said, and the dog looked up at him on hearing her wake-word.

I wasn't trying to challenge you, I said. You say she'd been "thrown down" a well.

Yes, with her litter.

And her litter?

In the end there was only her who came out of the well.

An insensible cruelty. An imagistic, insensible cruelty, I said.

Yes, but then some person did pull her out. Not me. I got her later, a bit later, once she was ready for me.

She's adjusted very well, given the situation. But, listen, you mustn't try to get around me by playing to sentiment. I lock the door at nine, or ten—actually, I can't remember when I lock the door, but I know there was a rule, and I agreed to the rule—

You can do whatever you want with the door. I don't come in by the door.

Fantastic. I'm excited to hear this.

I come in through the tapestry. Besides, it doesn't matter. I have keys to everywhere.

Listen, I'm exhausted.

It's the organ twisting. The Finns. It has a soporific effect. Famously. That shouldn't be news to you.

Everything is news to me at this place. Listen, do you know how to get ahold of Chef Anatole?

I know how to get ahold of everybody.

Will you ring up Chef Anatole?

No.

Give me his number. I'll ring him up. I'm not shy.

He doesn't have a phone. He was asked to relinquish it.

Come to think of it, so was I. Tell me where he's lodged, then, and I'll pay him a visit.

No, he said softly. No, I don't think so. I will share my Canadian cheese with you.

You have it on your person?

It's in my hamper, he said, and producing a hamper very much like the one I'd been given that morning, he lifted out a large wheel of cheese in a waxen rind, missing a quarter's wedge. He cut another quarter's wedge with a Leatherman and handed it to me.

What is this culture of hampers?

I make my own hamper before I leave at night. It allows me to come and go without notice, and to stay as long as I like.

Every night? Oh, no. You can't come here every night. Hamper or otherwise, I will notice. I don't sleep well.

Neither do I, obviously, or I wouldn't be here every night. Anyone who stares into the abyss has trouble sleeping. That has always been the case.

I haven't seen you on the grounds.

You've only been here one day, or two. And, anyway, I don't live on the grounds. Not on the immediate grounds anyway. I live on the mountain.

The mountain?

I think I said it clearly.

What's that like? Does that indicate that you've shown progress? The doctor lets you go further afield? Is it a cabin or something?

In the words of the poet Stonehouse:

> *On a 10,000-story-high mountain*
> *my hut sits at the very top*
> *I shaped three Buddhas from clay*
> *and keep an oil lamp burning*
> *I ring a bell cold moonlit nights*
> *and brew tea with pond ice—*

Where's the pond?

I am speaking figuratively. There isn't a pond. There are lakes.

"Lake" loses something, don't you think?

Lakes are much more desirable than ponds. And their ice is much cleaner.

Can you pour out some of that scotch? Whatever's left. Make one for yourself. The fire's nice.

Wouldn't you prefer a toddy? I have a kettle. I don't think whiskey helps with sleeping, he said, liberally pouring out the whiskey.

Don't have any then.

I don't have any intention of sleeping tonight, he said, and gave himself a similar portion. I've made peace with that part of myself. From his hamper he found half a lemon and a jar of honey and augmented the scotch with each. He topped up the cup with the steaming kettle and stretched out both cups toward me.

Left or right? he said. You choose.

They look the same.

They are the same.

Then just give me one.

Left or right?

Left, I said.

Sinister, he said, and handed me the cup in his left hand. Dexter, he said, and drank from his own cup.

You aren't part of Jaquith House, then?

(He was slow to respond.)

You're slow to respond, I said.

No, I am, I suppose, he said. The mountain is still part of Jaquith House, technically. My part of it, anyway, is part of the original estate. My studio is there. I make furnishings.

He swept his arms around the loft suggestively.

You made this furniture?

No, not these. These are obviously antiques. I made your chandelier. And fixtures. I weld also. And I cut the wood for the fires. All the fires of Jaquith House.

I like the chandelier.

Yes?

I think so. It's odd, though. I have to think about it. Are you being treated by Dr. Duvaux?

I would never let that man near me.

He's a well-reputed genius!

A specialist in brains. And their washing.

Are you a doctor then?

I live on the mountain. I make furnishings. I stock wood. Why would I also be a doctor?

I'm Helena, I said, in as ungracious an offering as I could affect. As you have already guessed.

My name is Lonnie, he said.

The doctor told me no one at Jaquith House was untrained. Exploring their own psychic crinolines. I'm not supposed to have the risk of encountering someone who will say damaging things to me.

Training rarely limits damage. I am trained in industrial design and fine craftsmanship, and I have degrees from several New York universities. And I hate alienists.

Everyone at Jaquith House seems overeducated to me.

You don't have to act as though I'm not being friendly. It's not anything personal, it's simply my way of being.

You are practically decorous.

I would think, given that you are in your night clothes, you might feel free to call me by my first name.

Have you been here as long as you say? You look younger than that.

You seem concerned with appearances. Are you sensitive about your disfigurement?

Do you mean this?—I flourished my claw—Not in the least. I'm quite happy with it. It helps me to maintain a firm grip on certain details of my new reality.

Scars can do that.

When you leave, Lonnie, you'll put out the lights and let the fire die down and that sort of thing, and slip out quietly?

I always do.

Through the tapestry?

Through the tapestry.

Then I'll leave you to it. But we may have to renegotiate at another time.

If you stay, I would read you more poetry.

Not tempting, Lonnie. I must make every effort to find unconsciousness.

You have lovely night clothes, he said.

I ought to, I said, convent made!

15

A PICTURE STORY

The tapestry told a story.
A Scandinavian locale was immediately apparent.
At the top corner, in laid work and in chain stitching, two sisters sat in contemplation of two caged birds. Around them their many admirers, seafarers, in dress uniforms. Across a gap of velvet, in an adjacent scene the same two sisters, now aged and decrepit, picnicked on a lawn, flanked by two tall long-haired dogs. These two as young maids were like golden lambs, picking violets in a meadow, the picture of fashion, observed and observing, even as they stepped from a barge, celebratory streamers whisked and puffed around them. And, as if let down on the ropes of a swing, they dropped into another scene, their trail couched in stout linen across the velvet. And there they appeared as old maids, in gray and dry bodies, in black velvet ribbon high at the throat, their birdlike lightness now a caricature of frailty, trembling in fits and starts like bodies composed of fumes, with white handkerchiefs in their fists, and tiny crystal buttons on their tunics. Another scene, at a ball, restored them to youth—what relief in bright silks—and dancing with a dashing privateer, a man made in threads to look so much like the two maids, who themselves were clearly identical,

indistinguishable really, two lovely maids in matching arraignment, and a man of their age so similar in visage, he was surely a brother. These same maids, first young, then old, then young, then old, in circling scenes through the streets and parks, the brightly painted houses of the port of Copenhagen periodically arising, and then giving over to trees filled with nightingales or to lakes on which swans drifted or to a sea becalmed, these edged the tapestry, the maids in an assortment of garden idylls, or in the safety of elegant rooms, strolling on stone or shell walkways, through ballrooms and parlors, astride horses, leading peacocks, flanked by dogs.

But at the tapestry's center another type of narrative swarmed, and lay forth the Napoleonic wars and the bombardment of Copenhagen on a September night, when the sky curled with flames, in scarlet silks, and consumed the bell tower of a kirke, which fell to ruins and slid toward the sea, where British frigates waited to capture the warships of Denmark in her own sound. But depicted in nearly the same roundel, the flames suddenly dispatched, the sea seemed swept with snow, and smaller ships of sea dogs and privateers, likewise glazed and frosted—two manners of white silk on white brocade against a black velvet background—their rigging coated in ice, these small light ships glided to port, and deposited the spoils of their pillage on the Copenhagen docks, stoneware and wine and spirits and coffee and sugar and silks, and the docks, now in morning's first light, piled with these riches, seemed to hang in space at the end of a sea battle under the guns of the Danish batteries, and so no clear progress in this careful history could be discerned despite the elegance and precision of the embroidery, and the Danish ships were pursuing and dispatching, and pursued and dispatched in no particular line, but in concentric circles of the narrative. All of these sea battles were all-at-once rather than in any particular order, all together the fire and the snow and the night skies and morning skies, the surrendering Danish ships and the victorious Danish ships, in the spray of grapeshot, with tholes bound with wool, boarding pikes planted on ships who appeared to be both retreating and arriving in their own conquest, and axes, broadswords, and knives and men swarming on decks, in the chain cables, on the figureheads, gaining and losing their ships, the sky was dark and the sky was also reddening in the east, though the east quickly became the west in the adjustment to the next battle, the harbor, the ramparts, a reminiscent rigging, and white silk on the dark waves, the same white silk of ice in the ropes now the white silk of billowing smoke, the riggings badly crippled, scenes so closely overlapped as to obscure the beginnings and endings of each individual moment, and even in their placement in the textile, they roiled. So much was the eye then drawn to the battles at sea that the narratives on the fringes were nearly forgotten. But, of course, circling the tumult on the sea, the young maids and their birds, the old maids and their picnic, the young maids and their suitors, and near the bottom of the tapestry in the corner overcast in shadows, the old maids gathered around the ghost of a hanged pirate, and indeed that pirate was the same boy who so resembled them in their youth, but now all of them were terrifically aged. And between each of these scenes a white frozen sea, and the sledges and horses and dogs that carried one across the ice, between these moments, as if between islands in a frozen sound, back and forth in time, the young maids and the old maids, and swans and gulls walked upon the ice, swans in all aspects twisting in space displaced from their frozen sound, swans that stood and gawked at the battle scenes at its center, though the two maids seemed never to take notice, so focused were they on their suitors, and on their hanged man, who seemed stitched in a silk faded from too much exposure to the sea itself, a translucent silk, tenuous and fraying, and near to the palest of these depictions of the hanged man, the ice was cut through with a jagged line of black, a line that, though shaped like a bolt of lightning, showed clearly that the ice was suddenly, or finally, breaking up.

You are close, he said, but you are over-reading.

Is someone there? I said. But there was no one. Was I speaking? I was.

No matter.

There were only two passages of text in banners to aid in the comprehension of this scene. At the top of the tapestry, in the leftmost corner, a motto in calligraphed gold-work read: *Let our house find a unity, a sympathy between windows and doors, each sound on a stair echoing across the floorboards of distant rooms.*

And at the bottom rightmost corner, the motto completed itself: *But let this not allow us to linger upon souls in hell lest they should return to our parlors.*

What a remarkable textile!

I wonder why I hadn't examined it before?

There was still the clicking of the billiard balls, and clicking of the toes of the dog on the saloon floorboards. I am, I thought, awake?

And yet, I had a sudden feeling that I would turn around and find David Trevor, as the gambler Doryan. And even without turning, I thought I heard David's voice, saying to me, Helena, you fickle bitch, your puppet is barely cold in the grave, and you are after your next conquest. Typical.

16

THE SEA AND THE BELVEDERE

A déjà vu. As though I was on one of my locations. Barbarêche was bright and familiar, as I emerged into the foyer that morning. But, of course, all barns are similar, almost identical.

A distinct draft wafted the edge of the tapestry. I pulled it aside and saw the passageway leading into the garage, and there, waiting in the corridor, was Dr. Duvaux. He wore a turtleneck and a woolen camp sweater, looking like something from a child's bedside lamp.

Good morning, Helena!

Good morning, Doctor. I was just on my way to breakfast.

He moved us back into my bedroom, and sat on the bed, below the modernist chandelier, feet dangling above the bed platform.

We missed you in the dining room last evening, he said.

I'm getting my bearings, eating is secondary.

Of course, I understand. I wanted to see how you were getting on in the barn, our caretaker mentioned something about a nuisance with some stoats in wheel housing. There's a small gap, I'm told, the doctor said, gesturing to the mill wheel. And the stoats sometimes sneak through. You really wouldn't want to wake up with a stoat sitting on your chest, I should think, Helena. I'll have someone look at it, if that doesn't feel invasive. I know you are a private person.

Am I?

It's what they say.

They would know best.

They might. A truly private person, one who keeps up such a reclusive lifestyle, is unlikely to know what is said. Of course, a person in the public eye said to keep a private lifestyle is a paradox. But then, they say, artists reveal themselves through their work.

They say a lot of things.

That they do. Helena, your work aside, perhaps you are a deliberately cultivated mystery? And I notice you're no longer a blonde.

Was I a blonde?

I could have sworn to it.

Well, Doctor. When in Rome.

Jaquith House is something of a holiday destination, I suppose. I mean that in the sense of a travel respite, rather than calendar holiday.

I am not much for vacations or holidays.

No? Holidays sometimes trigger the sufferer, because they tend to artificially pressurize family dynamics.

I cared only for Uncle Yiorgos. Anyone else was a gatecrasher.

It was your uncle who raised you, if I am correct.

I wouldn't say raised. Housed, maybe. Ferried, more like.

And yet you were fond of him?

He was a lecherous reprobate. I loved his spirit, and he could certainly throw a party. But he's long dead.

Ah, Helena the recalcitrant loner. We return to the myth. He leaned back on to the bed and gazed up. I joined him.

It's a nice furnishing, I said.

Do you think so? I find it fussy and a little absurd, really.

I met the maker.

I doubt that, said the doctor.

Why would you doubt that?

Infernal machines, designed by the devil himself. I really don't see the point of modernizing the cottages. If we aren't careful, we'll modernize ourselves right out of Jaquith House.

Who is the we in that equation, Doctor?

Those of us who are already on the edge of extinction anyway, I suppose. Though I don't complain. I don't wish to be young again. I've only ever wanted to be older, but I do notice a toll taken on the body.

Helena, I don't think you look a day over twenty-five.

Thank you, Doctor. I don't think you look a day over forty.

And yet, despite your youthful appearance, you have a wisdom about you. I'm very interested in the types of information you have picked up, without guidance, as a filmmaker. I think it could be very useful to us in unwinding your concerns. I am thinking of your war film, for instance.

I'm a magpie, and an assembler. I don't think there's much sense to be made.

You worked closely with a circus performer once, rather a famous one if I am correct? An acrobat? And a Frenchman.

Yes.

Perhaps you'll tell me about that.

Perhaps! Doctor, wouldn't you like to escort me to breakfast?

I would be delighted, Helena, but I can't be seen to play favorites. Since it's Sunday, and you have a car, it might make sense to go out to Les Roches Blanches—it's delightfully recherché. You'll find some maps in the maps cupboard.

Drive myself?

Yes.

The gate stands open on Sundays to encourage independence. Only on Sundays, mind you! If you are not feeling intrepid, you might track down Brigita to arrange for some buttermilk and sandwiches in the main house—she's quite popular among our aides-de-camp, very buxom but very exacting.

Doctor, about the tapestry—

Modern Danish! Very beautiful craftsmanship. I envy anyone who can work in such meticulous detail. They say it was woven by nuns, but I've always wondered about that. The subject matter I find a bit mature for the spiritually inclined, no?

I'm more interested in how one goes through it, and who goes through it, and at what times of day and night.

Well, it's very simple as you can plainly see, he said, and lifted a corner. Arrivederci. Mind the stoats! he said, and as quickly as he had emerged, Dr. Duvaux disappeared behind the tapestry.

And so I could drive after all! This was a welcome discovery, or a rediscovery, a former talent from my vagabond days reclaimed! The folding map I'd taken from Jaquith House made it appear as though the sea was practically lapping at the front door, and I ought to be able to get there on foot, but it was one of those maps where all the destinations are drawn in cartoonish three-dimensionality for tourists, so they pop up and off the map, and a roadside hut selling lemonade, for instance, ends up looking the same size as a Victorian hotel, and both are rendered down to the detail of the grain on their shingling. Roads, however, were barely noted as such and any gaps of space on the map not commercially occupied were simply elided.

As I drove, I found more and more winding roads such as the one I had come in on that first day—only I saw no large lake or small lake, and as far as I could tell, no little chalet ski village. There were only endless pines and hemlocks, and occasional shelves of pink rocks rising on either side of me where the road cut through the granite. The pinky of my driving glove flapped on my talon's grip as my Jaguar purred along neatly. Or anyway I assumed it was my little Jaguar, since it was the only car left in the garage and the keys were in the glove box. It had a soft top, and I let it down.

Further up the point, I pulled into the lot of Les Roches Blanches, a Victorian mansion that towered precariously on the bluff, overlooking white caps and granite polished pale by the sea. It would have been a glorious hotel in its era, jutting out on its point over the water, with sun on three sides, and surrounding porches with steamer lounges and men in straw boaters and piped jackets and women in lace frocks with yards of material in the skirts, carrying parasols, their hair thickly and elegantly arranged so that tiny hats perched just atop their enormous coiffure, trailing ribbons down their backs. And there would have been a croquet lawn on the cliff, just about where the parking lot was now located, and there would have been little changing cabins on the lee side, where a small beach curved out of the reach of the more glorious seaward waves. Bathing cabins dotting the shore, with donkey rides.

Now there was only what looked to me like a hut for selling inflatable rafts and fried dough. It was early enough that there was still a bit of mist floating around the cliff and up onto the decks of the hotel, and from the car lot I could see into the dining room, which was bustling and well lit.

Suddenly I remembered or returned to Weymouth in Dorset, that southernmost beach town on the English Channel, positioned so as to be nearly in view of Cherbourg, or to have Cherbourg in its sights. I had lived there once in one of my previous incarnations. It was in Weymouth where I had taken a short hiatus in the months after *Mechanism* debuted, when money suddenly seemed to be around me like a blanket in a way that it hadn't been at any previous point in my life. I had shed Emile, but I admit, I had not yet shed the residual grim feeling that accompanied thoughts of Emile—I won't say guilt. It was something else I had learned from Uncle Yiorgos: it never pays to draw anything out. In those days, when I was young, I often became attached to one of his lovelies: Jacqueline, the underwater dancer who taught me to swim, or Elsa, the clothing designer who made me my first suit, or Svetlana, the Russian actress who traded me swear words in several languages if I helped her practice English. When the lovelies were on the boat, life felt lazy, and decadent. When they were on the boat, they were so completely there, it was if they had always been there. And then in a flash, they weren't.

It happened the same each time, I would awake in the morning, and there would be the absence of all smells but the stagnation of the bay. No coffee, no bread, and the galley of the *Anjodie* would be bare apart from the stains and dregs of red wine, nut shells, rinds from stinking cheese, an ashtray overflowing with remnants of cigarillos. I felt immediately that grim feeling. Inevitably, I would find my uncle painting, smoking, unwashed, tousled, a coffee mug of Armagnac in his fist, and quite enrapt in his work. He was always filled with energy after the disposal of a lovely.

There's no coffee, I would announce, and nothing to eat.

It will come again in time, he said.

What happened to Jacqueline?

Just because someone thinks they want you, it doesn't mean you have to give yourself to them. Remember that, Élena.

I remembered. And he was right: after the dispatch of a lovely, there would be a few days, a few weeks while he plunged back into his work, while niceties were scarce, but in time, another girl would appear, and with her, champagne, smoked salmon, salami, and potato salad, or brioche and strawberry jam, each one embellished the boat in her way, and the grim feeling would fade. I remembered! And so I remembered what was the surest remedy to that grim feeling: a focus on work until the arrival of the next lovely! And I was happy to await my lovely in Weymouth. David Trevor was brand new to me then. He was finishing his run in Kleist on the London stage, and I was submerged in my work, finishing the draft of *The Tightening Knot*. I rented an exorbitant little ocean-view flat in the Bluette, a boarding house which was attached to the Hotel Basilic. Both structures, and the extensive grounds between, were owned by an Englishman called Potts, whose family had held them as a vacation property for two centuries, barring only the lend of it for two seasons to Winston Churchill. Both of Churchill's sojourns were documented photographically on the walls of the hotel lobby, which had opened for more base and genuine business when the family funds ran out after World War II. For reasons that were unclear to me, it was during that period that it had adopted a Mediterranean persona. Or disguise. But buildings gave away the game: from north to south an evolution of architectural attributes revealed the efforts of the hotel to thrust itself into a fantasy of southern climes. My small wing of stones and whitewash and thatch was the oldest remaining part of the original eighteenth-century structure, but as one panned left, the stone was slowly overtaken by the Victorian wing in plaster and lap, formerly white but in my era repainted a Provençal ochre, where the roof thatch gave way to slate tiles, and then eventually to clay tiles, and the dark slatted storm shutters gave way to sunflower calico, the evolution of the fantasia marked in each wing and addition. The slate bench outside my door was the only remaining bit of patio furnishing that wasn't mosaic and fresco. The worst of this effect culminated in the blinding neon accents of the Deco-period Hotel Basilic, a conjoined sibling structure. The whole sprawling compound was fringed by a fluid and undulating pink stucco wall, the only feature of continuity, and its gates stood open at all hours giving a picturesque glimpse into the hotel's corner of eclectic luxury. The garden was planted with rosemary and lavender hedges, umbrella pines, redbuds, and yellow mimosa, and Potts, in his lifetime, had even installed a few struggling pineapple-shaped palm trees. There was the very grand "restaurant Basilic," and the very un-grand café, Snack La Mer, specializing in several dozen unnatural colors of ice cream and phosphate beverages. Snack La Mer had oil-clothed tables perched dangerously over the narrow coastal road that ran between the Bluette-Basilic compound and the beach wall, and it served pastis, or Campari and sodas, or Diablo au menthe, alongside lemon squash and elderflower cordials. On the very bottom floor was a tobacconist who sold everything from beach mats to fountain pens out of the space of a kitchen pantry. The whole structure faced the water like a stage, just as the café customers, who, no matter how their table was located and despite the crippling sun, turned their chairs to face the turquoise waves.

Living in Weymouth was my first time on my own in such a seaside village. Uncle Yiorgos kept me crawling the Pacific coastline in my childhood, but as anchor-out types, there was not a dime to be spent on shore: a floating shanty was his preferred scene of debauchery, or a hot tub on a sloping Sausalito balcony.

The shore is a trap! my uncle often said. And I think he meant a trap for tourists, but it sounded quite a bit more ominous.

So, I had glimpsed those grand but decrepit hotels on the headlands, but I had little experience of them.

The Bluette was my first resort. The first of many as it turned out, since my life seems to have been a series of lost or last resorts. And although I was meant to be writing, the script was pretty slender, and I found that there was little to do in those first months. The slow-paced Anglo-Mediterranean lifestyle Potts was so desperate to achieve depended entirely on long lunches, coffees and teas, and walks on the quay. I aped what was modeled. I strung myself along daily walks, caustically moving from the safety of the Bluette, drawn to the water, or I perched on a bench high above the beach wall of the Hotel Basilic, in front of a row of potted palms, observing the scene. I looked out at the boats moored in the harbor and felt a familiar pang.

On Sundays, the lovely glassed dining room of the Basilic—much like the one I was spying on from the parking lot of Les Roches Blanches—offered a coveted French-style breakfast buffet of blood sausages, marbled salt pork, a potted terrine thickly coated in aspic, and stewed pig trotter served in a galvanized bucket. At the end of the buffet, a selection of mustards and mayonnaises were lined up, in white bowls, and a chip basket containing a mountain of tiny deep-fried bait fishes could be ladled into a paper cone and eaten standing at the buffet. All meals, no matter the hour of the morning, were accompanied by sparkling red wine and dark bread. The flavors being somewhat more northern than the standard Mediterranean fare (an indication that while the compound aspired to the Riviera, it was more practical to import goods from Normandy) gave it some novelty perhaps, though to my eyes the whole display was mildly stomach-turning. The guests gathered around the small Basilic buffet table in chaotic, swarming groups, planted firmly and unyielding, eating from napkin and hand and paper cone, standing up while swilling the good sparkling red wine until the entire spread was reduced to smudges and crumbs. They did not even stop for coffee, and none was available in the dining room until after noon. I horrified everyone by bringing in a paper cup of tea from Snack La Mer and asking the serving staff to toast my brown bread—and by the time I received my brown toast, the majority of breakfasters had meandered out onto the hotel decks, toward the café tables to take the sun, as best they could manage in their dark coats and scarves, because the weather in Weymouth was frigid most of the year. Here I went and sat at a table alone, with my paper cup of tea and my brown toast, working on *The Tightening Knot* and feeling the power of my escape from Emile while waiting for life with David Trevor to begin. It was perhaps the happiest I had been and would be since in this interim of possibility.

I could never get enough of observing the sea stretching out and meeting the sky, and shifting, through a startling array of blue and green shades in the course of the day, with the changing light. And I could remember, walking back from the market, I would first see the hotel rising up and then the Bluette, and I would rush past the entrance to my flat, and through the grounds and then down to the water, because I couldn't see the water until I came up and over the hill and through the stucco wall.

Now at Les Roches Blanches, I felt a bit snowblind, or something like snowblind, water-blind, because I no longer remembered a time when I could not see water.

The breakfast threatened me with its boisterous diners. In the hotel entry, some little bookcases with glass fronts ran the length of the room—no books, of course. A concierge in a smart dinner jacket with the air of a young psychologist approached me with his fingers tented before him.

How may I direct you? Are you in search of our award-winning brunch?

I looked past and beyond him, to a foyer space where a pair of dour Midwestern vegetarians had begun to shout brunch complaints, and before he could attend to any needs I might have, he was drawn immediately into their conflict. I sat like a stone on a puffed ottoman and regained my composure. The concierge returned immediately to my aid.

I'm so sorry madam, I apologize. Those persons are not even guests of the hotel.

Nor am I, I said. It made no difference to him however, for he thought I was some grandee in need of attention.

Those persons were simply trying to get out of paying for their brunch.

I suspect it's overpriced, I said.

It's no reason for them to treat me with such indignity. I have worked at the Savoy! he announced.

Don't worry, I said, and I winked. I can tell.

And so, while he mistook those doubtless well-landed Midwestern vegetarians for haggling skinflints, one thing was for sure, I was cosmopolitan! And for that I had his esteem. Of course, I couldn't remember the last time I had actually spent a night in a city, but what was I if not the product of too many cities, watching my expenditure not from poverty but from avarice, which was always respectable to a concierge. I was wearing knickerbockers and a light over jacket with a belted waist, and I looked like a young dandy with a feather in his hat. I took out a crushed morocco case, in which I carried a small cigar wrapped with a band of purple.

We don't allow smoking in the lobby, he said apologetically.

Don't we? I said. Where do we allow it?

Well, technically not anywhere, but... in the hair salon, he said, and gestured me down toward a subterranean stair.

I thank you for your time, I said, and tipped him five dollars. Then I took myself and cigar off down the stairs to the lower level which revealed a small floor of shops: a hairdresser's, a matronly dress shop, a golf club outfitter, and a bakery, which was the only one open, and a small number of customers were looking hopefully at a platter of weeping scones. What a ruse! I followed the hallway to the end of the little arcade, and as in all hotels what goes down must come up, and soon enough I was back on the ground floor and out on the opposite lawn of the hotel, where some children were eating ices across from a statue of a pioneer dressed in buckskins. A small rack of hotel propaganda materials as well as local tourist information was propped against the base of the statue. I fished out the hotel prospectus. Les Roches Blanches, I read out, is a delightful abode, exquisite and fair, with a beautiful view across its front lawns to the Casino gardens, and an antique lift to the highest point in the building, a belvedere and skylight modeled on Norman churches.

Lift? I said to myself, and reentered the ground floor, holding on to my pamphlet.

Once again in the main lobby of the hotel, I found the concierge, now nursing a wound of some kind over his lip.

Madam, I... he slurred through his handkerchief.

One question only, I said. Direct me to the lift!

He gestured behind him to a paneled column, lit with brocade wallpaper. Running alongside it, a narrow communicating stair, and above, a range of ombréed galleries opening out like the tail of a peacock. There an iron cage was fitted within the paneled column, and the concierge pulled a remote control device from a holster on his cummerbund and zapped the cage. A mechanized shriek ensued, and in a matter of minutes, the bottom floor of a lit lift box appeared just above eyesight, grinding through the iron column, with the lift operator installed inside like a captive squirrel. He was a teen or tween, perched on a small stool. He, too, wore a headset and headphones, though the headphones were around his neck like a travel pillow, and the headset was resting just over them wedged against his teeth. Everyone was so beautifully outfitted with communications gear. I wondered if the concierge's injury was preventing him from donning his own headset. The concierge peeled open the outer caging for me, and the lift operator peeled open the inner cage. There was only just enough room inside for myself, the lift operator, and the lift operator's head apparatuses. He moved aside his mouth microphone to address me. It winged out from his cheek like a Gumby arm, or a whisker.

 Which floor, Miss?
 Just once around the park, please.
 Pardon me, Miss, which floor?
 I'm a tourist, take me to your belvedere.
 Of course, Miss. Top floor! and he placed his hand on a brass lever, which resisted him, or perhaps supported him, but which I was quite convinced did absolutely nothing to actually move the mechanism of the lift.

 Up we ratcheted into the turret of the hotel, where the lift operator sought to release me first from my inner cage door and then from my outer cage door, though this was wedged or secured externally, so my complete release from the lift was only achievable after another quick communication on his headset summoning a chambermaid. She was dressed in a swinging sateen cosmetics smock and tasteful cambric undergown the color of hay—also in headset and caring a very large bolster pillow. As the chambermaid juggled her bolster and tugged at the outer latches, the lift operator continued to address her, whispering furiously, through his headset. What is taking so long? It's one clasp, he whispered furiously into his microphone, gumbying the bulb ever tighter into his lip crease. I'm trying, she whispered furiously into her headset even though by this point she was quite within earshot.

 But suddenly I was released, and the lift operator gestured toward the belvedere's panoramic view, and the chambermaid and her bolster stuffed themselves into his lift, while the two continued to argue into their headsets.

 In the air there was an artificial scent of flowering grasses, which puffed out from a little electric crockpot every few seconds with a hiss. Indeed the view was tremendous and panoramic, and the turret simply a glassed tube with the lift and connecting stairs for its spine, and I began to circumambulate, taking in the possibilities of sight, the sea stretching out, and the now minuscule lawn and beaches below in the gray sky, but as I circled, I knew I was back in Weymouth, and that I had begun to chatter—the folly of the castle, the peninsula fort, the beach with David Trevor jostling in his swim trunks, the sea a topaz yellow in the fading sun, and the great bay of glass, which allowed so much light to flood the belvedere, should it be opened to the air, as the one in the Hotel Basilic, bringing in a sea wind that sent things flying—menus, the *Financial Times*, *Hello* magazine—as it would have sent flying the veils and parasols of the Austro-Hungarian imperials, or the hat off the head of Churchill, there in the South of France, where Churchill had summered, that little hotel where I had retreated after the fiasco war picture, hiding from Corey, who awaited me in a brothel in Oslo, and I turned and turned toward the rocks, white and pale, the water gray and choppy, and there was the boat that turned and turned and the water slipping up and over its decks, the potted hibiscus sliding toward me, the distant jungle sliding by the glass, the water, the sea, the river, and Corey, waterlogged, a gash in his head, brazenly dead in front of me.

I was stopped blankly in my turning when my eyes seized upon a little sloganed placard, hanging on the wall. It read, "Les Roches Blanches: A distinctly historic character." I have always known there was enough power in a place to invoke a reverie, but there was equal power in a place-name to revoke it.

The hotel lift, the Victorian turret and its belvedere, these things were transporting. However, they belonged not to a distant place, but to a displaced era: the place was concretely in front of me, unyielding in its determination to exist in the real, despite all efforts to transform it.

PORTHOLE

I did not swipe the panel on the wall to call for the lift, but let myself down the connecting stairs, and allowed myself, finally to be seated in a dining room.

The sole was prepared with hollandaise, and I ordered two, and I picked over the flesh of this pair of delightful fishes until all that was left were the fans of their feathered skeletons and the leathern rind of a lemon that adorned them.

PART II

17

ODOR OF CEDARS

I scarcely recall the drive back from Les Roches Blanches. I felt sated for the first time in weeks, and yet also light-headed, like the wind in the convertible might be enough to lift me out of the driver's seat. I know I must have stopped along the way, or taken a wrong turning at some point, because the day was nearly gone by the time I pulled into the garage at the back of Barbarêche and parked my convertible next to a pale blue Deux Chevaux. As I alighted, Dominick, the tennis pro, pulled up on his all-terrain cart, blithely marked "the EZ-Go."

You might have just asked, he said. His manner was cool, and subdued. He was still in his tennis whites, and his hair was tousled.

What?

You could have asked to borrow my car. I might not have given it to you just like that, but I would have driven you wherever you wanted to go.

I'm awfully sorry—is it your car? I thought it was my car. The keys were in the glove box.

Do you leave your keys in the glove box?

I really couldn't say. I don't drive much.

That's reassuring. He laughed.

I went to breakfast.

For eight hours?

I lost track of time. Which do you suppose is my car then?

Are you sure you've got a car?

The doctor said I did.

Are you drunk?

Dominick had a lilting voice, but one that seemed to emerge from a trance, as if a part of him was asleep in a distant locale. I was charmed by his unflappable manner.

I should get a lesson from you some time.

Why? Do you play tennis?

No. But maybe a lesson would help.

I don't really give lessons here. I can take a look at you and tell you who to talk to in town.

You give lessons in town, but you don't give lessons here? Aren't you the tennis pro?

It's not a country club.

It was just a thought.

I came by the barn last night, I thought we might have a drink, but you already had company.

I did?

Yes.

Oh, the furnishings. Furniture-maker. Uninvited.

Lucky you. He only comes off the mountain to collect his packages or to see me. He can phone me, of course, if he wishes to see me.

I thought we weren't allowed phones?

There's a phone in the pool house.

This is absolutely excellent to know, Dominick! I found myself wanting one last night. I missed dinner and I wanted to get ahold of one of the chefs.

Ah! Of course. Anatole. I can see I am late to the game. I won't get in your way. But you shouldn't let him—from the mountain—get in your way either. He can be... too much, I think. My offer stands, by the way. Our drink, together. But, listen, if you take my Jag out again without asking, we might have a fight. I'm serious about that.

He let go of my shoulders and hopped back onto the EZ-Go with a warm wave of his hand, and then purred his way up the gravel drive, and onto the grassy hill behind the barn, and dipped out of site in the trees.

The sun was starting to decline, though only a little, and I wanted to walk. I already felt I'd been at Jaquith House for a very long time. I felt even, as I began to walk toward the western lawn, that I had walked there before many times, or that walking to the western lawn to wait for the sunset was a ritual.

Perched on a sandstone bench, sobbing, was Tina. She spotted me and looked imploring. I feinted left and ducked instead through a shrubbery.

An elderly woman was standing in front of me. She was small and dressed in a little denim suit with a western collar and short trousers that showed her translucent ankles above her buckled sandals. Her silver hair was cut short, with bangs that feathered back from her face, almost a schoolgirl's haircut. She wore large round glasses, which magnified the circles surrounding her eyes, and from these glasses dangled a chain, and then around her neck another set of large round glasses hung, also on a chain. Her whole face was overtaken by a smile of great shock, and she dropped a little black apparatus, just smaller than a phone, with two little microphones on the top. She switched her glasses to peer at me for a moment from the second pair, and then switched them back again.

Oh, my heavens, what were you doing in that bush? She spoke in a cheerful warble.

I suppose I was running away from Tina, I said.

Oh, that explains it, she said. I always run away from Tina. What did she do?

I'm not sure, exactly. I think she was about to confide in me.

Did you slap her?

No.

Did you want to slap her?

I wanted to run, and I did.

I always want to slap that girl. Come up to my room, and I will hide you, she said. I have sherry! You still have a branch in your hair. Is that real hair?

It once was. Where's your room?

I live in the tree house!

Oh, no, I said. I'm not going back that way.

Suit yourself, she said, and very slowly bent to collect her device from the grass.

Is that a tape recorder?

It certainly hears things, she said. Unlike me, these days. You should pick up your mail in the front foyer.

Pick up my mail? I've only been here a few days. Do I have mail?

I remember you.

Have we met before?

I remember you from the monastery! I do!

What monastery?

I bet you thought I was a nun.

Are you a nun? Do you mean the monastery in France?

I don't like nuns. I prefer monks. Do you still like ghost stories?

What? I said, and then, What?

Do you still like ghost stories?

Yes, I said. I like ghost stories.

My room is haunted!

Just your room or the whole house?

Yes. She's driving me crazy at night. She wears high heels. Or he, who knows. I know he wears heels is all. Come see me in the tree house! I don't bite. Lonnie can come too. Lonnie is always welcome.

I doubled back across the front lawn of the house, in a little jog, as the old woman waved at me with her recorder.

When I closed the yellow door of the barn behind me, I finally took a breath and leaned in against the boards. I locked the latch and checked it. It didn't matter, of course, there was no way to secure the tapestry. The door to my bedroom was open, and I thought there was the flicker of candlelight coming from within. Could Lonnie, the woodsman, already be at his game? The sun was barely below the horizon.

I smelled something before I knew what it was, and then all at once I identified the fragrance: Bave Cèdres!

He was stretched out in my bed, posed on one elbow, the sheets lightly draped over an improbably enormous erection. His hair hung loose around his face and neck, and his chest looked polished and practically glazed.

Chef Anatole! I exclaimed.

Look at what I brought you!

I can see perfectly well what you brought me, Chef.

You think you can, but take another look, he said, and drew back the sheet just enough to unveil the moist pink tip, which was, as it turned out, a preserved cherry atop a glossy bun.

Is that a brioche?

Aux fruit confits. I made it with my bare hands, he said. I'm very skilled with my hands.

I have no doubt.

Come find out. Eyewitness testimony. Hands on, you know what I'm saying.

Just leave the bun on the table and let yourself out.

Come on. I can tell you're interested.

I'm not disinterested, Chef. I promised the doctor I would not encourage—

It's good for me. The doctor would want you to contribute to my well-being.

Not true. There is no way this is good for you.

The doctor doesn't care what we do.

He does, Chef, he told me specifically not to indulge your—

OK, so what do you care what the doctor thinks? You're a big shot.

Yes, I said. I'm a big shot. But I'm not going to put you in pictures. I'm done putting people in pictures, especially ones like you.

What like me? There is not "like me." Look at me! He threw back the covers. He was definitely a specimen. The brioche told no tales.

Chef Anatole, I have no doubt that your talents are extensive.

This is just the beginning: Do you know what's over there in my hamper?

More hampers?

I made for you my absolute specialty. Hot chicken mousse. Nobody but nobody makes hot chicken mousse the way I do.

I have no grounds for comparison, Chef.

Do you want to know my secret? he whispered, his brioche bobbing slightly with the measured rise and fall of his breath.

Without question, Chef.

There is a farm nearby that is owned by a butcher—these chickens, these are the most beautiful, the most heavenly creatures. They practically sleep on silk pillows. They walk around on a hillside, they are so delicate, so beautiful, they are protected, they are untouchable, they don't know danger. They don't know anger—I go, I find my girl, I hold her in my arms, I speak to her softly, the last thing she hears before her throat is cut is the love of my voice, the calmness, the pleasure she brings me.

You have to do the deed yourself?

Most people they just pick their chicken and then let the butcher take care of things, but I like to be there till the end. I like to show respect. I think that is right, don't you?

And then you make her into a mousse straightway? Right there on the hillside?

No, you know, I put her in a bag. But when I walk away from that place, you know, when I get back to the kitchen, there she is hanging against my leg, in her bag, still warm. That is how fresh this chicken is when I go to disjoint it. Her spirit is with me: she is very tender. Not boring.

It is a far, far better thing she does, et cetera.

I'm trying to impress you, he said, gesturing first to his hamper, then to his brioche. Is it working?

I sighed. All of this and hot chicken mousse! I thought. Jaquith House was filled with traps.

Take off your clothes and come to bed, he suggested.

Not happening, I said.

He sat upright against the headboard and then slapped his hands against the mattress. What the fuck? he said. Dominick said you were asking for me. I had to switch shifts for this!

Dominick told you what? That's rich, I said.

You didn't ask for me? I made you a mousse!

No, Chef Anatole. I don't mean it that way. I did tell Dominick I was looking for you, I just didn't mean *this*. Necessarily.

That is harsh.

Chef, I'm just trying not to do everything wrong immediately,

and I'll admit, at Jaquith House the methods... I'm really trying to do things that are not—
Selfish?
I didn't say that, I said.
So you are trying to be selfish?
I didn't say that either. It was exhausting, all this language! Was this really the way of the world, to go on talking and talking and never a moment of peace? I sat down on the bed beside Anatole. Chef, I said, I seem to be the target of critique.
You should think about that. That's a punctuation.
What's going on around here? Is there any actual therapy happening at this place?
The doctor works very slowly. He's got excellent methods. But it takes time.
It doesn't seem to be working on you.
I'm better than I've been in years.
Really?
The doctor says I will find myself through my artistry! The doctor says I have a lot to offer people.
You obviously do have a lot to offer, but... listen, I don't know anything about it.
You're cynical. That's a defense mechanism.
I'm not cynical in the least. I think it might be worth considering becoming someone who believes in things other than celluloid, it would be a new Helena, but—
Like a romantic?
Romanticism is a sort of belief. Sure, I'd be willing to entertain romanticism, I lied.
You have to give it time. The doctor doesn't work like anyone else. You'll see. Once you settle in you'll see how effective it is.
Settle in? How long have you been here?

A couple of years, only.

Are you settled then?

I'm starting to settle. I can help you too. Just relax. Take things as they come to you. He reached for my hand and placed it on his thigh. I'm warm, he said.

Yes, I said. Tender, I thought. Not boring.

He took my hand again and moved it. He had softened somewhat across the course of our conversation. He closed his eyes. This softening, however slight, and however brief, appealed to me. I closed my eyes, and feeling him grow in my hand, I allowed myself to give way to the attar of cedars, and for a moment Corey had come back to me, not as he always did in the picture of my mind, waterlogged, a gash in his head, but warm, alive, offering himself without speaking. And when I bent to taste the skin that was before me, it was Corey's skin I expected—but this was, of course, a different taste, or it should have been. Or perhaps I couldn't remember what he tasted like.

No matter, I thought, and I continued with my eyes closed to taste the chef, who, as my mouth slid across him, had begun to mutter in another language, one that was definitely neither French nor German—it was a language I didn't recognize.

Much later, in the dark quiet of Barbarêche, the chef was gone, the sound of the brook was gone, and the recreation lounge above me was likewise still and quiet. The woodsman hadn't come again, with or without his dog. Chef Anatole had left me as well, but left the hamper of mousse and the little sugared bun with the candied cherry on top, which gleamed slightly in the moonlight. I threw on a wrap and let myself out of the yellow front door, to stand on the flagstones and look up at the moon, which was fully risen, nearly full, waning rather than waxing. I looked up to the main house through the darkened back windows, some few rooms on the third floor were glowing—more insomniacs, I wondered? The Syllabary was also lit and seemed to me suddenly a little haven in the midst of so many unknowns.

18

THE WAR PICTURE

Today, Helena, I would like to take up the subject of one of your films, I'd like to talk about *Silent Trenches*, the doctor said.

I was stretched out in a hammock, which looped the sequoia outside the Syllabary with an enormous tether. He sat adjacent in an Adirondack chair.

I had quite a nice meal at Les Roches Blanches yesterday, Doctor.

Don't try to derail me, Helena. I have only a limited time with each of you. *Silent Trenches*: it's my favorite of your films. What did you love about it?

Love?

Yes, the thing you loved most.

It was beautifully lit.

Fascinating. The professional's tutored gaze coming through! I never really think of those technical aspects; it interferes with the fantasy, I suppose. That's the difference between the professional and the audience.

A dim natural glow. You could barely see it. That's what I like best about that film—if I watch it in a room with the blinds up, it's like it isn't there.

Oh, dear. What a negative attitude!

Right now, I am interested in the other occupants at Jaquith House.

Do you mean Chef Anatole?

You know about that already?

He is an open person.

That he is.

Tsk, tsk, Helena. I did specifically warn you.

I'm sorry about that, Doctor. Not exactly sorry. Sorry to find that I am not sorry. But, no. Tell me about the little woman who lives in the tree house. Is she there now?

She is out for the afternoon with her walker, recording sounds.

A walker?

Not that sort of walker, one of my aides, who carries her equipment and allows her to take his arm, that sort of thing, while she is recording. Fanny records the forest, the lakes, the birds. She is recording the sound of the known existing world. It's a very comprehensive project.

Is she an artist?

She is an artist of sound, yes, and recording, and thought. But she is much more than that.

She thought we had met before. Has she worked in film, do you know?

I think she has always been an independent person, but really these are questions you should be asking her, Helena. The point of your interaction with the community of Jaquith House is interaction in and of itself. Such interactions should not be toward some epistemological end.

I interacted with Chef Anatole.

And I don't discount that. You'll think my motives suspect, Helena, but in your way, and in his, there is something even in that type of interaction that might contribute to your health overall.

Both of you. I won't discount that, no. But I do think it is rather cheating? Don't you?

I don't believe in cheating.

Helena, if you don't want to talk about your films. Perhaps you want to speak about your upbringing. Your uncle had many lovers, I believe you mentioned.

So many lovelies.

And were you fond of these women? Did you grow close to any of them?

Did I grow close? I said. And, I thought, I grew. They grew. In close-up. And I have a portfolio to prove it.

Anyone in particular you recall?

Jacqueline, who could hold her breath under water for two minutes while keeping her visage absolutely perfect, unstrained, unaffected, beautiful, and floating. Elsa, who dressed me as a Victorian dandy and instructed me in the best manner of holding a cigar, a cane, a snuff box, and a cigarette case, so I could get a job on Saturdays as a page boy in a revival cinema. Svetlana, who, while playing the role of Anna Karenina in a language she neither knew nor understood, had nonetheless translated the feeling of the part from the language of the original, and timed it perfectly to pair with the words she recited. Carlotta, who read my fortune in tarot cards and saw there a death by drowning. Laure, who worked in a flower shop in San Francisco and arrived to the *Anjodie* always with bouquets of over-blown roses, shedding their petals, heady with a perfume on the edge of decay. Fernande, who was escaping a jilted lover who anchored his skiff at a distance from the *Anjodie* and shouted across the bay, pleading with her to return to him. Germaine, who lived on her own boat and drove a water taxi, one which delivered so many of the others to us at regular intervals. Irène, Madeline, Juliane, Colette, Eve—

Helena?

Yes, Doctor?

Did you remember anyone in particular?

Wasn't I talking?

Not at this moment, no, you seemed in a faraway place.

No names, Doctor. It never pays to name the lab rats.

A curious analogy. If you don't want to talk about that, he said, then where does that leave us? Back to your war picture: I read this wonderful article by a young film critic about the final scene in *Silent Trenches*—I have it here somewhere…

I suppose I should be grateful that some young person has wasted a part of his life taking my films seriously. But—I am not grateful. For that kind of attention.

You say that as if you were wary of being pigeonholed, or harshly interpreted, or attributed some political credo.

That is the problem, Doctor! My work is more—

Visceral?

Yes. Exactly, Doctor. And more—

Cosmological?

I can see that.

That's just what this article says! There, I've found it finally. And yet, to my way of thinking, *Silent Trenches* has a kind of radical message, doesn't it?

Doctor, I have never been, nor will I ever be, a political filmmaker.

Now that's a start, Helena. That's a fine start! Future-tense verbs. We're getting somewhere. And I don't think the political discounts the visceral, or the cosmological for that matter. A masterpiece, this article suggests, let me read it out and just focus your eyes on the light coming through the needles of tree, such a clear day, see the way the shadows pattern…

"*Silent Trenches* is a film of people watching other people, the camera becomes all-watching eyes, egalitarian and roaming. Désir avoids the static—and implicated—single gaze. She rejects the law that viewers can only identify with one hero—the tired nineteenth-century notion of cinematic perspective which still holds sway today—she refuses the closure that makes the camera enclose a space or imprison a character, instead she makes the camera assume multiple roles, in the same way that the characters are interchangeable..."

And the doctor continued to read in his studied, even delivery, so flat, so even—a mesmerist's reading voice, it occurred to me as I lay in the hammock—but by then I was already truly faraway, and lost in something like sleep-not-sleep.

I was not a political filmmaker. *Silent Trenches* was the accidental exception to this rule. That fiasco war picture!

The story went this way: during the First World War, an officer of mapmaking, called Saint-Luc (played by Corey) is shot down during a routine reconnaissance mission. He is captured and imprisoned in a château or a schloss, geographic location unclear. Suffering from amnesia, shellshocked or affected by mustard gas, his faculties are compromised. In the ambulatory yard, he comes under the influence of a spy called Dun, with whom he eventually escapes into the snowy wastes. This was the basic end result for the film; a somewhat unresolved and ambiguous approach to narrative, and therefore it lent itself to interpretation. Scene. Fin.

A deviation for me, this film featured not one, but two actors. Here is the beginning of the end.

The original concept for the film was quite different; the escape sequence into the snowy waste, which became the ending for *Silent Trenches*, would have been the midpoint of the film as originally envisioned. Across the second half—should such a second half have been realized—the film would follow Saint-Luc exclusively. Having escaped the château, he awakens in the shelter of an order of Carthusian monks, silent ascetics, in a remote mountain monastery. Dun the spy has died in the transit over the mountains. Saint-Luc regains his faculties through the silent rituals of the monastery, tending garden plots and beehives. The war would progress—much as it did historically—the monks under threat from occupation by invaders. And so it was according to the original concept, that in the effort to protect their silence from occupiers, the monks end the film (the film that would have been, the film-to-come that never came) in a bloody battle with the encroaching military, with Corey as Saint-Luc in their frontlines, in the trenches of their own design, the transformed frames of their vegetable gardens.

I still have a vivid image in my mind of this final moment in the film, as if I shot it. Corey rising up out of the framed trench of the snow-covered, frozen vegetable plot, in smoke or mists, in the white robes of his order, in a gas mask, leveling his rifle, the monastery in the background, the Alps rising above it.

In the film in my mind, he levels a Karabiner Kurz, model 98, with a walnut stock and a stripper clip above the magazine. What a harrowing and beautiful rifle! I know this is historically inaccurate—but it is the gun I see in my mind, and I would have fought for that gun, to the bitter end. I would have had my reasons.

Narratively the whole thing was a bit of a stretch. An ambitious plot, to say the least, and the violent resistance of the monks was probably romanticized, and likely controversial as well: research has never been my strong suit. I think in images.

I labored over the second half of the script—leaving the first half of the script in the prison chateau as little more than a rough sketch—trying to justify the logic of the final violent action without any speech, and no matter how carefully I worked, in this voiceless mode, I risked making a statement in which I might become invested, and the film would be an inevitable failure.

Beginning that film, my ideas were forged and unshakable. It was, as it turns out, to be short-lived, this unshakable confidence. I was coming off the small success of *Walkway* and indulging the window of autonomy the film studio offered and indulging in the cinematic fashion of that moment—toward sweeping, dramatic, historical pieces patched together through montage. This trend seduced me not as a mode to embrace for the rest of my career but as a mode of conveyance, a means of smuggling in some of my most preferred film elements: male-dominated worlds of silent, grim engagement, potential violence in all quarters no matter how antithetical, exile in a remote, harsh terrain—cold, dark, frozen, violent. All my favorite things.

Everything that could go wrong with the film, however, did go wrong, so very wrong. Worried about time, I plunged into the project while many elements were unformed in my mind. Corey was in low spirits and had not recovered from the immersion of *Walkway*. I had pulled him away suddenly to Grenoble in midwinter so filming could begin on this next project. I can't remember from what exactly he was pulled away, another love affair, another crumbling marriage, or was it the death of a sister? All of the above? His particular scandals blur together in my mind.

The château in Grenoble was a refitted luxury hotel, perfect for our eccentricities, accustomed as it was to the purpose of tourist spectacle. It could be stripped down to its original austerity quickly and restaged just as quickly. The mountain monastery location needed for the second half of the film, however, became impossible to secure. The few sects willing to allow us inside their walls to film were wrongly placed geographically. When a compound in the Vosges mountains was finally booked, it was so Romanesque in construction and crawling with so many Benedictine nuns, we were limited to very obscure angles and only a few interior spaces. Construction began on a sound stage and interior sets to make up for this, and I was once again faced with my own resistance to sets.

More delays, more searching for locations, all of which continued to drain the budget of the film before the film had begun. I had scripted two equestrian scenes inside the monastery (fevered hallucinations by Corey as Saint-Luc) but there was the problem of getting the dressage animals from Doncières up to our Vosges location, worse still to work with them on sets. Just as we began resolving the horse transit problem, the nuns got fed up with the details of our contract, and the general dissoluteness of our crew. They reserved the right to slam their door in our faces.

This was the first real devastation. Corey was terrified. The response of the nuns triggered some deep superstition, and the focus on his character was evaporating. And with my concentration now turned toward the logistics of the horses, I resolved to shoot equestrian sequences at a riding school in the Touraine. This meant another relocation. I was not happy, but that, for me, was easily hidden. Worse still, and less discreetly managed, Corey was despondent.

I did what I did best: stalled and lied to my crew. We delayed our departure for a week in a grand hotel and vineyard in Chinon, hoping that eating and drinking madly, to the detriment of the budget, would have some cheering effect on Corey. It was the sort of thing that worked wonders on David Trevor: lock him up in some luxury suite, ply him with drink, entertain his fantasies, and most importantly gaze upon him—gaze upon him unblinkingly. A few days of this, muttering the right flattering phrases, and waiting for all other impediments to fall away, which of course, they never do.

With Corey, my approaches were still experimental: I had not yet mastered the correct technique to trick him out of himself.

I can see you have already formed attachments with the locals, I said to him.

Does it bother you?

Your French is strange but effective.

Better than yours, he said. Did you teach yourself?

I don't remember. (... Jacqueline, Collette, Fernande, Iréne...) Did you teach yourself?

I thought we agreed, no history. But if you want to know: I was a porter at Les Halles.

Yes, well. And I picked it up from distant relations. So, we are very much the same, in that regard.

Very much the same, I think, he said. Such types who drift and absorb and reflect back. And we are both good mimics. It's useful, don't you think?

In your line, it is.

I was never meant to be an actor, Hel. Did you know? It was an accident.

I've heard the rumors.

Oh, yes. Of course. That they found me in a rented suit.

You know me, Corey. I don't pay attention to past lives.

Oh, no? It seems to me that you only pay attention to past lives. Selectively.

If you mean that I work with history subjects, yes. That's no secret.

You are lost in history. You look like history.

Another insult?

On the contrary. It's to your credit. But, you admit, you have tunnel vision.

My vision thus far is paying your rent. And the rent on your suits.

My face pays my rent, he said. And the rent on your suits.

Then we are both frauds, and we were lucky to find each other. But I think it is also lucky that there is a camera between us most of the time.

You think that when you want to think that.

I mean it in the bigger picture. No pun intended. But we all need a vacation sometimes, don't we?

Your horses are waiting for us, Hel.

But you don't see the point of the horses, do you?

I don't see the point of any of this at the moment, but I don't want to work at not working. Do you?

Never, I said.

And with that we were off to Touraine, and the next set of setbacks.

Setbacks upon setbacks. Filming at the Grenoble location was suspended before it began—too much snow, difficulty delivering materials, equipment, and trailers, and zoning problems. Next, a plumbing fiasco at the château that put everyone into the eighteenth-century outhouses. Finally, or penultimately, a heavy wet snow collapsed one section of the rooftop that I particularly needed for my escape sequence. There was no choice but to focus on shooting Corey with the dressage horses in Touraine.

What would I do with all this horse footage? That was a problem for the editing room. But the editing room was rapidly becoming automatized, it was not even a place but something that happened inside the mind of a machine entirely. Becoming, to me, a robotic prosthesis, which I feared. The camera was the only remaining device that gave me confidence. I just had to move forward with filming, even if there was very little to film.

Now the most devastating fiasco hit us solidly. I lost my other actor: Alec Cornwall, who had miraculously agreed to play the secondary role of the spy Dun. This great British actor of the stage who'd transitioned to film late in life but with considerable ease was an ideal figure for the illusive Dun: silver-haired, slim, elegant, and reserved, my private Laurence Olivier. We were waiting for him to finish a film in Mallorca, so by the time he arrived in Grenoble, we were already in the process of relocating to the dressage château in Touraine. There, he was not needed. An avid and accomplished skier, Cornwall decided to stay in Grenoble and take in the local sport. For the first time in his life, he was in a skiing accident. He broke both legs and had to be airlifted off the mountain.

Cornwall's hospital incarceration was indefinite—his true age was an industry secret, though I would guess he was sixty at least—having him back on his feet and able to scale the roof of our château seemed unlikely, a month's delay at least.

I convinced Corey to spend a day with me apart from the crew and his entourage to review our footage. The rushes were lackluster. I was scribbling changes even as the images flickered across the viewer, and Corey could no longer watch. I found him smoking outside our hotel, though he had claimed to have quit years previously, if he had ever smoked at all.

I think we should run through a few changes before tomorrow.

Hel, what is this film?

You liked yesterday's script changes, you'll like these—we just need to reconfigure.

It is becoming avant-garde.

And what if it is? I thought you wanted to be taken more seriously.

"No more Borsalinos and tommy gun gangsters," you said. "Finally, the path of a true samurai."

Because of the monastery, the warrior monks, the vow of silence. Where is any of that?

You have to trust me.

The character is an airman, a pilot. Not in the cavalry, not in some sort of spaghetti western.

There's no point in discussing this, Corey. We shoot the film, we edit, we make decisions later. I am not going to mount a case every night that there are changes.

I feel removed from the world. I don't go out, no one sees me—I am worried. There's been more of that very unkind gossip in the press about my business associates, simply because of that unfortunate suicide attempt.

How dare he whine to me about his personal problems? Actors should have no lives beyond the frame!

I said: Surely, no one still cares—that was months ago. How can anyone even remember?

It keeps coming up. I know it won't go away—normally it doesn't bother me, if I know that I am working and my work is coming to something. But is it?

The monastery is still a problem, Corey, as you know.

But it is the heart of the film, conceptually.

I know! I wrote it! You must stop this. The location will come together, I have the very best people working on it, I said, and gave him a firm shake of the shoulder, like a good father.

But he was not wrong. Of course, the film was becoming avant-garde: all narrative structure out of reach. Truly the material was difficult, but I had counted on Cornwall on the set by then to rally Corey, who needed a stern and confident papa. I could wear the pants, most days, but it was taking a toll on both of us. This constant veneer of composure and logic. If he continued to brood, he might also try to escape the film.

I had to find a way to move forward with the filming. I gave the crew a day off for revelry and then summoned Corey to our little dark wine bar.

I've decided to recast Cornwall, I said. We can't wait for him to recover. I think we have to knock off here and go to Grenoble and sort out things.

How will these things be sorted out? Corey asked. He could barely lift his head, his performance of acute fatigue was so studied.

I've talked to production, and it's quite easy: he'll have to be replaced.

I don't want to hear this. You know I looked forward to learning from his methodology.

Yes, I know. The part of the spy must house a professional, I agree with you completely. Someone from the stage is absolutely necessary. To do anything else would be to combat cliché with cliché. I don't want to combat clichés.

You want to trade in them.

Fair enough, Corey. I know you're upset with me.

This is gutting.

Absolutely gutting, I said. I am asking you for your advice.

Someone known, but not necessarily recognizable. He must have something in his eyes that would cause Saint-Luc to follow him implicitly, despite misgivings. He could not be too distinct. You know—he mustn't be vulgarly handsome or anything like that.

God forbid.

He would need to blend into a crowd—he could become invisible.

We are in total agreement, Corey. There is a Scottish actor I have in mind. He's very authentic—symmetrical scars on either side of his face—I saw him in two productions in Edinburgh.

Too young!

You know the actor I'm talking about?

I'm speaking of myself. (He held his head in his hands.)

You really shouldn't be worrying about this, Corey. The studio has lots of ideas. There are lots of possibilities.

You've spoken to production?

Of course! (I had not.)

Swear it!

I swear it. Rest assured, I am in complete control of this film.

I no longer believe in control; it is contrary to the better belief systems.

You'll pack up? We'll do this together?

I already notified Valasquez. The bags will be down shortly.

And as if by magic, the slender white-suited Valasquez appeared at the top of the stairs with a collection of contemporary valises.

Ah, Grenoble! Perhaps the truest of river cities. Looking back on it now, I can blame even my love affair with a river on that fiasco war picture. Beautiful Grenoble, where the dark river Drac, catching the light of the Alps, snakes its way toward the river Isere like a procession of lanterns. The city itself is a city of remnants, of Roman walls, of leper hospitals, of the garrisons of religious wars. Remnants of baronetcies and comital land parcels, remnants of Huguenots and the pillaged tombs of the dauphins, remnants of a centuries' old glove industry. Great glove rivalries went on between Grenoble and Grasse through the late Middle Ages, through edicts and the revocation of edicts of the sixteenth century, until a Protestant purge finally gave Grenoble the monopoly on gloves, and the number of glovers trebled prior to the Reign of Terror, and one can only assume that when heads rolled, the gloves worn by both the aristocrats and their executioners were all made in Grenoble.

For this reason, I always wore gloves when in the city.

Alec Cornwall was in traction from his skiing accident in a hospital on the Ile Verte. I sent Corey out on an invented errand to an address across town. I sent my driver on to the hospital to await me, but walked to think and prepare.

I crossed a cemetery, where lepers and dignitaries were buried together. The most spectacular tombs were those of the manufacturers of gloves. Walking among the glovers' tombs, I steeled myself and practiced my severance speech for Cornwall. It was very short, very clear. My dear Eck, I would say. We have to face facts. I've got to replace you. I've got to keep filming.

When had I become so tentative? The Helena of *Mechanism,* the Helena of *Slipcase,* even the Helena of *Walkway* would have fired him summarily for even looking at skis while under contract. While Corey had finally given me my most vital playing piece, something had gone soft on the edges: the need to keep him, the need to prop him up was making me second-guess my every move.

In the hospital, Cornwall had a suite of rooms on a floor that was reserved, full stop. I was given a special code to enter into the elevator and released into a deserted and dark hallway. In the spirit of my wandering among the tombs, I was wearing the funeral kimono my tailor had refashioned into a jumpsuit. A dubious but formidable look, and the stiff black silk rustled as I moved through the corridor, and my boot heels rang on the polished concrete.

The sound returned me to film images—the dark long hall, shoes echoing in the empty expanse—always precursors to an assassination in the hospital bed. The appearance of the professional assassin was imminent: but was I the professional? Or was I the professional's target?

I had to pause and lean against a wall. I had a friend who was an intellectual sort of filmmaker, trying to make a perfect film of immanence. No one knew what this meant, apart from him. He tried many methods—all failures. He had yet to make an immanent film. I was suddenly seized by the idea that this moment, awaiting the professional, in radical ambiguity... the assassin-as-immanence might solve my friend's failure.

I stopped. I had allowed myself to think of another project! With another person. I had allowed myself to think of another project when my own project was in complete ruins. When we are alone and failing alone, we dream of collaborations with other failures.

I rounded a corner into a buzzing and well-lit nurses' station, where Cornwall's fashionable wife, twenty years at least his junior, was on the phone ordering in oysters and champagne from a bistro. She waved me in. She feigned to kiss me on one cheek, then on the other. She mimed a gesture of approval for my clothing, and I mimed a comparable gesture to her. I thought, this is a superb woman, and I left her to her ordering.

I found Cornwall in his suite of rooms, bare-chested, looking tan and fit, albeit splinted to the waist, stippled with silver stubble, his blue eyes lit as if from inside his head, and an enormous whiskey glass in his hand. On the settee beside him was David Trevor.

Oh, for fuck's sake? I said.

Helena! It's sweet of you to come see an old man, Cornwall said, I'm the most impossible wreck.

I'm so sorry, Eck. Will you walk again soon?

I was walking earlier today! That's why they've re-splinted me. But don't you look wonderful!

No, it's you who looks good, I said. Apart from the splints, of course. And you're clearly well attended, I see. I gestured to David Trevor.

I'm barely off my skis and this rascal turns up angling for my job.

PORTHOLE

Don't be ridiculous, Trevor said. He's my uncle.

Your uncle?

Obviously.

Are you related to everyone in the theater, David? I said.

Just the best-looking ones. And the most degenerate.

Yes, well, Cornwall interrupted, David will have a good perspective on that bit. Helena, darling, I've made a real mess of this mess, I know. Can you forgive me? I was so desperate to get a chance to really, really... he waved his cocktail to finish his thought.

Can you give us a minute, David? I'd like to talk business, I said.

He has a morphine pump and a pitcher of manhattans; I don't think he's in a state to discuss business. Come some other time.

Cornwall said, I hope you've learned to ignore his one-liners, Helena—his mother had him in *Good Night Bassington* at age six. Darling, but truly, if I didn't believe so strongly in your vision, this wonderful opportunity to really, you know, give something, well, genuine, in this difficult medium—I'm so cynical, darling, so cynical, but, really, I'm also so hopeful that I'll be in prime condition in a matter of weeks, but... he plunged back into his cocktail.

He'll be on his back for months. He's practically eighty, David said.

And I still look better than you, David. Kidding, of course! Helena, I can't tell you how happy I am to be part of this wonderful vision—war, intrigue, ethical dilemma—it's perfect for me. I know that I could, could have brought it a... and a rare privilege to a humble stage man, a man of the footlights, such as myself—but I'm worried... I fear...

What rot! said David. His ego is massive. He knows you're flailing, and he's got another project in Morocco on the hook. Your film sounds awful, Helena. I suppose you wrote it? More of your macho bullshit and hackneyed dialogue? Only with some sort of pseudo-religious dick-waving thrown in?

Eck, you see the problem I'm facing. We've got to keep filming, I'm afraid. I've got to replace you.

Of course. You've got to find someone else. Though it pains me, I will yield.

I spoke to the studio, and I think there is some hope... I began, but, of course, I hadn't taken a call from anyone in weeks. I really hadn't thought at all about what to hope for, and for that matter, couldn't even remember what I had rehearsed to say to Cornwall when I was walking among the tombs. I must have imagined something, but what would it have been? I twisted my hands in my black gloves. My memory was going, as was my ability to hold on to the truly horrid aspects of my career, given the lure of the fantasy of other, hypothetical horrors.

I mean, Helena, why not take David?

(My composure in the past weeks had become a thin veil even at the best of times.) I said, David? He's too young! He's too vulgarly handsome!

Thirty, forty, fifty—what difference does age make to a true actor?

What is this about, Cornwall? Is he really your nephew?

He's like a nephew, darling. He'll manage easily.

You called me out here, with him waiting—did you also throw yourself down a mountain?

I didn't call you, Helena. You'll recall you came here on your own. I had no idea that you two would even turn up in Grenoble. You really could try to be reasonable. With David there's no surprises, no concerns. David is such an old pro. An old young pro.

I won't have him, Eck.

She won't get a chance, David said. I wouldn't touch this doomed project for love or money. I go into rehearsal for *Private Lives* next month.

Drop your ridiculous posturing, David, Cornwall said. You couldn't throw a stone in London without hitting some hack playing

Elyot; it runs more than *The Bald Soprano*. When you're sixty you'll be playing Elyot at the Old Vic, and I'll be playing him at the Young Vic, and I'll get better reviews. Take the part.

I'm not offering it to him. I said, He's all wrong—wrong everything, and he's impossible to work with. I won't subject Corey to him.

That affected little prima donna! David said. Don't be absurd. He won't notice the cast has even changed, he'll be glued to a mirror or a whore or his team of catamites. He'll be sculpting his midsection—

He's a professional. He's not typecast.

He's a manikin with no past, present, or future. He's a pretty little blank. And his hobby is fucking the wives of oligarchs. It's a miracle someone hasn't poisoned him already.

I don't understand your obsession with tabloid gossip, David, given the way you've been left out of it your whole career.

How lovely for you to have some flaccid little toy to twist and bend to your will.

A versatile actor, you mean.

A limp dick!

For Christ's sake! Cornwall shouted. You're both spoiling my morphine. David, enough playacting. Helena, you know he's not wrong: you've got yourself in quite a difficult spot. Given my contract, I could shut down this whole production for a year. I'm generously offering you a release. And I may have fallen off a mountain, but my ear is still to the ground. You've got no location, no footage, and a script that wanders all over hell and back. The whole thing's a pretentious nightmare and a political embarrassment, and you're wildly off schedule anyway. Now you've lost an actor, and frankly the strength of my name on the picture is the only reason your studio has let you run this thing so far aground. Take David to your castle, shoot your miserable film, and get out of this fiasco while you can.

The two of you can continue to yell profanities at each other and do whatever else you do off set, and it will be like old times.

I value silence! I screamed.

If I do it, I will do it as I like—I won't take direction from her.

Little change that would be, I said.

I'm not joking; I won't let her bully me.

It's a minor part, David, said Cornwall, and buzzed for his nurse to usher all of us out of his suite. At reception, Cornwall's wife gave me a thumbs-up.

I was beside myself. I didn't even make the elevator. I raged as quickly as imaginable down the stairs and out of the hospital. I raged and gestured wildly for my driver, as if I were filming myself. I could hear David following me. His shoes were Swiss and bespoke. They were ones I'd bought for him. I'd recognize the ring of those heels anywhere.

On the sidewalk, David caught the door handle of my car and opened it for me. My driver was waiting, behind his darkened glass. Inside was serene and leathern. The scene was over.

Where are you staying? David asked me. His transformation to the sympathetic, the concerned David was always swift and seamless.

I'm at the château. Corey is with me.

You can't stay there. It's really inhospitable. I was there with Eck before the accident.

And did you break his legs for him?

I mean it, Helena: it's truly cold and damp. You can't sleep there. The roof collapsed.

Stop pandering, David, it's pathetic.

Then stop the Nick and Nora act. I don't know who you think we are fooling. Your boy wasn't even there to see your scene. And everyone knows you love me.

I do not know it.

Well, Eck does in any case. He knows you called me.

David, stop trying to get around me. Yes, I need you. Only just this once. But there is no way I am going to let you do to Corey what you did to little Emile, wedging him out of a career like that.

You did that to little Emile!

No, I was seduced by your matinee idol routine, your swagger, your charm...

My talent, I think you mean.

Your shallow tricks.

Helena, not even you could believe that. Anyway, Emile's career is made now. He should thank us. And, in fact, I think he does.

Career? A career is only what the outside sees. I am here on the inside, in this abysmal film!

And so, I'm here to help.

Help, yes. Maybe. But I will not let you push Corey out of his place.

On your lap?

I mean it David. This is a cameo, less than a cameo. It's a walk-on. The minute the film ends you are back to Terrance Rattigan. Are we clear? You know we both do much better with an ocean between us.

I understand completely: once more, only. With feeling! And what fun we'll have. I'm at the Shackelton Lodge. It's beautiful. There's a pool in a room of sloping glass. The mountains beyond. I have an oversized bed, and there are wooden beams—you can fall asleep counting them, just as you love to do. Do something because it's fun for a change, and stay with me. But there's no roadway. You'll have to come up on the cables. Will you think about it? You know I'm good for it.

If only you had similar prowess on set.

You are terrified I'll outshine him!

No one—absolutely no one—should dare to *shine* in any film of mine.

Always the dour auteur, Helena. Come up the cables, tell him you have to brief me on the script. Tell him he is the star, but I am the needy, helpless extra. Tell him whatever you want. Tell him the things you tell yourself.

Eck's wife is extraordinary, I muttered.

Isn't she? We were an item, you know, in the Pleistocene era. I was still a schoolboy. But it was ill-fated. She always did prefer the elderly—even then.

David, you will say nothing to him, do you understand? Nothing—I heard myself saying, but the old familiar capitulation had already taken hold of me as the car pulled away from the curb that day in Grenoble. The door was already shut. Somehow, I was still holding David's patterned scarf in my hands. What did David say as the car door closed? I can't quite remember. Something like: Helena, I'm going to be so good. So well behaved. Helena, I get along with everyone. Wait and see, I'll charm the pants off your little thug.

I knew Corey: his icy posture, his stoicism, his refusal to register threat, his puppyish devotion to actors of the stage. David Trevor was the one thing that would push the film forward, my lifeline. It was a gamble, to be certain, and I could not help but fear that the two of them together would be my final undoing. Not one, but two actors? As Uncle Yiorgos knew so well, you must never let the lovelies meet, lest they bond and turn against you.

19
AN EXPERIMENT IN THOUGHT

His fingers snapped.

Helena? Are you with me?

I awoke, but I was not rested. I felt that I had lost sleep, that in falling into memory, falling into a recounting or reorganizing of time, I was taking time from elsewhere, from the future. Where could it come from but from my sleep, I wondered?

Was I speaking?

A little experiment. To cut through the mists. How fascinating the true story of how you cast your second lead.

There was no second lead. There was a small second role.

Reviews suggest otherwise. A roving perspective.

I let the camera lead, it has a mind of its own.

A wandering eye.

I had lost the plot. Somehow with David, I had a collaborationist. The film was emerging: its lines of force, its intention...

That sounds natural, and organic. When a lover returns to your life, a lover you have perhaps never resolved entirely in your mind.

I don't have lovers, Doctor. I have actors with benefits. I am not in a nineteenth-century novel.

Oh, no? You are on a nineteenth-century rest cure. Isn't it possible that your imagined fixation with one actor might have been, as it were, a distraction from the total fixation with another? Why, Helena, I do believe you are close to tears!

You won't get that sort of satisfaction from me, Doctor.

I loved your war picture. Dun the spy is the real hero of the film, and we do love heroes. He draws up your inept, confused pilot just when he is most likely to be murdered by his captors, and then he carries him. He literally carries him! There is excitement and suspense and intrigue and a dangerous climb over the rooftops toward freedom. I thought it was a thoroughly uplifting story of a man who is both heroic and charitable, despite being cynical and world-weary.

That description just turns my stomach, Doctor.

That's it precisely. It's a pure, selfless gesture of entertainment. And that finally is what you wrote and what you filmed, isn't it? Besides, it strikes me as rather natural that your audiences would follow David Trevor, who, to be perfectly frank, is just *such* a better actor. And where is he these days, Helena?

I don't know, Dr. Duvaux, nor do I care.

I find that very hard to believe. And in any case, I certainly *do* know where he is. But I won't tell you unless you ask me. We shall end there for today. Wouldn't you like to take Tina out for an ice cream? I'll have the gate opened.

Definitely not, Doctor. I'm going to spend today on my own.

And why not? I asked myself. Why not alone, why not walking, apart from everyone else? To walk was to think, that much I remembered. As I strode with purpose across the western lawn it was toward thinking I was striding, a thinking that put the mind straight, rather than a thinking that tied the mind in knots. I had come to Jaquith

House believing, mistakenly, that I would find a way inside my thinking. But the problem I kept facing was one of getting outside my thinking. I reckoned that because I was never in one place for such a sustained period of time as I might be at Jaquith House, I could now begin working concentratedly on the thinking as I might work concentratedly on a film script, and so the idea was to put myself into a place where I might uninterruptedly concentrate on my thinking, and thereby gain access to it. That was wrong. What needed to be done was to get outside my thinking. I oscillated between the desire to get outside my thinking and the desire to come inside my thinking, so that I was always in a state of amnesia about my thoughts as I had often been in a state of amnesia about my films once the filming began, because of this same struggle with movement and interruption. Movement interrupted by other movement at tangential angles to the original path of pursuit. Was that thinking? Even looking at the footage from filming, once I was filming, I didn't always recognize it, only the faces rang a bell—and to watch the footage as in periphery, this was the only way it could be tolerated. But when I attempted to sit with it, uninterrupted, I was suddenly trapped in the extant film, or the extant part of the unfinished film, unable to get outside it or unable to get inside it enough to get to the next open space where a scene might occur, where another structure had been built, a structure that might be another château or might be another body of water. This was the problem of the war picture: a dwelling on process, unable to enter it, or a dwelling on process, unable to escape it.

Whatever had happened there, in the hammock with Dr. Duvaux, whatever happened—and perhaps many things happened, and took place in the hammock, but I know I experienced the duration of time—*that* was thinking. But it was not a forward progression of thinking, that which I pursued now as I strode across the western lawn, but a regression of thinking—which is to say, thinking as remembering. It was the remembering that was the worst part of the thinking, that was perfectly obvious. Knowing that remembering is painful, that was not new information, that was old information, even the remembering of the pain of remembering was banal. So, as I strode with purpose it was toward an unraveling, an unsnarling, an unremembering, a striding away from one kind of thinking toward another kind of thinking, which I supposed was toward an unthought as much as toward a thought, one which erased rather than inscribed. Away, away, I thought as I passed the curve of the front lake with its geyser lying dormant, toward the line of trees to the west, where the land was starting to slope away from Jaquith House. I could see the tennis pro driving, in the distance, on his EZ-Go, with two gentlemen also dressed for tennis, perched behind him on the cargo rack. He was waving at something or someone, even approaching me, possibly he was gesturing toward me. It was hard to tell, however, since the tennis pro seemed to need both hands to control the steering column of the EZ-Go and since I was now striding so quickly I could only look over my shoulder and catch him in glances. But it seemed he did approach me at the slow speed of an ATV heavily laden with tennis enthusiasts, and while the little EZ-Go was trying to climb the rather steep incline of the lawn toward the western tree line, I was outstripping him with the speed and energy of a woman who has no known destination, but nonetheless must reach it. The EZ-Go was slower than me in my purposeful striding, and the tree line would be reached before the EZ-Go caught me, and before the thinking of the hammock caught me, and then I would be in the trees. But where would that be? The tree line wasn't even dense, not even dense enough to hide me from the tennis pro's sight, and not dense enough for me to escape into it, away from the doctor, or the tennis pro, or the two sportive charges of the tennis pro, or the sound of the grinding of the mechanism of the geyser inside the front lake. The trees were spare, and the slope was exposed and open and would not hide me from anything, nor would my next line of thinking erase my last line of thinking, the thinking of whatever had just happened there, in the hammock with Dr. Duvaux.

How do we—if I may say we—come to this?

I will say instead, How have I come to this?

I turned now here, on the edge of the line of trees, and I began to gesture wildly at the tennis pro, a sweeping of the arms, leave me alone I mouthed, go away, go in the other direction—I did not shout. I don't know why. I only mimed, and the EZ-Go continued on its way, I realized not toward me at all, but up toward the house, perpendicular to me. Perhaps I had not even been seen by the tennis pro, or his passengers. I had been gesturing wildly, silently, demanding to be left in peace, but what was actually taking place was that there had never been any intention of the others to find or include me, or address me in any way, they were simply on their way to enjoy something playful, and they were probably even capable of enjoying that playful thing, and here was I, raving silently. To anyone watching, any viewers in their seats in the theater watching this particular disastrous film unfold, what I had done was mime a desperate attempt to make contact, which, of course, had gone nowhere, gone unnoticed. I paused in my stride. I had come alongside the tall fence that seemed to be made of twine. I touched it, and a shock of electric popped into my fingertips numbing them instantly. Not a huge shock—but enough to make me think it unwise to try and cross it, and as it deterred the deer from entering the compound to eat the hydrangeas, the roses, the tomatoes in the community garden, or the apples in the orchard, it had deterred me from progressing as well. I walked along the fence, and continued at my high pace, thinking now only about the electric fence and what it conducted and how much it conducted and what real danger it posed, and how if it posed any danger how could that danger be other than momentary, and as I continued to linger on the obstruction posed by the fence, but in fixating on the fence, I realized that at least now I was thinking about the fence and not about whatever had happened in the hammock or the war picture, but I walked on and in very little time at all, I had come to a corner of the fence that barred my path not only from a western direction but from a northern direction as well, and I imagined a day in which I paced the entire length of the fence around the immediate compound of Jaquith House, which might take some time but would still be finite. It did seem that the only thing that my mind wanted was to continue to stride forward, and this electrical twine was between me and the infinity of trees beyond, the slope beyond, possibly even other properties beyond me, containing other personalities whom I had not yet failed and who had not yet failed me. It seemed to me that the war picture was gaining on me, Corey, too, was gaining on me, and that there was me and my memory and a skein of electrical twine, and I was on the wrong side of it. That much I knew. And so, for these reasons I reached out and snatched at it, and caught it mercifully with only the flat of my palm rather than the hook of my fingers so that it was only enough to knock me to the ground, which it did, and perhaps it was the ground that took me further into darkness, or perhaps it was the reverberation of the shock moving through me, but a cloud quickly overtook me and, suddenly, I was free of thought, for a good long while.

20

THE VANISHED LADY

It was late in the day, and I was walking quickly along a beach, between the water and train tracks, somewhere above the dunes. Sometimes the trains passed, though rarely. I'd been walking for an hour or so. The tide was out at this time, very far out, for miles it seemed. I continued walking along the beach. It wasn't a beautiful beach—it was difficult walking on stones, and mud more than sand, and there were dead fish and beached jellyfish, and far too many gulls. An industrial manufacturing strip ran along the other side of the railway, and a series of surplus supermarkets, and I remember looking up at a café on a balcony of the larger supermarket, just beyond the railway, thinking, How? Why? It was an improbable seascape promenade. And yet, I wasn't bothered. I was walking, walking briskly toward something.

An island in the distance with a castle on it.

Where was I? Let me think. It was obviously a popular tourist destination. I walked faster and even at times ran along the beach. It took a great while to close the gap between myself and the castle on the island, and even when I came level with it, it was so much further out to sea than it looked upon approach. Between the beach and the island was a little cobblestone causeway, only a few feet across, and by the time I reached it, it rose a few inches above the level of the sea. As long as the tide was out, I would be able to cross to the island, and so I started and went across very quickly, because I thought, I will want to get across and be able to enjoy the castle and still get back before the tide comes in. The crossing was longer than I thought, or perhaps I spent longer at it than I realized, because I was looking for a special stone that was shaped like a heart and embedded somewhere on the passage.

Other tourists were crossing over and some were crossing back, at the end of their day. Little children were being carried on the shoulders of their parents and many were crying and refusing to go on, the causeway was a bit of a trial. There we were marching along the trial of a causeway. What a pleasure! I crossed, looking intently at the cobbles but being torn between looking out to sea while standing in the middle of the sea, which is a rare treat, and looking intently at the cobbles trying to find the heart stone. I never found it. To be honest all the stones looked a little heart-shaped.

I had only just stepped foot on the island, and I was barely in the shadow of the castle, when I saw the posted timetables for the tide, and indeed the causeway was closing in ten minutes! You needn't worry though, I was informed at the kiosk, because there are regular ferries, and if you are on the island after the tide comes in, you just take a ferry. I turned around, without seeing the castle or any of the gardens, because I realized most important was crossing the causeway on foot, and especially crossing as the tide was coming in and covering the cobblestones. Then the water passed over your feet. However, it came in so quickly. At the midpoint in the causeway, it was nearly to my thighs. No matter, I looked up to the distant hills, it seemed, one village over, and I said to a companion, That church tower marks where we are staying, and I think it will take us at least two hours to walk back.

PORTHOLE

I can't see it, where is it? my companion said.

Can you see the orange awnings of the supermarket café? Look straight up the mountain, and you'll see the church tower.

Will it really take all that time? she asked. Can you hear seagulls?

You said you enjoyed walking.

Did I? I probably did.

I enjoy the causeway. I said.

What was the cause? And what about that clicking? Do you hear the clicking?

Clicking?

Can you tell me what that clicking sound is you hear?

What clicking sound?

Don't you hear a clicking sound? The sound of tape in a machine, maybe. Can't you hear it?

What tape? I'm on the shore.

Like tape flapping on a reel?

That's not tape. That's film. Film isn't tape. That's the sound of film in a projector.

Bingo! You are waking up, she said. Finally. You had me worried. But you're right, it's film. What about this, what's this sound?

The striking together of something thin, maybe small sticks, or wooden chimes?

Oh, that's very close. Shall we do another, or do you want some coffee?

Why is it dark?

It makes it easier to hear.

Is that true?

They say it's true. All right, I'll put up the blinds, she said, and I heard the sound of a cord, and a thin circle of light began around our feet and then grew a bit and a bit more, and the cord continued along a pulley, and up went the black shades, and up the light came along the circle of the room, which was an apse of some kind. I was laid out on a rosewood settee in a round room of windows, with a ceiling of pale pinewood. Beside me in a basket swing, suspended by a long chain from the center of the ceiling, was Fanny, the sound artist I had met in the shrubbery, still dressed in her denim western suit, her legs dangling above the floor.

The Syllabary turret! I thought. I've had a knock on the head, I said.

Wrong again, she said. You've shocked yourself silly.

I've what?

You were trying to escape!

Oh? I suppose I wasn't thinking.

You were thinking, you just weren't caring very much. You tried to rip through the electric fence. I watched it all from the window.

How did I get here?

Never you mind about that.

How long was I out? Was it you talking to me just now?

We were playing a little game. Just some bits and pieces of my hobby. I was trying to wake you up. What if you had a concussion?

I had a dream—something odd about a castle on an island.

That's fanciful.

Yes, it was fanciful, but also tawdry. Did you call the doctor?

I'm not a snitch!

Right: you thought I was trying to escape.

Weren't you?

No, not exactly—I, well, I'm not sure. We aren't prisoners. Are we? I went to a restaurant yesterday. I'm fine now. I'm sure. I'm excellent, in fact. I'll have that coffee, thanks. Actually, I'll have a brandy, and then a coffee.

You had a brandy. Do you want another?

I drank a brandy while I was sleeping? That's a precedent. No, don't tell me. Yes, I'd better have another. I don't think the first one counts. And then a coffee. Do you have a machine or something?

I have a whole kitchenette!

That's swank.

I've been here forty-two years!

Good Lord. You must be healed of your sufferings by now, I would hope.

Not consecutively. And not always as myself.

Oh, I see.

I doubt it!

You're right. I don't see much. The woodsman said something similar.

Lonnie is an old soul. He isn't older than the doctor, it's just that he was here before the doctor, because of his mother.

Was his mother a doctor?

Oh, no. Not Lonnie. His mother was a weaver.

Was she a sufferer?

She suffered.

Fanny poured out the coffee into two tiny cups of rose-colored porcelain rimmed with gold and placed them on saucers of exactly the same design. Her little kitchenette on the floor below the apse was part of a work studio that looked out onto the giant sequoia, and the hypnotist's hammock.

Indeed, it was a homey spot, this Syllabary, with the feel of a tree house. The table was round and rough, but hand-painted with a giant lavender trumpet blossom, bearing little resemblance to any flower in nature.

Some table, I said.

Bloomsbury, Fanny told me. Painted in a group. The hands of Virginia Woolf probably touched it—well, or at the very least, Clive Bell.

The kitchenette's narrow counter was tiled in clay, and the floor much the same, burnished and well worn, but not well cleaned. The whole of the small space smelled of pine planking and hot coffee.

In the work area, a long table was arranged with a series of microphones and puff screens, a small computer and a larger monitor, and two small speakers, nests of snaking cords and cables. A large wooden easel was heavily laden with clippings, one overlapping another, and some coming together into a collage.

Is this your production studio? I asked her.

Well, yes. I suppose. Coming from you that makes it sound official.

Do you make tapes? Or records? I have a romantic notion that sound recordings are always pressed freshly on vinyl or inscribed onto albums, or something.

Oh, no, everything is digital these days.

That's very boring. What sort of things do you find to record at Jaquith House?

Everything. Lake water especially—as it strikes against things. Wind in the pine trees, moving through water under the dock. It keeps me very busy.

What do you do with your recordings? Are you in the music industry? Or film?

I have been in all the industries! But no more. Now, I save my recordings. So I have them. I'm totally deaf on one side. Soon I'll be deaf on both sides.

What will you do then?

I'll read lips. I'm teaching myself now. I will also learn sign language. But I will hate being deaf. There goes my pastime! I'll have to focus on my clippings. I use the easel to hang my clippings. I just love clippings. Do you see those drawers: all clippings!

There was a tall cabinet filled with many rows of small, deep drawers rather like a card catalog or an apothecary's store. Each drawer was labeled, in a tiny script I couldn't quite make out.

Another sort of archive? I asked her.

Any occasion you can imagine, and I will have just the right clipping. Say I go to a dinner somewhere at someone's home, and the dinner is fantastic. I go to the clipping drawer for "dinner party" and pull out a clipping, and I can write my thank you right on it. I have so many clippings of dinner parties, I can usually find something that looks so nearly like the meal that was eaten it is almost as if I photographed the meal itself. Isn't that clever? she asked.

But you don't take pictures yourself.

Oh, no. I never take pictures. I think it spoils the fun.

Yes, pictures spoil fun. That is for certain.

And memories, I think.

Yes, probably that as well, I said.

Clippings, however, are perfect.

So, are all these files of dinner parties?

Oh, no. Let's say you wrote me a letter and said you were very sad because you had just been attending a funeral in Cabiria. I could go to the file on "death" and then go to the travelers file and find a photograph of Cabiria, and I could put them together and write on the back. Or I wouldn't even have to write on the back. That would maybe seem more solemn to just send the clippings.

I don't think Cabiria is a place, Fanny.

It's the name of a place.

It's a name, but I don't think it's a place-name.

It's in Sicily.

I don't think so.

Isn't it? That's a shame. Well, you would know best.

Would I?

World traveler! Just name a place, and I'll find you a clipping.

I thought. Aubusson, I said.

Oh, obscure! Well, I have a way around that. You tell me something about the place.

It's in France.

I guessed that much! Je parle bien français, thank you very much. North or south?

Sort of dead center, really.

Mountains?

Not particularly.

Rivers?

Not especially.

Any celebrities?

None that I know of.

Famous battles?

I imagine so, but I don't recall the specifics. There are some Roman ruins.

That hardly helps. Industry?

Now you're on to something. It's known for its carpets. And tapestries.

Ah! I see exactly what you are after. Just hold on, she said, and in opening a little cupboard produced a collapsible stair, which she uncollapsed and quickly scaled. Deep from within a drawer at the top of her catalog she pulled out a long glossy photo card. Sheltering it to her chest, she quickly descended and dashed a note on the back.

Here! she said, and presented it to me. It was a photograph of *The Lady and the Unicorn*. "All this and more! Best regards, Fanny," the note on the back read.

This is *The Lady and the Unicorn*, I said.

Yes!

That's in Paris at the Cluny.

I know that. I've seen it a dozen times. That's why it says "and more."

But it isn't even an Aubusson tapestry. Is it?

Give it back, she said, and amending her message handed it back to me. "Nearly this and more," it now read.

I see. I suppose that does clear things up. It's really more of a photograph than a clipping isn't it?

Your point being?

It must have spoiled someone else's fun and memories when they took it.

Yes, but not mine.

You're mercenary regarding your clippings, Fanny.

I should hope so! Besides it was probably staged, so it doesn't count as spoiling.

I wonder about that.

Oh my, you've got to go! she shouted at me suddenly, and began to hustle me out the Dutch doors of the syllabary.

Right this second?

Absolutely. It's nearly time for supper. I've got to go, she said, and pulled the doors to and locked them.

Are you going to the dining room? Perhaps I'll join you.

Oh, no, never.

Where are you going?

You are a nosy creature. I've looked after you all afternoon, and that should be plenty for anyone. But don't worry, I'll have you back, and we'll have a dinner party in the kitchenette. I'll send you a clipping to confirm it.

And with that she vanished down the steps to the courtyard and into the shadows of the dusk.

And I was left alone to consider the dining room. Which I walked toward not by walking toward, but by walking below and around.

The terror of the dining room, in that moment. The idea that I would have to overcome so much—it's quite embarrassing to confess, given how formidable I was in my life prior to this, my new incarnation. At Jaquith House, I found myself rearranged. I could say now that each new thing was a horror. I thought, Perhaps it is the coming and going that is so unusual. The coming and going of myself and only myself. Wasn't I always coming into a meal with some other person—someone from my cast or crew? If so, it was a new and separate production, this going into a dining room at Jaquith House. And the dining room at Jaquith House, which should have been on the ground floor, and was in many regards on the ground floor, in effect was not on the ground floor, because it overlooked the valley, and any spectacle beyond the enormous glass windows was on display to the natural amphitheater of the field below, from the stage of the dining room itself. But for what audience? There was no one but me in the recessed field, and once I was no longer walking there, looking into the great glass window at the spectacle within, there would be no audience for whatever spectacle I was about to enact in the dining room.

But wait, I thought, there had been so many meals I went to alone. How many dining rooms entered all alone, across the course of my career? As many entered alone as entered accompanied! Why, I wondered, did being at Jaquith House make these old things, old habits, become new things, or call them into question? They were new things, all, yes. Even things that had been old things somehow became new things: for it was certainly an old habit of mine to enter a dining room alone, one that my memory had just at this moment nearly robbed me of—many hours alone in a dining room of a hotel in the hours between service, working on a script, listening to the activity in the kitchen, or watching the wait staff dressing the tables with starched cloths, folding napkins, appointing wine glasses, laying out and spacing cutlery. In fact, my eccentricity to prowl dining rooms in the off hours was well-known. I had haunted and prowled dining rooms and bars my entire career. At this thought, I began to rush, to run nearly, into Jaquith House, and toward the dining room, imagining now how I would push through those doors, in a whirl, in a state of dishevel and flushed skin, having rushed across the damp recessed field—the cuffs of my trousers now soiled and pasted in wet grass, grass covering my patent boots, one of my braces off my shoulder and flapping, my foulard unfurled—I would push violently through these double doors and stand in the bright haze of the dining room and begin my spectacle. Why not?

But there was no need to rush, as it turned out, because when I arrived at the dining room, the doors were open, and the room was mostly empty. Only a few individuals spread loosely across separate tables. I rushed in, nonetheless—only there was simply the silent rushing of damp trousers, and the silent hush of having come to halt on the carpet of the landing of the dining room in my plimsolls.

ENTR'ACTE: PRAWN'S SAGA

I spotted an open table and made my way, but was halted by a matron in gray linen. Her hair had been arranged into a roll at the back of her head, a roll so pronounced that it suggested a quantity of coiled hair that was frankly inconceivable, even on an eccentric head of hair, a roll of hair so exuberant it could only be false, augmented at its core by half, if not three quarters, by a ring of dense sponge. Over her breast plate dangled a saucer of silver on a beaded chain, and it was this decorative breast plate that I confronted directly as she darted into my pathway and blocked me from my separate table.

Ms. Désir?

Madame Concierge?

The doctor has you booked into the dining car for tonight.

The dining car?

If you will follow me, please. She grabbed a slice of paper and draped her arm in a cloth. She escorted me back through the smattering of separate tables. The rest of the diners were unknown to me.

The matron in gray linen walked me past the bubbling buffet table and then suddenly gripped the molding in the wall and a little hidden door, papered into the contour of the wall, popped open to reveal a passage: into the passage we went, past a luggage rack, and into a narrow carriage lined with windows and passenger seats, and indeed, it did seem as though we had entered a train carriage, and there was even a bit of swooshing and rushing wind, and it seemed a slight vibration to the car, and a slight *clickety-clack, clickety-clack*, and we continued through two connecting doors and through a stamped-tin foyer, and past a series of sleeper compartments and a pair of toilets, and sliding open the final door, I arrived in the dining car. It was exactly as I might have imagined and also entirely empty except for George Prawn, the sufferer of the taffy jowls and the bright blue eyes who I had met my first morning with the chef. He was waving at me warmly from a booth mid-car.

How wonderful of you to join me! he announced as I slipped into my bench.

Is this the Orient Express?

More of a Transatlantic! You can have the chicken or the fish. I'm afraid the railcar menu is slightly limited.

I'll have the fish, I said to the hovering matron.

An excellent choice.

And you?

I've already ordered. Forgive me for taking the liberty of requesting a Dom Pérignon.

That hardly bears apology. But I really must go, you see, I've spent the last half hour anticipating and celebrating my power to eat alone.

But you've only just arrived!

Yes, but I think there must have been some mistake.

Oh, not at all, not at all, I was hoping for a guest.

Strange luck, I said.

There's no luck about it. I tipped Brigita twenty dollars to seat you here.

So that is the famous Brigita?

Osteopathy—you've heard.

Yes, the doctor warned me. I understand her techniques are subtle.

Yes, she worked on my back recently, and I only felt the hovering of her hands at a great distance and then a popping sound and my fingers have been completely numb for three days.

Was that the effect you were seeking?

I wouldn't have said it was at the time.

I've heard of this type of therapy—the tiniest gestures can create some substantial shift in the alignment of the inner skin.

Well, yes. Perhaps there was some substantial shift, though I have only noted the substantial shift of money out of my pocket.

Brigita is a free contractor?

She offers a limited selection of services for the household, but if you go off menu, it adds up very quickly.

Happy endings?

Nothing like that! Or, well, at least nothing that I know about.

I'm sure it's all medicinal, I said. But you were unconvinced?

Let's say that I am reserving judgment. My physical ailments are contestable.

How do you mean?

Well, they may not be physical in nature. Some say.

The doctor?

Who knows what that man thinks, or if he does. What is your opinion of him so far?

I have no opinions. But your sojourn is ongoing, Prawn, am I correct?

Oh, yes. Indefinitely.

What can you tell me about the forms of psychic exhaustion of our fellow sufferers?

Anything you want to know.

What about the tennis pro?

Pills. But if you ask me, wealth and boredom.

What about Lonnie? The woodsman from the mountain.

The caretaker? I know nothing. I've seen him building fires in the main house and collecting his mail. Does he have a very large dog?

He has a very medium-sized dog.

I've seen him with the dog.

Fanny seems to know more about him. What can you tell me about Fanny?

Who is Fanny?

The recorder of sounds, a collector of clippings, an artist. The little old lady in a western suit. In the Syllabary.

Do you mean the tree house? I thought that was uninhabited.

Did you? You know less than anyone it seems, Prawn. I've only been here a few days, and I know the Syllabary is very much inhabited.

I know of no little old ladies, he said, and as he laid his linen napkin in his lap, Brigita appeared with our cold salads and our colder wine, a jar of potted herring, and a loaf of dark brown bread. Outside the glass of the window there seemed to be a fog obscuring our vista, a vista that I imagined could only lead back into Jaquith House. Everything seems to loop upon itself. But how convincing the whooshing and jostling, and the sound of the tracks below us. And how good it was to be in the railcar! Prawn offered me my champagne glass.

What? No caviar, I asked?

You have to order that in advance, and I'm trying to leave things to chance. Here's to us.

To the sufferers.

Exactly. Where were we?

What is the story of Tina?

Oh, please, not very interesting. Depression. Anxiety. Insecurity. Fear of failure. In short, youth.

You're so sure of your diagnoses, Prawn.

Don't you think the doctor gossiping about his patients is a bit unprofessional?

I find everything about Jaquith House unprofessional, I said.

And yet you are here, he said.

I have never really thrived at professionalism.

This place takes it to the next level, doesn't it?

And yet you are here, I said. Why do you bother if you distrust the doctor's methods?

I don't know if it is as simple as that. He never looks at us. Or he looks but he never sees. There are days that I feel like death, that I look like death. He tells me I look fantastic. He sees nothing. Anyway, I'm gathering evidence.

Evidence of what?

I'm not sure yet. I know what's wrong with me; I just need to figure out how to solve it. Or if I can solve it.

By yourself?

We have only ourselves, Helena. May I call you Helena?

May I call you Prawn?

We have only ourselves, and only this one life, he said, and as Brigita returned with our entrees, he snatched up my claw and began to stroke me between the knuckles. This was made difficult for him by the preponderance of my onyx rings, which he adjusted about to gain more pliable surface. What would I say if I burst in at just this moment and saw myself gripped in the paws of Prawn? The me that I once was, that is.

Brigita scurried away with no comment. Perhaps she was used to such shameless seduction attempts in the dining car.

What are you suffering from, Prawn?

He dropped my hand. Do you really want to hear about all that?

I absolutely do.

Then prepare yourself. I am about to embark on a long saga.

I was a successful man, in a respected profession, Prawn began. You, who are a creative person with bohemian leanings, might not respect it, but most people thought me successful, or at least not a failure.

You were a banker?

Close, but not quite. I worked as a broker between banks and realtors in property dealings. This could be large parcels of land, or it could be large businesses or large buildings, but the larger the better. I did not buy anything directly, didn't sell anything, I simply brokered buying and selling. You could call me a middleman, but I developed a Rolodex, as they say. You can take your Rolodex with you anywhere, you keep your clients, no matter what. Do you know what I mean?

Roughly. The studio always handled all my contacts. The studio is a collective. Independence would have been a mark of financial failure.

As it turns out, there were aspects of my personality that served me as a broker: I listened, you see, and I was empathetic, and so I could guess what people wanted me to say, and I could carry out things within reason, in the least precarious way, financially. It doesn't sound very hard, but you would be surprised. This listening made me trustworthy. I might fail to broker the sale, or they might ultimately lose money on the transaction, but it rarely was the case that I was held responsible for these errors or failures since I was saying, and doing, to the best of my ability, as my clients wanted.

A yes man.

Well, I suppose, to some degree. And I was good enough at it that eventually I could consult, and there was an even better living to be made in consultation, and so I was even less connected to the selling or buying, and less connected to the actual exchange, and made my living on the theoretical. Intuitive projections.

I thought this sort of thing was done entirely by robots these days.

You aren't far wrong, but there will always be humans involved and humans will always want some other human voices in the mix.

Until there are no more humans.

I suppose. Perhaps from your more bohemian standpoint, I'm a problem, but I believe in free trade.

You take me and my bohemian nature to be very leftist, Prawn.

Isn't it? Well, it's what I expect from artists. In any case, I had no reason to feel bad about my career. I had a great apartment. I had a very nice office, on a hill, with a view. I made my own hours. I left time to do things like walking to lunch, or personal errands or playing tennis at a club where I was a member. Everything was in walking distance.

This seems like a practical arrangement.

I was a bachelor, in a small place, but top floor, very grand. My neighbors were all middle-class people, professors and mathematicians and accountants, and we all had balconies overlooking our own secret garden.

You paint an idyllic picture of this lifestyle you inhabited, Prawn. Are you about to tell me you were lonely and dissatisfied in your bachelor's garret?

No, nothing of the sort. I had a girlfriend. She lived in another city, but she was successful also—and so she had no interest in moving, so we visited, and took some vacations together. I never felt strongly for her, but I did enjoy her company, and there were occasionally more local women who I might have over for dinner, or a drink, or a brief encounter, and this was neither here nor there for anyone. All the parties were perfectly satisfied with the arrangement.

All parties satisfied.

And so my days were set: I walked from my office to my club along a known route, and walked to lunch along another known route and returned to my office by a third route and to my apartment by a fourth, et cetera. Do you know I could make all these walks through gardens? I mean to say I never had to walk on a street or alley. These were semi-public spaces, you see, but you had to know the way to enter through gates, et cetera, so in effect they felt like private gardens.

Desire paths, I have heard them called.

When I was working, I was focused, and when I was out with a client, I was focused on that, and it seemed to me that I only noticed my life when I was walking to some location. And then suddenly, I would feel very tired, almost as if I couldn't walk a step. I became obsessed with recuperative strategies for my depleted energy.

What sort of strategies?

Anything restorative. A cup of coffee or sugar bun in the middle of the afternoon, or maybe leaving midday to walk on a beach.

I suspect it didn't work.

Not really. What I need is a vacation, I thought: a resort-type vacation where I could just sit and enjoy myself and not think for one minute about work. Do you agree?

What do you mean? That people need vacations? I'm sure that anyone working in a regular field needs a break, of course. I have lived my life on a permanent vacation, I think, so I view things differently.

Really?

In many ways, yes. But in other ways, no: it's the opposite, and I have never not been working, so perhaps I am never on vacation—filmmaking is not quantifiable in that way. It bleeds over. The grimness bleeds over and poisons everything.

Aha! My noncreative existence is closer to yours than you think! So you can see where I am going with this, Prawn said.

I'm not sure I can, I said.

Well, it's as you say—impossible to separate out, and yet the instinct is there to try. So, I was making a good living, and my lifestyle was healthy but not decadent, and I had money to spend on a week or so in a paradise. And I would go off to these amazing places, gorgeous beaches, sailing in the Mediterranean, or the Caribbean, or the fjords.

Yachting in the Baltic?

That's the idea. One year I spent an entire week just sitting on a dock in the middle of a lake watching sunsets and sunrises. I would read books and attend shows, and eat at good restaurants, and take in views everywhere along the way. But this became difficult for me, and can you guess why?

Traveling is complicated, and exhausting.

Yes, there is that cliché. But for me, it had to do with repetition and routines. You see, when I was little, my family went always to the same places. This was my upbringing, and so this was how I approached my own restoratives, I couldn't help it. The first time I went to a place, it seemed like the best place in the world, and I felt certain that the place itself was key. So, a few months later, I would return again to the same resort, same beach, same hotel, same restaurants, and it would feel even better on this second visit, because it was familiar. I returned to work, and for a time all I could do was think about getting back to this place, this place that was going to be *my* place for recovery. I tried to think about this ideal place as my reward for work.

That can't last! Resorts are notoriously one note, really boring ultimately. And the clientele! And traveling is exhausting, as I said.

Yes, you were right, and you are right, and when I returned to my apartment I was more exhausted! I would flop in bed.

You needed time away from time away.

But I still needed time away from work as well. This means three types of time were needed to conduct my life: time working, time away from working, and time away from time away, as you put it.

That's quite a lot of time.

Exactly. More time than anyone has.

Certainly more time than anyone deserves.

I kept trying to make things fit.

Reasonable idea.

Was it? I found it unreasonable, as it meant that one third of my time was spent working and two thirds of my time was spent not working, and I think no businessman alive believes this is a way to make money. But I thought it was *the place* that mattered, you see. If the work itself could be moved around, then the location fatigue might be alleviated.

Jet-set international entrepreneur?

I know it sounds conceited. I mean, what about the everyday person tied to a place?

Modern global times.

It's just not a feasible lifestyle to deliberately disconnect yourself from a place in order to connect yourself to a rotating buffet of places.

Some of us come pre-disconnected.

Yes! And for me it was surprisingly easy in fact. In my travels, I had come to know a few new people and got to know their business, and they got to know mine, and without my even trying, my Rolodex expanded across new cities. So that meant moving work into travel, to some extent. I could just go to a place for a month and settle in there and continue to work.

A month is a good stretch, a feasible stretch of time, as you say. Practical.

I'll give you an example of what I mean—I liked London.

That hardly makes you special! That is a city that wears her charm on her sleeve. You can certainly fill a day walking around from place to place lunching and considering the historical buildings.

Exactly, so I might spend a month there, and in that month I would work, but I would also be walking to and from very different places, and so it would enliven the work, and also I would make some little trips into the countryside, or the coasts—I could come and go to Scotland or Wales or even Paris fairly easily—and those places jazzed up the working.

And this was helping?

No, I was exhausted all the time. And I was miserable, I think now I can say I was miserable, but at the time I just thought I was agitated, I was malcontent. The London plan seemed to be operating, but inevitably a month felt a little long to be in a place that was not my home. I walked all the time, sometimes an hour or two a day, and I would pick these curious pathways, so that I had to cross through a restaurant patio and then go down an alley behind a kitchen, cut through a cathedral garden, et cetera, so I could come out on a particularly hidden road.

I love this about cities. There is always a vein that everyone travels, tourists and residents alike are so fixed on these direct routes, they don't want to get lost or lose time, and if you go just one street off the main path, you are completely alone.

Yes, but I was growing exhausted by these paths. I had to have breaks in the walks, a glass of wine in a park in the afternoon, or I'd go into a library or a museum and just sit in the foyer reading or checking phone messages or something. I still felt the basic concept was correct, and so I began doing the business in a few other cities: Hong Kong and Toronto, especially. I still thought of my little apartment and my little office on the hill as my true home base.

And where was this little home base?

Oh, not so far from here. Anyhow, things thrived in their way. But I had become frenetic, more desperate, because so much was hanging on the stability of financial exchanges, which were by definition not stable, and not likely to occur on fixed timetables. And there I was, obsessed with the calendar year. I would spend most of a summer, for instance, away from my home, but maybe also December or January or February had to be parsed out. I never had permanent living arrangements in these other places, mind you, but I had places that I regularly might rent, and so I could also begin to think of specific offices or apartments in those other places as familiar, and walking to and from the train to the apartment to the office and the route from the apartment to the lunches or to the tennis courts, et cetera, developed in all these places, so it felt like I was living several lives, really, at a very high pace.

And the woman with whom you were involved?

In the beginning, she tried to keep up. But the nature of her job was rooted, and so she was less free. I don't think she resented me entirely. I think she resented the way I handled things, so that I was less and less in the city where she was rooted, and more and more in other cities, and because there was evidence that my failure to be in her city was not tied to my job, as she originally believed. If I could do my work from different places, why didn't I just do it where she lived? I think this is why things fell apart.

I understand this resistance. May I ask why you did not make this city of hers one of your work bases, one of your work-homes away from your work-home?

I don't know entirely, but I think it was the city itself that was the issue. I didn't find it restful or exciting, and I didn't find it particularly conducive to work or brokerage of sales either.

Some cities are good for neither work nor leisure.

You see my point!

It would be hard not to, Prawn.

It was not her fault, but I didn't think it was my fault, I thought it was the city's fault. Places, you see. I was still fixated on place. She didn't see it this way. I should have wanted to be near her, and she me.

And this relationship dissolved?

Quite literally. I think we just simply stopped talking, and that was that.

You became a truly free agent.

I suppose so. I had even less to tie me to any fixed location. I had no children and, by this time, no parents left living, and though I still thought of my little office and my apartment with the balcony and the secret garden as my home, this was an arbitrary feeling, given that I was not there much more than I was away. Do you follow my thinking?

More than you might imagine, Prawn, I said.

And you may remember the thing that I said about how this all came about, the fact of my walking—office to lunch to club—and the feeling of exhaustion. And then there was the feeling of exhaustion from being in the sun on a beautiful beach, and drinking too much beer or eating too many rich foods, or it might be the exhaustion of being in a cool, moist climate so quickly after coming from a tropical one, and perhaps I forgot to confess this, but in order to afford myself so much time traveling, I needed to fit what was a normal year's work into a matter of a few months here and there, and so during the periods of work, I would not do anything but work, sometimes days of fifteen or twenty hours, and all of these hours full except for the periods of walking, and I continued to work through lunch even, and sometimes instead of playing tennis at the club, I would walk on a treadmill so that I could continue to work. So the pace of my work life became intensified dramatically, so that I could afford to be able to take my cures.

You were not then a wage slave in the traditional sense?

It amounts to the same, of course. I would finish a period of working, and within an hour or so of my final deadline, I would be in an airport lounge beginning to live restoratively, and I would live my restorative life nonstop, without consideration of work until another working period began again, et cetera. I was moving from place to place, but moving also from work period to work period, and from rest period to rest period.

You wear me out even just describing it.

Yes, it's all very obvious in retrospect. I got tired of each place more quickly, I could be only one or two days working in a place before losing my grip, and then I would go off to somewhere else and find that within one or two days I was already tired of that place. I would go from place to place and feel exhausted by the place and unable to enjoy it, even a place that was so idyllic that many people would live their whole lives dreaming of taking a short vacation to this place, and if they should be so lucky to do so, they would remember it and talk about it for years afterward, and probably show slides of their vacation to their neighbors.

This is a very particular kind of angst.

Isn't it? Name a place you've always dreamed of living.

Montmartre, Pigalle, circa 1930.

I had an apartment on the Boulevard de Clichy!

Not in 1930! Pigalle is just club music and digital screens these days.

Oh, I see. You have a different sort of problem with time than I do. No, I am not romantic in that way. Or at least, I think not. Too bad, it might have served me.

I doubt it. It has never served me.

Maybe this was the problem: a failure of the fantasy of a place. When you live somewhere for any length of time it stops being mysterious and exciting and just becomes sickeningly real, and a grind of some sort. I would come home from these places, desperate to be away from them, to get back to myself, and I would find, within twenty-four hours or sometimes less, there I was by myself walking along one of my known routes—apartment to lunch to tennis club to train or bus station—and I would be immediately exhausted. And I felt hunted. I was scared to be spotted going about my life in any way that could be seen as regular or routine. I had developed a certain fame for always traveling. People expected it of me, and I didn't want to disappoint my reputation. I also wanted to work uninterrupted. My work periods had become so concentrated that to even stop to have a conversation with another person, or to see a friend for a drink, would put me behind.

It would seem difficult to carry on relationships.

It was impossible. I was so often away from home that my friends began to feel that they were being neglected, and so when I was home, the expectation was that I would see people right away upon arrival. As I built my Rolodex, I built my social ties in other places, and so these friends and business connections were all tied up in it. My time with anyone was brief. You see, I thought all my time at leisure was my social life, and all my time working was my working life. So to add work to other places was also to add social life to other places, and so it became impossible to come and go without always feeling that I was obliged to see someone and catch them up on my life thus far.

You are a people pleaser. This is your real demise.

Not by nature, as you might have noticed, but I agree, there was some of this.

It's a tricky role to play.

But if people thought I was not around, people didn't miss me or ask for me. If I was away in London, I was not expected in Hong Kong or Toronto, et cetera, and so if I were away from a place, I could conduct my business nonstop without worrying about my social responsibilities to the place. And so I began to imply—if not say outright—to my friends that I was in one place, when I was actually elsewhere.

Further complications.

Further and further still, for it meant that when I was in a place, I had to live secretly.

The only way to avoid such things is to travel in disguise.

I didn't go that far, but even in my home city, I took hidden routes. I'd get into and out of my office using the janitor's elevator. I would enter my club by a fire escape door, and I used an executive locker room but only in the dead of night. I couldn't see anyone—if I did, it would upset my work.

And was this the case for your periods of leisure?

More or less, though with a concentration on leisure. I tried to arrange my social encounters as if by accident. I planned nothing in advance and gave no warning. I hoped, and I was usually right, that others would fall in line because I was so busy. And they did. They felt singled out to be on my agenda: I would call someone up suddenly and say, "I'm only in town for a day—are you free?" And they would immediately agree.

People are often unselfish in this regard—the very busy or the very mobile personalities are thought to be worthy of accommodation.

Oh, so you do this sort of thing also?

I am a recluse. I never seek society.

On that we are different. I don't trust myself to be completely alone if I am not working. Leisure time also needs people—if not you start to feel unpopular. So there you have it! That is my story!

What is your story?

I mean simply this feeling that settled upon me when walking from place to place that I could never be seen to inhabit my life, least of all by myself.

You couldn't stand that feeling?

I could not stand it.

Wherever you went, there you were?

It is more that wherever I went, I would know the place, and if I didn't know the place, I would soon know it, and while I was learning it, I wouldn't have time to notice.

Boredom. The effect of living a spoiled existence.

Well, you could reduce all of our disorders to that. I mean why are we at Jaquith House, really? None of us have anything serious going on: we don't like to molest children, we haven't murdered anyone, we don't hear voices telling us to pull our own hair out—this entire house is just made up of people who are dissatisfied but who are well-heeled enough to be able to experience dissatisfaction as a paralysis.

Better not to linger on it, Prawn, it will get you nowhere—when you were working you were fine.

I don't really know. When I was working I thought only of the time when I would not be working.

And when you were not working?

I feared the return to work. It was so relentless. There were days when I would wake up and know the number of things that had to be done, and also know that it might not be possible to do those things in that amount of time, and yet there was no choice.

And then you went off on those wonderful holidays anxious and apprehensive of a return to work?

More or less.

Or dissatisfied and unable to feel content even in luxury?

Yes.

And so Jaquith House.

Well, there was a rough patch just prior, and a sort of crashing halt to the business, but yes, the upshot was Jaquith House.

And would there have been no way to simply give up all the zooming around and enjoy the place you lived and worked and perhaps work in a less frenetic way and live in a slightly more relaxed way?

Do you know, I have often asked myself this. I liked my office, I liked my home, I even liked the moment-to-moment transactions of my work. But no, I don't think so.

And you hoped the doctor could correct this dissatisfaction?

Honestly, no, I didn't. I don't think it is possible.

And yet you are here.

I am here. But this is probably just another kind of avoidance. I suppose the difference is that the avoidance is sustainable here in a way that perhaps it would never be if my whole life hadn't stopped.

That life is completely gone?

I would say so. Things went a bit haywire in the end. But I made off with a lot of money, so I am not in any real danger.

I thought you had no reason to feel compromised? No apologies. In the end, I bent that rule. But I was desperate, as I've said. Anyway, it made my exit definitive.

I envy you that.

Aha! Then the doctor is also trying to rehabilitate you occupationally?

I think that's the primary goal.

Yes, the real problem is having a career that people think matters. Then someone is always invested in you keeping at it. When you work in some horrid cube and you want to quit, nobody questions that. But a fine career, a valued career, and you are shackled to it for the rest of your days because it's someone else's fantasy. What do you think about your future?

I have no goals.

We have rather similar stories, in the end, I suppose, said Prawn.

There's a part of yours that is missing though. May I now tell a saga? It has to do with an accident that happened near Thunder Bay.

Ah, go on.

It only occurs to me because you have listed Ontario as one of your haunts. It's a famous story. It involves a gentleman named Stach, who owned a seaplane. He had also come to purchase an island in the middle of Lake Huron, one that had a tower on it.

A tower? Like a lighthouse?

I've always imagined it that way. He had a wife and some children of mixed ages. They often went ahead of him to this island—a treacherous half-hour journey by boat on the unpredictable lake. Sometimes the wife and children were alone for weeks. He worked very steadily at his trade, as you can imagine, to be able to afford adventurous vacation homes in the middle of Lake Huron.

What was this man's trade?

I would like to say banking or stockbroker, but I think he began more simply in manufacturing some sort of good. Tent sheeting, for instance, something that is uninteresting, but you imagine it is practical.

Tarps.

Yes, or power washers of some kind.

Hydraulics. He's just the sort of man I would have in my Rolodex.

I guessed as much. In any case, he bought the seaplane to come and go from Toronto. Less pressure on transit by boat.

Waterfront property is a sinkhole. I watched it ruin more than one businessman. That's where I was smart: never own places. Visit places, rent places, but never own them. Too much private property is the absolute downfall of a businessman.

But perhaps this philosophy is why you were never content? You were unmoored. He meanwhile was punished for this desire. Yes, he crashed the plane and demolished it completely.

And the moral of the story is that when you get yourself in a twist about work and play you are sure to get yourself killed?

He was not killed. Though he was sliced from stem to stern, he did survive the crash.

How?

He was too tough or too rich to die, they say.

And the tower on the lake, and the wife and the children?

They are together still to this day. They have some much larger cottage, on some much larger tract of land, in some even more desirable lake location, and all their children and grandchildren are swarming around in swim trunks, on paddle boards and in speed boats, and they have their own cottages and balconies and hot tubs as well on this tract of land in this even more desirable lake, and the husband still comes and goes by seaplane, and the wife has a set of three Hungarian dogs, who bark anytime a boat arrives.

Good lord. Another seaplane? How do you think he managed to get in one after the accident?

I have no idea.

And what does any of this have to do with Thunder Bay?

Oh, I've forgotten. But I do think the lead-in with Thunder Bay improves the saga. I'm only interested finally because of the wife.

What about the wife?

When she tells this story, she often says of this time of her coming and going with infants in a precarious boat to a tower in the middle of the water was the happiest time of her life.

How depressing! Do you think this has something do with having children? Or do you think it was because, for her, the joy of it was simply in the difficulty?

I think it is because to be so rich is sorrowful.

Do you really?

That is my bohemian interpretation. The interpretation you were hoping I'd give you.

But they were already very rich when they had the lighthouse.

Yes, but not nearly so rich as they have become since.

You think my suffering is somehow tied to my wealth more than to my comings and goings?

I'm not a doctor, Prawn. Plus, you told me that you were better equipped to diagnose yourself than any doctor.

True.

Though, Prawn, I am curious as to how you can allow yourself to sit still at Jaquith, if you couldn't allow yourself to sit still in all those other places.

I've thought about that a lot. And I don't have a clear answer, but I do think about this one element: how rapidly time seemed to be going by me. All those appointments in my diary, meetings set months in advance, everything prearranged, but I could never wait for anyone or for anything. I don't mean I was impatient, or that I was demanding, obviously there were plenty of times when I had periods where I was waiting for deliveries or for a car service or for a client to arrive, but if I waited—you know, in a line for a coffee or for a plane or because the trains were delayed—there was always something to be done, work to be done in those interims, and devices to help me do the work. So that wasn't ever really waiting. At Jaquith, I find I am waiting for something: I'm not entirely sure what. Recovery, I suppose, though I don't believe in that. Understanding, maybe. And it seems to me that in this waiting, time has opened up, and it sometimes feels infinite. Or at the very least, suspended.

And what if nothing comes? No recovery? No understanding?

I don't know. But I am confident something will. I suppose that's the difference between those of us who jump off buildings and those of us who don't but probably should—this confidence in waiting for something: that it will arrive. Like you, tonight. I knew you would eventually come into the dining room, and I knew we would have a long conversation—but somehow, I was aware of the waiting for that in a different way than I was on the outside. Very different.

We were finishing our coffee at that point. I realized we hadn't seen Brigita for some time. The evening had passed in a blink! Just then, a train whistle blew, and something struck against the window of the railcar and lingered: What was it? A packet of tea? An envelope of yeast? The waxen wrapper of a Canadian cheese? It was sullied and damp as if it had been cast out in the rubbish. A phrase of some kind was printed on its opposite side, reading backward against the glass, and while I couldn't quite make it out, I felt it significantly to be a clue to a mystery that had not yet been posed.

PART III

21

THE FLESH DISCARNATE

I don't know what made George Prawn tip Brigita to seat me in the railcar that evening, but I felt my spirits somehow improved by our chat—or I thought, I am noticing that before my chat with Prawn my spirits were low, and now I am not aware of this feeling. Of course, I had not been aware of this feeling of lowness when I was marching through the fields outside the dining room. I had been aware of feeling anxious, regarding the dining room, and feeling taxed, as regarding having shocked myself on the fence, and feeling hazy, regarding the several brandies in the Syllabary, but I was not feeling low, I would have said "not." So the feeling of improvement after my conversation with Prawn was perhaps not an indication of an improvement of feeling, but simply an awareness, by which I was now seized, an awareness of a previous state of being that was less desirable than the present state. The present state might be the median or norm, and the previous state might have been an aberrant dip or trough, but at the time I hadn't been entirely aware of any trough. This problem of feeling a change in my mood not as an active or ongoing happening, but only as a past event, a loggable shift, this was rather typical of me. But I thought this made it somewhat hard to know, for instance, if the feeling I was feeling (one of improvement) was indeed a change or if the feeling indicated a change which had occurred earlier and already passed—for instance, I had been feeling reasonably "myself" and then I had begun to feel low, and this feeling of feeling low was the change, the shift, and now it had passed and I was, essentially, back to myself. It seemed odd that I rarely had the thought "I'm feeling low," but instead often had the thought "I must have been feeling low," a thought that seems somewhat useless in retrospect. The reality of my existence at Jaquith House was that I was feeling low, I wouldn't have been at Jaquith House if I hadn't been feeling low, and so the idea that I would have moments where I felt otherwise was notable. And yet, why, then, did I never say to myself, "I am feeling low"? Instead, either I said to myself—in a surprised way—"I must have been feeling low" or I said nothing to myself, which led me to believe that perhaps these dips or troughs, these lows that had passed or been endured, might actually be significant changes in which not only was I feeling low, but I was feeling lower, and in fact, as evidenced by my being at Jaquith House, I was always feeling low, so to say so would be obvious. For to feel myself was to feel low—myself was low. If I was feeling myself, I was feeling low, but if I was not feeling myself, I was feeling lower. But this makes no difference, really, because I was no more aware of feeling low in a given instance than I was of feeling lower in a given instance. I was only aware of feeling low or lower *in retrospect.* Was this a kind of mechanism of denial, I wondered? Or was this a kind of powerful optimism that allowed me to weather the lows or the lower lows and emerge unscathed?

    I pondered this as I strode away from Prawn, who was still sitting with his coffee in the railcar, and as Brigita led me back through the tunnels and out to the dining room, which I saw had emptied out almost completely, with the exception of Little Tina, whose eyes were locked on the galley door as I passed through it. Little Tina, it seemed, was also resigned to waiting at Jaquith, though I wondered if it was for me or for Prawn, and perhaps it was precisely this knowledge that allowed Prawn to remain in the safety of the railcar, for another moment of suspension—for instance, smoking a cigar?

Meanwhile, here was Tina, waiting. She was perched on the edge of her dining chair, her legs pegged around each other like a clothespin, a clothespin capped in clean white sneakers, and she had her phone in her hand and was waving it. How natural to see the youth with their phones, so natural that for a moment I forgot such devices were contraband at Jaquith, and that in brandishing her phone at me, with a slight tinkling of her many gold bracelets, and a slight clicking of her many gold rings on the surface of the phone, she was in violation of a rule, and that in violation of that rule, she was performing her passions already, even with no audience, a landmark of her generation. It was nearly admirable, I thought, because I had been seized by this sense of magnanimity following the recognition of having recently felt low and having been unexpectedly released from my trough by Prawn. It was nice to see Tina showing a bit of spirit: a rebellious, antiestablishment spirit in the brandishing of her phone. This spirit was preferable to presenting herself as a wounded—ongoingly wounded—youth, her capacious handbag at the mercy of any stronger or madder sufferer. Instead she was beckoning me threateningly with her contraband phone, looking rather like one of those famous posters from May of '68 of a protesting youth hurling a paving stone—was this phone the paving stone of the current age? Could one say, I wondered, *sous les portables, la plage?* If only I had been carrying my notebag!

But even as she beckoned me, I sailed past undaunted, and she did not launch the object at me.

So what! So what if I was throwing a career into the sea, I wondered, as I passed through the grounds of Jaquith House, in my newly elated state. What if I was? It was my career and my sea, both were entirely of my making and imagination. I could jettison either at any moment. I was the director!

Film takes its toll—I've always known that, I thought. David Trevor had said this much to me the last time we met. Film is unforgiving—David told me, it would turn on me. And what else had he said? In my new state of elation, I felt a sudden opening of heart that allowed me to think of David Trevor.

Keep it brief, Helena, I told myself!

The last time I had seen David Trevor, it was an unremarkable scene for us, really, in many ways. I remark on it now only because David's unremarkable remarks tended to collect in the quiet spaces of mind just at the moments when I dared to feel less low! But it was too late for brevity of recollection, and the voice of David Trevor was suddenly there, back in a wave, in a surge as I strode across the western lawn toward the safety of my barn.

The last time I had seen David was in London. Shortly before Corey and I began filming *Sanguine Season*, before the boat.

Often before I started a film, I went somewhere disconnected from the script, disconnected from the next location, so that I could walk in a neutral city and prepare myself for thinking. A change of place! Maybe this was why I was so taken with Prawn's saga. There was so much of it I recognized. London was a neutral place for me. I had not grown up there, I had not filmed there, nothing had failed there, in theory or in practice. In London, I went out in the morning and walked a giant loop along the South Bank starting at Tower Bridge, past the Globe and the Tate Modern, the film institute, past the book venders under the Waterloo Bridge, where Jean-Luc Godard famously screened his director's cut of *Sympathy for the Devil* on hanging bedsheets, in protest of his studio's release of the unsanctioned version. I crossed the river at Hungerford footbridge, walked through Charing Cross station, up Shaftesbury Avenue and past the booksellers on Charing Cross and in Cecil Court, striding on into Bloomsbury, past the museum, toward Euston and the library, and up to St. Pancras and the beautiful bars and hotels surrounding it, and then I walked back down again, through Covent Garden and the West End, the Strand, through the City, St. Paul's, across the Millennium Bridge, and then back along the river bank to Tower Bridge and a small hidden street of wine bars selling Spanish ham on tables made from wine barrels. Here, I regularly rented a cramped and unassuming flat.

I loved making loops in London, and sometimes I went as far north as Camden Town and then followed the canal to Regent's Park to Baker Street, through Fitzrovia, through Piccadilly Circus, into Fortnum's and the arcades; I just made loops like that, stopping in pubs every so often to drink or sit unnoticed. Aimless wandering really, which, I suppose, was intended to clear my head for the serious thinking that would come soon enough when I was back at work. This was the part that I understood most in Prawn's saga. What was missing from Prawn's saga was the actual thinking, or more precisely the product of the thinking, which in my case would have been a film. These poor people who have no justification to clear the world for their own thinking! Of course, their careers end in sorrow. But the risk of clearing the world for one's own thinking was the displacement of so many other thoughts—where would they go? Perhaps that was where I had gone wrong. I was not thinking in order to produce films. I was producing films in order to purge my thinking.

I had been in London most of a week, making my loops, clearing my mind, preparing for thinking, when suddenly, walking through

Covent Garden, David Trevor's picture reared up at me out of a marquee, spoiling my walk, spoiling my plans for the afternoon, which of course weren't plans further than the plan of walking aimlessly. It was so typical of David's effrontery.

I went immediately into a wine bar close by where the lighting was Caravaggesque. I rang his phone to shout down the voice mail, but—he answered instantly.

How dare you interrupt my thinking! I shouted.

Oh, so you are in London. I heard you were in London, he said.

From whom?

You'd like to know. Came to see me in *Discarnate*?

I didn't come to see you.

Then why are you phoning me?

Why is it impossible for you to keep a country or two countries distance between us, as agreed?

I live in London. I was born in London. And I'm in a play in London. You can walk around procrastinating anywhere you want. Find another city.

I didn't know anything about your play.

It's *Blithe Spirit* meets *The Duchess of Malfi*. A real bloodbath. I'm excellent. Read the reviews.

Who do you play?

I'm an angry young man, in a sense.

Playing to type?

Hardly—I'm quite cheerful these days, Helena. Your war picture lined my pockets nicely. And now I have the pick of the West End.

Flowing locks and puffy sleeves?

I look like a million bucks, actually. I have a new trainer—my body is spectacular. A doctor completely reset my hairline. I'm getting younger every day.

Me too. Infantilized by the weight of filming.

The weight of being infantile while filming, you mean.

I'm always looking for someone to lift the load, David.

That must be your obsession with my broad shoulders. I thought you were just shallow, and oversexed.

To my detriment, David.

Speaking of, did you bring our playboy with you?

No. He's in Bolivia. We start filming in two weeks.

Some kind of gaucho adventure?

Nothing like it.

I can't wait for you to see me. It's going to destroy you.

What's left to destroy?

That's shockingly honest of you, Helena. Come see me anyway. See the one who got away, and away, and away! he said, and hung up on me.

He had left me an excellent box seat, a pass to his dressing room, and a bottle of blanquette de Limoux, called Longue Durée, well chilled. To his credit, David Trevor always hit just the right chord at this sort of thing. But I wasn't having any of it. Except, of course, that I was, somehow. Why had I come? Force of habit, I suppose. I spent so much time berating and insulting David retrospectively in my memories, the opportunity to bring the reruns into live audience performance was too tempting. I came at the last possible second, of course, and got scolded by ushers and crept into the shadows of my box.

The play opened suddenly. The lights came up on an ordinary, bourgeois living room in the stage tradition of the thirties—which is to say, equipped with a long Chippendale sofa in olive leather. The fringed corner-cup of a billiard table visible in the background. On the sofa lay David Trevor, shirt open at the collar, sleeves rolled, bandaged wrists, tended by a young girl, maybe a maid, maybe a governess, maybe a sweet cousin—who could say. These plays were all alike.

David had arranged for my exceptional seat so that I could see him quite plainly. Indeed, he did look younger—partly, I suspect because he was meant to be younger, and was made up so. At forty-two he was playing twenty-five still, something which is only permissible in the elegant haze of the theater, among men. Next month, he would be forty-two playing seventy-five. All logic of time and duration were collapsed on the stage.

David Trevor gazed emptily into space as if somewhat anaesthetized. The girl caressed his bandages as a wolfhound strolled onstage, approached the sofa, and sat politely at his feet.

The girl we would soon find was called Egri, Trevor was Val, convalescing from a suicide attempt, and the staging was high Bloomsbury, interwar.

EGRI
Val, here is Ollie. (*Motions toward wolfhound.*) We've been walking in the park. He does prefer to walk with you, of course, he's come to see how you're managing to brush away the cobwebs. We must get you back on your feet. You gave us quite a scare. (*Caressing his bandages.*)

VAL (*fixed gaze, tonelessly*)
Who's there?

EGRI (*warbling, anxious*)
Oh Val! The seasons are changing, soon it will not be summer at all, and we'll be trapped inside again, although I hope it will not be as severe as last winter...

The first sequence continued. As if the bandages didn't indicate as much, the play was quick to fill in any doubts in the audience's mind with a monologue of highly convoluted backstory in the sing-song of Egri. Val, a failed suicide; Egri, the impoverished cousin living in service to the family, in love of course with Val. A sinister auntie, Bordoah, soon to be revealed, was a medium, and a mesmerist.

The last clamors of the first act came in fair predictability: more insults and cryptic nihilism from Bordoah channeling ghosts; Val, the half-spirit, fainting in front of the guests with moans and tremors; gasping and heavy-handed interpretation from stage-left Egri; quips from the stock characters—a tennis pro, a patroness, an aviator, a motorist, a colonel, a debutant; disparaging remarks about the Huns from the military set; and then—and I suppose this was the moment David was so excited for me to witness—Val's full seizure, a collapse on the stage, thrashing, moaning inaudibly. Distressed pontification and indignation from Egri, until various members of the party slumped into submission, first the debutant into the arms of the tennis pro, then Bordoah into Val, then the colonel into the aviator, and then Val into Egri's arms. A set of dominos. Darkness, curtain, and for me, finally a cocktail at the bronzed tiki bar in the second-floor lobby.

Needless to say, I was grateful for the reprieve. There was a crush around me, a perplexed but enthusiastic buzz from the crowds, then when the lights flickered, I remained on my plush stool. The bartender refilled my drink without asking.

Second act starting, Miss.

I'm skipping it, I'm afraid.

I can stay with you for ten minutes, but I'll have to move you across the street, then, Miss, to the cocktail bar. I'm intermission only.

Across the street? Is that what it's come to in the West End?

Well, we're not on for full staff on a weeknight.

I'd better stay here. I'll have to go back in for the final bit. I know one of the actors.

The ushers won't permit anyone in after the second act begins, I'm sorry to say. And I'll tell you, it's a very violent play, very shocking final act—so they must respect the suspense.

Stage violence is never shocking. There's not a single thing that could happen in that play that isn't one of a hundred clichés already telegraphed.

There's a twist! No one is who you think they are. I don't want to spoil it for you, but you'll regret not finishing it out.

Are you also an actor?

Aspiring.

And you think this is a good play?

Oh, yes—it's got it all, right? Bit of drama, bit of horror, young lovers and all that.

Can you see yourself in the lead?

Oh, that's above my station, I think. Give me time, though. David Trevor is fantastic, I think. And a really lovely, lovely man if I may say so—very generous with all of us.

Bartenders especially, no doubt.

Do you know the gentleman in question?

I'm just making guesses. Actors, you know. You all have a terrible reputation.

Oh, yes, for our sins.

That's a wonderful cologne, what do you call it?

Are you asking for your boyfriend?

For my grandfather!

Bave Cèdres, it's called.

Essence of the forest.

Shall I top you up then? I'm afraid I'll have to be elsewhere.

I felt the bottle of Longue Durée in my cape pocket, cool, damp—no matter, I told the bartender, I'll wait in his room. I showed my pass, and with not even a bit of surprise, he directed me below stairs to a stage doorkeeper, who, on her break, was devouring a plastic box of leaves and moist grain while hunched on a sateen bench. She seemed reluctant to walk me back, but a quick recap of my professional relationship to Trevor cleared the air beautifully. I felt powerful in my shearling cape, tuxedo corset, and Zouave trousers, costume props all. I often felt my most powerful in dealing with set directors, stage mechanics, and stage guards. It was as if I was operating from the inside of a play in which I played the director. These were the only personalities in the world of the theater who might be ingénues yet, and not completely disavowed and disabused of the romance of the creative genius. Not yet—if they were young. Not yet, but certainly soon.

Can it be said to be sleep if it arrives after several cocktails and even more of the Longue Durée? I can only remember the uncomfortable closeness of David's dressing room, his things scattered around haphazardly, a very large duffle bag of soiled clothes wafting with his particular odor. Whiskey bottles and smudged wine glasses and a dressing gown with cuffs crusted in some industrial, theatrical filth. A few odd untouched books—a historical novel, a book of aphoristic Marxisms—and a basket of exotic jerky and fashionable seeds. David hadn't touched grains or sugars since we began working together: I had instilled in him a sense of the power of bodily vanity.

    I stretched out on the small sofa, uncomfortably wedged below a shelf of lights, and in the heat and stillness, I stopped noticing the dressing room, the lights, and then nothing again until I awoke to find a woman straddling me. It was the medium from the play! Still in her turban and veil, though now covered in an enormous amount of stage blood.

I beg your pardon? I said. Am I in the wrong room?

The auntie quickly had her hands in and under my leathern shell: You who would look death in the eye and claim not to notice it, she intoned—you who would deny yourself even your softest kindness. You who will deny yourself even the soft pleasure of homeliness, of conjugate bliss, of familial—

Madame, run your scenes elsewhere! I am not who you think I am, clearly!

And I am not who you think, if you can think, if your feeble mind will let the spirit enter you, as you know it wishes, she continued—and as the beturbaned matron lent ever closer to my face, and with her hand already entering the waistband of my Zouave trousers and right away into my lace underclothes, which served as no sufficient border at the best of times, and in the petroleum gleam of the synthetic sateen of a stage caftan glinting, I felt her powerful mesmerism, and I began to be moved by the spirit much in sync with the motion of the hands upon my body, and then the veil lifted only slightly, and her mouth was upon me, a strange familiar flavor, a warmth, a spice, and what was it, and where was it—I had the moment of transfer back to one of the many great round beds of the Blue Lily, when youth was still upon me, and the offerings of all mouths and all legs and the dark long hair, and women and men of all manner and form slipped one into another, and all of that motion and spreading and liquid embrace seemed to obscure the otherwise tawdriness of polyester and florescence and deodorizing sprays and vinyl in place of animal hide, that gorgeous cheapness and tawdriness of the Blue Lily, and this mouth in particular, which bore that common trace of rye whiskey and bitters and anise seed toothpaste, but still: This is not the Blue Lily! I shouted.

Helena, you spoil every approach. You just can't stand it when anyone else is on top.

David!

In perpetuity! he exclaimed, and doffed his turban as he collapsed back on the sofa beside me. Without the veil, the eyeliner was obvious and crude, but I could not deny it: the mimicry and cadence of the voice, the movements, the pose, the carriage of the shoulders, the position of the fingers on the hips, even from this close distance, the fingers themselves weighted in agate and inlay. How had I ever been fooled?

I thought you were an actress—then I thought you were a prostitute, I said.

And this erection? This now-dwindling erection?

Anything is possible at the Blue Lily.

Anything *was* possible at the Blue Lily, he said. Sadly, those days are gone. In any case—what did you think of my play?

I only saw the first act. Then I went and had a drink and talked to the bartender.

Helena—you missed everything!

I saw the séance and the bit with the seizure. Were you already into the turban by the seizure?

Only just, but yes.

I didn't spot the swap.

Not at all, not even for a minute?

Not at all.

You're so gullible, Helena. Even schoolchildren can spot a cheap drag show. It's sweet, really. You're so desperate to believe the spectacle, it's like your life depends on it. But I think you're a shit anyway. You knew I was going to be fantastic, and you couldn't stand to watch.

I knew the play was going to be awful, and I left. You can't help a play like that, David.

Reviews strongly suggest otherwise.

Perhaps, I'll come again tomorrow. No need to sulk, I said, and groped beneath his caftan.

No, I think the mood has passed.
Close your eyes and think of the Blue Lily, I said.
There's little point in trying to resurrect the dead, Helena.
I abandoned my campaign and lent back onto his fainting couch.
I was there recently, I said. At the Blue Lily, I mean.
It has changed, but it will always have a little spark of something from the past, no matter what. Don't you think? That's what I told your boy anyway.
Told my boy?
Helena, you'll have to forgive me for contributing to that little subterfuge, but he was desperate, and I don't know, I felt I owed him something after *Trenches*.
You sent Corey to the Blue Lily? You?
I did.
But his entourage found me in Cassis.
You always use the same hotels. You're not exactly hard to find.
 And his speech at the Blue Lily—
Oh, Helena, what was I going to do? He actually phoned me. No one phones anyone anymore. I honestly think he can't order breakfast without your direction.
And since when do you care about such things?
I'm a people person, Helena. What do you expect? Anyway, I figured I owed it to him after what happened.
I'm surprised he would even talk to you.
What did I do? I was a consummate professional—I coached him like a father, like a brother...
Like a lover?
Don't get us confused, Helena. I can't help it that the reviews didn't mention him. He obviously wasn't bad. He just wasn't memorable.
He made me negotiate.
It doesn't matter—it all worked out for the best, didn't it? He

got his next part, you conjured up your next film, and you are all off to Bolivia. "Thank you, David."

He thought I was throwing him away.

Weren't you? Why didn't you? You always do.

I'm too tired to start all over again.

Keep telling yourself that. You adore him. He adores you. Be pleased!

I compromised. I made promises.

All he wants is to do the odd film on the side, Helena. So he has a safety net when you cast him away. He's not really stage material. He didn't know how to present it without upsetting you. I just gave him a few strategies. That's all.

Everyone is lying. Everyone is always lying.

Does it matter?

I suppose it doesn't. Though I don't care for you two conspiring.

What was the film option he was after? I did wonder. He was so tight-lipped.

Something ridiculous. It will never happen, I assure you. I'll bury it.

I did tell him Helena would never collaborate.

I have enough voices in my head, as it is. So, David: Are you going to turn up in Bolivia and scotch my film?

Not possible—I've got at least eight weeks' run with *Discarnate*, and then it's *A Doll's House* in the spring.

Torvald?

Naturally.

Will they age you?

I don't think they will have to. I may look thirty-five, but I feel sixty in spirit. Actually, it's a relief, really.

I thought you were getting younger?

Oh, what do you expect me to say? God knows, working with

you aged me at least half a century. Although working in film took its toll in general. You can't be blamed for that—not entirely. It's an unforgiving medium, Helena. You'll see—one day it will turn on you, and you'll be in the same boat with all the rest of us.

That's quite a soapbox. Are you done with film then, David, if for some reason some misguided director wanted to endure having you in their blockbuster? I suppose you'd tell them to source their needs elsewhere?

Oh, I wish. I'd love to be brave enough to tell someone to go choke on it, but my life is expensive, and my morals are shaky. That said, I'm quite happy taking a break for now, but perhaps I'll try again once I'm truly agèd. The *late* forties. You know how it goes: venerable stage actors wanted for comic book villains, science fictions, and to play Nazi war criminals.

Gods in Valhalla.

Right. To be elderly on camera is to be supernatural. But not yet, Helena. Let me have my fun while I still can—I told you: the stage values me, and it's easy, it's less total than film. For the time being, or as long as I need to, I'll milk that for every drop.

So, you're the one leaving me.

I left you years ago. And you left me—that's what we do, we keep leaving each other. It never gets old.

I don't know about that, I said.

I know you don't believe me—you never believe me. Why should you? You always get your way with your films.

And why shouldn't I?

Helena, you've been so spoiled you can't even see how spoiled you really are.

Actors are the spoiled brats.

You didn't even sit through the second act of my play.

I was having a drink!

I left you a whole bottle and a private box! You could have got drunk in the box.

I'll try to come tomorrow.

You already know the punchline.

It doesn't matter. It will be easier to watch your performance if I know what I'm looking at.

Maybe. I am curious what you will think of me. And the technicians are brilliant! Wait till you see how they deal with the corpses. But some of the dialogue is real schmaltz, I grant you. You could have written it.

It would be shorter by two thirds if I had.

Shall I clear the box for you for tomorrow, then?

I'll try to come, David, but I can't promise. I'm trying to keep my mind clear. You know how it is, I said. But I'll try, I said.

I didn't, of course. I left London for Bolivia the next morning. I was anxious to get to Corey, anxious to begin *Sanguine Season*, suddenly. And for that matter, David didn't send tickets, or champagne, or anything that suggested he thought I might turn up. He didn't even try to keep me out with him that night—he left me in his dressing room and went out drinking with the cast, young Egri, now in leather miniskirt, clinging to his jacket sleeve.

22

THE MORAL OF THE MENDER

By the time I flipped the sign on the door at Barbarêche, my reverie of *Discarnate* had emptied me of any of the triumph of having braved the dining room and communed with Prawn. My reverie of *Discarnate* put me in doubt even of my doubt. Was I so easily manipulated by ghosts of the past? The spirit shall not move me! I exclaimed in the voice of David Trevor's medium.

Hello there, I heard from above me. Are you rehearsing an operetta? (It was the woodsman leaning over the upstairs banister.)

I am not! I said.

Come up then, I've lit the fire, and I brought you a present, he said.

The billiard room was warm and aglow, and the white and pink dog did not even remark on my arrival, so comfortably had she situated herself in the middle of one of the sofas. As I sat with her, she moved her head to be in better range of stroking.

Well? What were you shouting about?

I wasn't shouting about anything—I was exclaiming to the spirit realm.

Have you missed supper again?

No, I have not. I had fish in the railcar with Prawn. And do you know, despite my bohemian ways, I found him to be quite a comrade.

Because you feel your profession let you down.

What do you know about my profession? I thought you were an ascetic living on a mountaintop?

I only know the movie you made about war.

Of course. Everyone knows the war picture, even the man on the mountain. Everyone knows the one I would prefer to put behind me.

I thought it was noble. But perhaps you wished it would make more money.

It made a ton of money.

You wished it would have made less money. Artists always hate the work audiences like most. It feels too easy.

Too seducing.

What about the one where your actor died on the set? I would think that would be the one to put behind you.

Ah, here we go.

Was it negligence?

Clearly you have the full dossier. No secrets among sufferers, I suppose, or their caretakers, whichever you are.

The war movie is wonderful. I remember so much of it, and I never remember movies—I sleep though most movies, my back injury makes it impossible to sit upright for long periods. I fell out of a tree once. Now sitting is so painful that to watch something I have to lie flat on the floor, and then, usually, I fall asleep. But I remember the movie you made about war, because I was lying flat, and then there was that scene when the soldier was walking in the yard with the spy, and he doesn't yet know for sure that he is a spy, but he suspects him, and they are walking along together and telling the story of the king mouse who has a phantom limb. And then the soldier says,

"Where did you come from?" and the spy says, "You won't like my answer," and then he tells him he came from the sea, and at that moment I stood up, and I watched it standing from there on. That is an amazing moment.

That's two scenes, actually.

No, really? I remember it as one.

Yes, because it should have been one. It makes better sense the way you remember it. It's simpler, more direct. My film suffered from embroidery.

You think you are going to solve something about the mystery of the castle, and the chain of command, and who is safe, and who is dangerous, and who we are supposed to trust. But no. He is from the sea. Did you write that?

Yes.

That must please you.

That's a curious idea.

That actor was wonderful. What was he called?

David Trevor.

He played the spy?

Yes.

Has he been in anything else?

Not much.

That's too bad.

He's all right, he works on the stage, he'll never starve.

And the regular soldier was called Saint-Luc? That actor was very good at looking moody and not saying much.

Yes.

Where does it all come from?

If you start with a body, everything is contained there. Breath, gesture, and then memory of the gesture. Or I stole it from somewhere. I don't mind really that all my ideas come from other places.

That's lucky, then, if you are always stealing. Will you still make movies?

I think I've come to the end of that.

How can you be sure?

In the same way that once I looked forward and thought, I'm going to make films. I was resigned to the path that had opened up in front me. Now, I look forward, and I think, I will not make any more films.

What will you do instead? Now that you aren't making movies.

I am going to try to do the least possible.

That sounds tragic.

No. Not at all. For a long time, I suffered from trying to do the most possible. Now I will try to do the least.

A new philosophical position.

I suppose so.

That makes sense to me, as a recluse on a mountaintop.

One thing I know: when you are dealing in film, you are dealing in movement, with moving things. I want to sit still, and sit with an image. I don't want to chase it.

The tapestry is still. But it is also moving.

The one downstairs? It is certainly moving. It's basically a revolving door.

Do you want to hear the story of my mother?

Yes, I think so. Fanny told me something already, but I've forgotten what... Oh, it was that your mother was a weaver.

You saw Fanny! That's auspicious.

So, she is alive.

Very much so.

Then why has Prawn never heard of her or seen her?

Is Prawn alive?

I think so. He told me the saga of his failures as a sort of stockbroker. That sort of tedium is unique to the living.

The walking dead of banking, the woodsman affirmed.

I suppose we're all half absent. We the sufferers. The doctor seems at least "among" us.

He's not even half a doctor!

And so what? I said. Do you expect more from a doctor than anyone else?

What's clear to me is that he profits on everyone pretending to believe his stories.

I like stories. I think I will stand by the doctor.

But you've barely spent any time with him.

Time in Jaquith House seems to operate by its own rules. But I've noticed something.

What?

Pauses. Breaks in my chatter. I hate to say it, but something might be taking effect.

And you attribute this to the talking cure?

I've been talking for months, so I doubt it's that.

Ah, but perhaps now you are listening. Do you want to hear about my mother or not?

I do! I definitely do. I seem to always ask the wrong questions. And then make the wrong speeches. When Prawn—

Stop! Listen now.

I nodded.

First, she was not exactly a weaver. She was a mender: she mended tapestries. Or her family did, and she did also, and she embroidered all her life.

Tapestries like the one downstairs?

Very much like the one downstairs. Second, she never slept in her entire life. Or nearly never—she could not tell night from day, she said, one had invaded the other.

An insomniac!

Third, she lived always close to water. In particular, she lived always close to a river. When she was little she lived in a large white house called Choosey. The river water was needed for the dyes, for the tapestries.

She remained there all her life?

No. She did not always live by the same river, but always beside a river, even though as a child she nearly drowned. There were periods of time where she was kept elsewhere, but those were the darkest periods, and she always returned to her place beside a river.

A river has a way of appearing, disappearing, and then reappearing across one's life. Like a mill at the end of a causeway. Like a sluice gate, or a canal lock.

A looping thread, he said. She sketched these images often, and landscapes of waves like hills rising up, and for this she was also known as an artist.

What did you want to tell me about your mother, Lonnie?

Just those three things—for now.

And the tapestry downstairs—did she make it?

Her hand was in it, certainly, but for mending only, when she was a child. You can see the very bottom corner: she was so small she rarely worked above the bottom edges. But you can see one very elegant shoe—that has her touch.

She was a sufferer.

She was the original sufferer.

So, you do have a long history with this place. And to think the doctor told me this tapestry was modern Danish. Was she Danish, your mother?

She was in no way Danish, and the doctor is not a doctor.

Yes, point taken, I can tell you have a painful history. But that's what Prawn said, also.

You're obsessed with this Prawn!

I thought he had a handle on things—I can see why you mention your mother to me: we have several things in common.

You have at least three things in common.

Except that I don't mend things, Lonnie. Can you show me the shoe you mentioned? And then I think I will have to go try to find my way toward sleep.

You never learn anything from anything.

That's almost certainly true. What would you want me to have learned?

You could be doing something with all this time you have not sleeping.

I'm doing something—I'm here with you and your dog. I'm doing the same as you. But yes, I used to do things with those shapeless hours—there was a time when I filled those hours with ease. That's wrong, though, I shouldn't say ease. I filled them with something, though it wasn't easy. But now I don't. Lonnie, did you once have a little model boat?

Most children have toy boats.

Tell me, did it end well for your mother? All her hours in the night of embroidery and mending?

I don't want to talk about the way things ended; I have to separate her from the way she ended. I only wanted to talk about the three things. But I will show you the shoe anyway.

It might not have otherwise presented itself to me, this elegant red shoe of the crone at the bottom of the bottommost corner scene of the tapestry hanging in Barbarêche, though the shoe itself was an image of—a representation of—embroidery, being as it was, an embroidered shoe. That is to say, the shoe was floral tapestry of red-toned silks. Is this so unusual? I suppose not. It was on the foot of one of the twin crones and extending up her ankle and into a similarly patterned stocking. It was on one of these crones who had once been a young maid. Though for the mother of the woodsman, small enough that she could reach only the hem of the hanging, her eyes perhaps only just above the line of the fringe, there was only the crone to gaze upon. What a difficult task it must be to mend an image of something that you can see only in part?

Surely, the story of the tapestry had no bearing on the craftsmanship in the embroidery, and thereby the demands it made on the work. Form should always lead, mind you.

The crone, whose embroidered shoe was extended out as she lifted her skirts and petticoats, and she was reaching a toe toward the edge of a pool of water, or the rim of a lake, or the edge of a sea—who could tell? Such was the ambiguity of the overlap of scenes. What difference did it make if I couldn't figure out the meaning of the story? What a relief to find such crisp precision in these otherwise frivolous accessories!

Lonnie, I asked, as he shined a small flashlight on the corner of the tapestry and studied it with all his quietness and all his stillness. It was the very corner I had seen the doctor escape through only a day or so before—oh, how the time blurred in Jaquith House, how it blurred and stretched out all at the same time.

Lonnie, I asked, do you want to spend the night with me?

Are you making a pass?

I am.

Why?

Why not?

No, I think. I am sorry, but I decline.

Are you sure about that?

I'm not sure, but I decline in any case.

Suit yourself.

I am sorry to say no. On another occasion I might answer differently.

Well, it's deflating, I'll admit, but nothing that should concern you. I haven't had to hear no very much. But I may have to get used to it.

Then you aren't upset with me?

Not at all. Don't give another thought. But tell me, what is going on in this tapestry? Is it a historical saga or something?

It's the story of a sailor who goes to sea—Lonnie gestured to one panel—He drowns—he gestured to another panel—but then comes back as a ghost, later—a final gesture.

A sailor's ghost! And yet the whole thing is just covered in women. Who are they? I asked.

The sailor had two sisters, as the story goes. They are very popular these sisters, but once the brother is lost at sea, they grow into spinsters waiting for his return. For a very long time, he doesn't return. And then he does. But as a ghost. I think it is hard for them to get on with things as long as he keeps hanging around in the parlor. But then there is also a war—which you see here. But I forget which comes first.

The order of things seems negotiable.

Yes. Do you like stories like that?

A bit hard to follow, but I don't mind.

Who will you ask in my place tonight? Dominick?

The tennis pro? Certainly not! Why would you think I would?

He's my brother. And I suspect it is my mother you want to be close to.

Dominick? Your brother? I would never have guessed it. I thought he was Italian.

An affectation. But also, different fathers.

He seems—lighthearted. And, forgive me, a bit blank? You are night and day apart!

Yes. I am night and he is day.

What a romantic. You really should stop while you are ahead, or I'll make a second pass, and it seems like your guard may be dropping.

It would be harder to turn down a second time, I admit.

Don't think I don't know that. I'm well-seasoned at casting for the couch.

But don't ask him about my mother.

But she's his mother also?

We know different things about her. In that way, she was different mothers. I think it should stay that way. For everyone's safety.

Aha. I'll keep our conversation under my vest.

Are you going to ask me into your room a second time?

Oh, no. It seems like taking advantage. I already got you to confess so much. And I won't call your brother.

Or the chef?

Or the chef. Tonight, anyway.

Well, you know where to find me.

Do I?

Just follow the road up the mountain. There's only one.

One road?

Yes. And one mountain.

I see. And you know where to find me, I said.

True. Well. Until you next fail to sleep, he said.

Until then, I said, and I closed him out into the hallway and left him alone before his mother's shoe.

23

THE POST AND THE PADDLE

Fanny had been correct about the delivery of my post. Just behind the rose-glass door in the back entrance to the main house, a series of cubbyholes were marked with the names of the sufferers. There I was, plainly identified by my codename, and inside my box was a small stack of letters.

The first item was from Fanny as promised: the clipping was a magazine photo of an outhouse with a large rooster perched on the seat of the facility. The caption in Fanny's script: "A chicken in every pot!" On the back of the clipping: "Come in one day's time to the Syllabary for dinner and bring the things needed to make the dinner. I will do the rest. P.S. Invitation required for admittance."

The second item was also a postcard invitation.

This invitation overlaid an engraving of visibly aroused demons—penetrating several ecstatic nubile figures. The card was unsigned, with no return address. In place of RSVP was scrawled: "From exalted mysticism to raging Satanism is but one step. Xoxo."

The third item was a little piece of paper from the studio. It was an unassuming note, inconsequential on the surface, but one that collapsed time and space in an ax blow and drew together the seams of my story before and after boats.

It was a memo reminding me that a film option was about to expire. Locations in Madrid and Barcelona. What, if anything, did I want to do about this option? the note asked.

At the bottom of the memo was printed, in a font without serif: Hoping for your swift recovery!—Best regards, YOUR STUDIO FAMILY.

Ah, Franco's Spain. What an escape. Where the charge of absolute control, fascism, and tyranny was being lobbied at someone other than myself. My paid vacation awaited, if I could simply return to the warm embrace of my studio and learn to work well with others.

I'm no fool. I know it was time I was looking for at Jaquith House. Time and ghosts. But time, for me, could be accessed only through the camera's lens—so how would I make this journey, this fantastic journey through space and time without my lens? Such historical regression suddenly felt very sci-fi to me, and I felt an uncharacteristic dampness crossing my face, like something in my visage had cracked.

I have no memory of leaving the mailroom, and the little boxes, but suddenly I discovered I was walking up the hill, along the main lane that crossed in front of Jaquith House. I walked for some time below apple and plum trees, now past their fruiting as the season was certainly on the turn, and I crossed the meadow that separated the orchards from the fringe of the woods. I knew that if I continued I would eventually find the road that went up the hill to the woodsman's cottage.

I heard the sounds of the quick-moving water from the stream diminish, and the sounds of the mechanisms of the farm fell away, and all that remained was that particular sound of wind in the pines and the popping of the electrical fence that I knew I must get beyond. While the fence itself lay almost invisible, so carefully woven into the underbrush, the complicated keypad announced itself singularly in its shining steel encasement, and I remembered that there would be no way to exit without asking for the code.

I hated to ask for things. Better that they offer themselves of their own accord.

But making out the parameters of the keypad, I saw that the gate in front of me was slightly agape, as if a failure in the mechanism prevented the movement in any direction toward opening or closing, leaving the tiniest and most rigid gap through which to slip. My contours were fluid enough, and with some difficulty, I got through.

Beyond the gate, I went into the damp, fragrant air. A peculiar climate.

And there I was on a dirt lane cutting through pines and cedars, pink granite rising now from the forest moss. The trees were not so dense as to shut out light entirely, but the day was gray enough, and the light uniformly muted or it carried itself as if all the different shades of the forest derived from that one color. The whole landscape, somber and grave, seemed almost imperceptibly to drift. I broke a twig from the hemlock, and its leaves were dark and unusually spaced and spare, and its aspect was almost black, and as I passed along this lane I saw the opening in the trees, and all at once I was on the edge of an enormous black lake, its narrow dock stretching out from me for a few feet only. It was still early enough in the morning that mists were lifting off the water, but anything beyond the black lake and the lifting mists was difficult to discern. There was land in the distance, but if it was the far edge of the other side of the lake or if it was an island freestanding in the middle of the water, I could not yet tell. But I fixed in my mind the notion that it was certainly an island, if for no other reason than that I desired it. Locked now in meditation on the land in the distance, the possible island in the middle of the lake, I lost track of my mission toward the home of the woodsman, and I tried to remember the last time, if there ever was a time, when I had visited an island on a lake, and it was then that the tip of a green-black canoe, the color of ferns, cut into my line of sight from out of the mists, Dr. Duvaux seated in its canvas shell! A life jacket hung loosely over his piped sport coat, and his feet, I noticed, were bare. He approached the dock and reached out a hand to the edge.

Grab on, if you don't mind, Helena, but when you climb into the canoe, make sure to step in the middle.

Into the boat?

The lake is quite calm, as you can see, and as long as you keep your weight low there's little risk of capsizing. If you behave foolishly, however, that's another story. Are you going to behave foolishly?

Doctor, who could say?

The doctor, lodged in the back of the canoe, gestured toward the front bit of the canoe and the taut netting where I was expected to perch. I had never been in such a beautiful canoe! It's curving bottom like the inside of a ribcage, in red and white cedar, gleaming and slipping with shipped lake water. I gave none of this away, of course, but stepped carefully and quietly onto the central spine of the bottom of the boat and took my seat. Dr. Duvaux nudged my back with the end of a paddle.

Do you know how to paddle?

I can manage.

We'll see soon enough. So many of our guests claim to know how to paddle. Few do, in actuality. Here we go: shoving off. Quick and stable and tandem, perfect for one of our chats.

I thought I might get the day off today.

After that business with the fence yesterday, Helena? I hardly think it would be responsible for me not to follow up.

You know about the fence?

I know about everything that happens here.

Is that an island in the distance?

One of many on the lake. And there's no need to turn around, Helena, I can hear you quite plainly. It's an effect of the granite rising from the water. You see it brings our voices back to us, so there is no need for you to face me.

I'm no stranger to water, Doctor, I said as I spoke toward the island. You don't have to explain every aspect of physics.

You could be taking out the boat yourself if you made a bit more effort with the community.

Sir, yesterday was simply packed with society!

I fear the wrong kinds. I hope you don't believe everything you hear in a dining car. Or over a billiard table for that matter. Tabloid gossip can be so misleading.

I agree with you there, Doctor. Are we going to the island?

Which island are you inquiring about?

Which island, which island! I shouted. The island directly in front of us, the island we are headed straight for. The only island in sight, Doctor!

Oh, no. That's all wrong.

All wrong?

There are four islands in front of us.

Are you speaking metaphorically?

I am speaking geographically, Helena. Topographically, as well, I suspect. There's a cut between the two larger islands, but we are coming at it from a forty-five-degree angle, so you are not able to see the gap. You will see it, if we continue on this course. But that is no matter, since the island we are going to is to the right of all that. Do you see those three trees, the single upright pine, and the two little cedars curving toward it?

Growing out of that jutting rock?

Gilbert is the larger of the two. We shall land there.

And the smaller?

Sullivan. Yes, mind yourself when we alight. There will be bushes that look like blueberries. Some of these are blueberries, and some of these are masquerading as blueberries. So we must be careful only to eat the honest berry.

Is this one of those therapeutic practices, Doctor, where I relive the trauma of the accident so as to purge it from my body?

Just tell me how it feels to be in a boat again.

Well, to be honest, this little thing really has no relationship in my mind to the boat in question.

Ah, look, the cut in the islands!

Suddenly, the land before us broke apart, and continued to open, as the channel of dark water emerged into view from over the gunwale, and though the channel had always been there, indeed it had been hidden from sight due to the angle of our approach, and now as it opened and widened before us, it seemed impossible that I had ever seen these two islands as one island, so wide was the channel that separated them. It was plain to see that even a small steamer could pass through, and that each island now seemed much larger on its own than the two together. The doctor adjusted our course, and we passed not through the channel but across it, toward the two small outcroppings of Gilbert and Sullivan. I wanted to enter the channel. Through the mist, I saw a boathouse covered in moss and sinking into the waters slightly, or so it seemed, from my distance, a ruin of a boathouse, or one at least in serious decline. I wanted also to know the names of these two larger islands. But the doctor, who seemed now to be recovering his composure, had begun to chatter about one of the myths of the lake involving the slaughter of one set of indigenous peoples by the ghosts of enemy indigenous peoples. As he drew close to Gilbert, just inches below the bottom of the canoe, shining and golden, there was a flat slab of granite.

PORTHOLE

The doctor said, Helena, disembark.

I stepped out onto the flat granite and slid suddenly nearly knee deep into the lake. But my bootheel caught, somehow, and I staggered up the slab onto Gilbert.

You're wearing shoes! That's hopeless. You get what you deserve.

It's forty degrees, Doctor.

In the air, Helena. Not in the lake. The lake is much warmer than that.

There was barely room on Sullivan for both of us to stand adjacent. The doctor paused before a shrubbery and began to examine its fruits. I perched on the edge of the water on a rise in the rock and snuggled into my sweaters and looked across the brief stretch of lake that ran between Gilbert and Sullivan. There were definitely what appeared to be blueberries on both outcroppings, and some other shrubbery that had a dark berry, but which looked, to my thinking, nothing like a blueberry. I could almost jump between the two islands, and in better weather wouldn't even have hesitated to pass. I nibbled on a tiny fruit. It tasted of very little, but it wasn't unappealing.

The doctor stood with a hand on one hip. And thence the rust-eaten weapon doubtless played its deadly part, he intoned.

What's that, Doctor?

I used to be able to recite quite a rousing ballad about the historic local massacres. I'm afraid these days I can only recall that one line.

You have so much else to hold in your mind.

It must be utter hell to be in charge of a whole film production, he said.

It was. It must be hell to run an entire asylum.

Yes. But worse still as you grow old.

That's a cliché.

Unfortunately, but it's also a truism. Our days are numbered.

You look the picture of health, Doctor.

The house, Helena. Our days are numbered at the house. We are—I am—an obsolete breed.

That must be why you and I get along so well.

This is harsh reality speaking. I'm speaking to you from a place of honesty and fear.

You seem to have a thriving business. There's no shortage of psychic exhaustion.

It would seem so, Helena, but I've been a bit lax on collecting fees.

Oh, I see. Yes, of course, you European geniuses would drop the ball on the bookkeeping. I should have seen that one coming.

Helena, do you fear shame? Do you ever fear the notion that you will have failed?

I have failed. Everyone knows I have failed.

Here, we are at the mercy of our landlords.

There are several?

There are two who are key. Brothers. Half-brothers. Who never agree on anything.

Oh, dear.

It's always been a selfish enterprise, I admit. But Helena, I ask you, is it wrong to want to keep all this respite for ourselves?

I've never been much for ethical positions, Doctor, but there is the issue of the deserving poor. And the undeserving poor, I suppose.

Helena, realistically, we both know that a loss of Jaquith House will not result in a betterment of the lives of the deserving poor. Or the undeserving poor. Merely more land will become available for the undeserving rich.

I may be rich for the moment, but there is something about having extracted it from thin air and celluloid that gives me a certain satisfaction. Like spinning gold from flax. Something diabolical.

Is that a spark I see in your eye, Madam Director?

There are aspects to my career I would miss, I don't deny it. There was a time when I thought I actually could be what I appeared to be. I bought into the script.

By that logic, all you need is a new script, and the belief will follow.

I wish it were so simple, Doctor.

Do you? Well, you know me, Helena. I advocate simplicity above all. But then what I advocate will soon be of little interest to anyone. Shall we start back?

Didn't you want to chat about the accident, Doctor?

Helena, I think you can see my heart is not in anything today. But, Helena, what did you find in your mail slot today?

As if you didn't already know.

Pretend I don't.

An invitation to a cabal, and an invitation to a civilized dinner party.

Proof of great popularity, I should think. I would like to attend a cabal! You must keep me in mind as your plus one.

Noted, Doctor. But I'm not really accepting off-campus social engagements at the moment. I've decided to take the advice of Chef Anatole and try to settle in—even if our days are numbered.

But who invited you to this cabal?

I have no clue, Doctor. The card wasn't signed.

And can you make no guess?

I cannot.

That's a pity. So many little mysteries. Nothing else then in the mail?

The letter from the studio.

Yes, the letter from the studio. Was it of interest?

Not particularly.

Oh, Helena. Then indeed we are not much good to each other.

Oh, that's fine, Doctor. There's an ambient accumulation. I mean, I must have been feeling low, but I am feeling much better at the moment. Even though it's very cold here on Gilbert, but I am glad to have seen these little islands.

If only you had come in July! Or the previous July. The previous July was gorgeous. But then, I imagine, you hadn't experienced your psychic trauma then. Where were you two Julys ago?

Stealing time. Stealing time to make up for wasting time. Or wasting time, in order to later have an excuse to steal it back.

Come on then, back into the boat, he said.

I did as instructed, and he climbed in behind me. We paddled back toward the mainland shore, which stretched, it seemed, for miles. I wondered how far the house of the woodsman was really. If I had continued on my path I could have walked for a day running parallel to the mountain along the lake but never ascending. Perhaps my notion that he came and went on foot was false. Surely, a little pickup truck must be in play? But all the modern technics of Jaquith House seemed hidden behind the scenes.

In the canoe, everything was especially peaceful.

The doctor returned me to the dock, hauled himself up first, then hauled up the canoe and strode off without comment. How quickly our trip to the little islands had ended, and now, as the day was warming and clearing, I could see very far. I thought I could see the two islands we had just passed through, but now, they had reformed into one property, so I couldn't be sure where one began and the other ended.

I abandoned my search for the little road up the hill to the woodsman's for the time being, and I returned to the path back down to the compound. What did I want with him in any case? More distraction?

PORTHOLE

In passing through the gate in the electric fence, I saw that it was standing open, left for me, I assumed, by Dr. Duvaux. Only in crossing back into the compound did I notice that I had been clasping my mail in my fist the entire time. It was soaked with water and stained with the juice of honest berries: two invitations and one ultimatum.

24

THE SPANISH OPTION

In the case of the Spanish option, my acquaintance with the novelist Augustin Caraterro began long before that day at the Blue Lily. And it had nothing to do with Corey, not as such. Not as the invention he had presented to me on the day of the auditions for *Walkway*, the Corey I would work with for the next five years. But, I admit, a draft version of him had been involved.

It was around the time of the editing of *The Tightening Knot*. David had returned to London for a production of *Heartbreak House* for twelve weeks, where he was ambitiously aging up and putting on weight to play Shotover. I was anxious to get on to the next thing, but also a bit at loose ends, as always after coming to end of a project. We would soon be starting *Slipcase*, with David in the lead as Doryan the gambler, but I was not yet sure, and there were always other projects in the works, other seducing projects. And if I still felt hope for the films to come, I was already tired of myself and my writing. Before thinking about *Slipcase*, I went to Portugal for my walking and unthinking. There I met the novelist Augustin Caraterro by chance, or by process of elimination. Derelict artists naturally pool in the filthiest crevices.

Augustin was a known quantity around town, known to be arrogant and provocative in social settings, drawing on the persona of the matador (which he had been in his youth in Spain). He had begun to work in film himself, scripting for other directors, and already had an excellent reputation for scripting. We knew so many people in common, I was not put off brash demeanor. Quite the contrary. I saw it for the protective guise that it was. He was certainly not yet the famous figure he would come to be as a filmmaker—in fact, given what I know of him now, it is hard to imagine he ever felt any insecurities about his talent: but this was the discovery I quickly made in our meetings in outdoor cafés along the Douro River. His bravado and arrogance fell away as he talked about his aspirations. He wished to adapt his first novel, an underworld noir called *Madrid Plays*. He had struggled with adapting it himself and felt too close to the project.

I learned much more: He was a student of philosophy, and an autodidact. We shared an obsession with the reading of faces, interpretation and divination via the lift of the eyes, the dip of the chin, et cetera, the potential to be found in the mime. He had seen *Mechanism*, and I remember now that we spent so much time talking about Emile's performance, Emile's choices. Yes, I would have said Emile's choices, Emile's performance—I may have taken credit for the film, but of course, I would have said to Augustin that the drifter Kestrel belonged to Emile.

Madrid Plays was a roman à clef, and as such made him feel vulnerable. He was looking for someone with more experience to option it, and made no pretense about his thinking that I was the person to do this. Truly what he hoped for was a collaboration, which he thought would ensure his first film was a success. My studio connections would allow for freedom of choice, of movement.

What was in it for me? I asked.

The novel itself was very good, and it fit with my genre, he told me. Besides, he needed my help with an actor who he had targeted to play the lead, an actor at that time entirely unknown, inexperienced, and who needed to be brought into hand. This was the bait that he offered.

It was a mere flirtation—in every regard. I was—and this is truly diabolical—completely absorbed by David and our next project. I had no notion of adapting anything. Nonetheless, Augustin and I continued to meet. Our little brainstorming sessions were a pleasant distraction as I waited for David, who, when he finished his run in *Heartbreak House*, would need to be packed off to fitness camp in the high desert to peel off the Shotover weight. There was time.

And what about this untried actor? I inquired.

For the lead, for the character of the thug Alberto, he had found someone who had a kind of pan-European blankness, someone, he told me, who was swarthy and cutthroat but with an effete and aristocratic profile. A protégé, he said.

He is a Spaniard? I asked. Surely, Alberto must be a Spaniard. To cast anything other than a Spaniard would be a disaster.

It is not necessary, said Augustin. It is perhaps better if he were not, *precisely*, a Spaniard. I am a Spaniard, and I cannot understand the mind of Alberto.

But you wrote Alberto.

I wrote the story of someone who believes all that he has heard of the story of Alberto, but I did not write Alberto.

I see your point, I said. And in fact, I did! I confess there was something exhilarating in having conversations with someone who worked in my field. In this case, a field that was not defined by medium, but by one's relationship to the gestation of a medium, and of course, I was intrigued by the idea of this non-actor he had in mind, who would supply the interiority of Alberto.

If I got involved, I would need to get a feel for the flavor of Madrid's criminal milieu, I warned him. His style as a novelist—baroque renderings, rambling prose—was difficult to translate into film, I said. We would all need to spend time together—myself, Augustin, and his would-be actor. Clearly, he was quite enamored already with his protégé. I recognized the pattern. But he needed help to regain the upper hand, and I was known for precisely this. They were staying together locally, the time was perfect to begin.

The option was easily secured for a small sum, the studio was intrigued with the concept, and the idea of an international collaboration. I thought, I will work with Augustin's actor, and I will rough out a script until I decide what is next with David. What seemed impossible was that something genuine might open up or that, in working on this project, I would see somewhere in the depths of another man's mind, a version of Helena.

I had rented a small apartment in Porto, along the cable car lines, a seedy little apartment, but quite high up on a hill, with a clear view of the wine cellars and the outdoor cafés, and a view of the Douro River. Below my window, at the bottom of the hill, an old man grilled sardines all day long in a metal drum and served them along with port and tonic cocktails.

Augustin and his protégé needed only to follow the river to find me. I met them at the bottom of my hill, in the smoke of the sardines.

He was calling himself then by another name, one that neither of us revisited in our years after *Walkway*. I agreed to call him only by the name of the character he was meant to play, the thug Alberto.

We drank port and tonic with the other tourists and ate sardines and talked about *Madrid Plays* until evening, when we drifted up to my apartment. I took notes all the while in shorthand.

I felt a kindred spirit in both the writer and his protégé. Their intimacy was unquestionable. And they had considered every external aspect of the thug Alberto together. But the interior of Alberto was still inaccessible to both. When that night, Augustin collapsed from drink and the exhaustion of the burden of discussing a book that was too much a part of himself, I urged him to sleep in my bed, while I took the opportunity to examine the interior of the thug Alberto with the man who would perhaps play him. This was only natural.

I said to the protégé, now offering me his undivided attention:

Could the thug Alberto remain silent on the screen? Alberto is an outsider, someone always on the margin in his underworld milieu. In a sense he has everything in common with the community of the underworld, and in another sense, the milieu is made of those who have nothing in common to begin with, being held together for mercenary purposes only. No one can be trusted, everyone must be sacrificed if need be, there can be no attachments.

There are attachments, extraordinary attachments and sentiment, the protégé told me.

Well, something holds the underworld together beyond racketeering, smuggling, and contraband—yes, I agree. If you were able to understand this, or capture this, how could you possibly hope to give voice to Alberto's silence? Because truly, Alberto must remain silent to hold his delicate place within this community. These mysterious attachments—this aspect is precisely what must be communicated through the slightest adjustments of his eyes, his lids, his lips, within his silence. It will all depend on you, the actor, if you become the actor, I said. Everything always depends on the actor, but also, nothing depends on the actor.

And you know actors very well, very intimately, he said.

An exaggeration. Tabloid stuff.

I'm not sure how to find this depth, he said. I have never worked with anyone like this.

I have, I said. It will be simple. Here is what we will do: as we begin to imagine the script, one of us will play the part of Alberto, and the other will play the part of someone else, someone close to Alberto or someone in the milieu.

Which of us will play Alberto?

For now, we will alternate. We will take turns arranging each other until the communication is complete.

How will we know?

We will have to know—the communication must not fail.

Do you really believe such a thing, he asked, that communication is so simple? We don't even speak the same language, Augustin and I. Alberto and I.

Don't worry so much about Augustin. I speak rather good Spanish, actually, but I just cannot write this script in Spanish.

The thug Alberto grew up speaking Catalan.

They speak Catalan in Madrid?

He grew up speaking Catalan.

But Alberto the thug is from Madrid?

So they say, he said.

Yes. I see. So they do. Then we'll communicate that.

I don't believe language is so crude, so flat. Alberto's language is the language of poetry. It can't be used simply to pass information, like a bus schedule, like a weather report.

No, of course not, I said, and I remembered the collection of dialects on my uncle's boat: Greek, French, Spanish, Polish, English, Portuguese, Russian—everyone spoke almost everything and yet very little direct communication ever took place.

How can I put it? I said. Something will be exchanged. Something ineffable will happen—something of note as Alberto offers his silence to us. And we will script this and write some lines around it. But only a few!

How could an actor possibly work under such fascism? Because it will be fascism, surely, to force someone to follow the choreography invented in a hotel.

The best actors thrive under such fascism, as you call it.

At a remove from the world? he asked.

We are not removed from the world. We are making the world.

Such arrogance, he said.

I hope so, I said. I will need photographs of you—you will have to be patient with me.

I'm sure this will be a great honor to have my face so cared for by your camera. His accent was such that "honor" sounded to me like "horror," and this struck me at the time as ominous, and strikes me still. And yet he yielded.

We began with the modeling, the gestures, the subtle physical adjustments of Alberto, first the protégé as Alberto, as I positioned his chin, his shoulders, while I asked him to express for me, with his eyes only, the nuances of Alberto the thug. I took pictures, I took notes, I softly manipulated his body and asked for stillness, which he was unable to provide. At that time, he couldn't stand to be touched or to be adjusted. We switched, and I played the part of Alberto, and asked for his direction, his adjustments, but he found it all foolish. He might become angry, I thought, he might become petulant and break the spell. But he gulped port and sweet red wine and instead called down to the café owner in bad Portuguese, who answered nonetheless and provided several bottles of a dry Duoro, and he even conjured a few small bitter Spanish beers.

The truth is that I wasn't remotely convinced by anything we were doing, it was a game, to fill time. I dashed off some lines on a page hoping to convince him that a script was coming from our role-play. He seemed unconvinced.

He clutched his brow, he massaged his eyes. But as things go, in such proximity, when I had put on the men's clothes of Alberto, the hat of Alberto, as I sipped the small bitter beer, and its flavor held on my breath, I relaxed. And so, too, did the protégé. He began to understand how to move and adjust my body, to take my head and turn it gently, and he photographed me. I lifted my dark glasses and revealed the full effect of my eyes. He moved my chin, and my neck, and I let him go on taking pictures, but then as he began to follow his way down my limbs and torso with his gentle, almost timid touch, I responded, but it was not with a gentle touch, it was with the strength of Alberto. He recoiled initially, but then I knew, as I watched him, turning the camera on him, that he felt suddenly the desire and cruelty of Alberto, but only in response to whatever desire or cruelty I gave out as Alberto. And so when I put down the camera, and finally our bodies fell together, as, of course, is inevitable in such a context, and he began to enjoy my body as I was enjoying his, it was, I felt, because he was finally able to truly enjoy the body of Alberto, as was I, and we each made love to Alberto the thug with complete voracity and with violence.

Perhaps there was only mechanism to our lovemaking. If passion is a mechanism, if desire is a machine. In the hours afterward, there is always the impression on the skin of the lover's body. There is the imprint, the impression on the lips and eyes, the stamp of the machine. There is the heat of the mechanism at its core in the body, and in the groin, along the thighs. And then hours pass, and there is only amnesia, or worse still, an artificial nostalgia.

I can say this word "lover" of Alberto because he was not yet an actor.

When it was over, we dressed, and we returned to the script. He was able to be still, finally, and he began to reveal things to me that he suspected lay hidden in the character of Alberto. And so it began.

In the morning, when Augustin awoke to find us at work on the script, he was delighted at the progress. He spoke alone with his protégé, and I could see both had come to an understanding.

A few days would pass, or a week, and I continued to play with the script. It was not long before I felt the need to see the thug Alberto, and I would summon him—sometimes with Augustin, sometimes alone.

When he came with Augustin we would begin in awkward collision. Our triangulated meetings were erratic, driven and punctuated by Augustin's restless movements: shifting about in the uncomfortable chairs in my rented flat. Despite our productive immersion in the thug Alberto, despite new confessions on Augustin's part regarding his understanding of Alberto as he witnessed our role-playing, he clearly felt more and more anxious about the trajectory of the adaptation. He made enfeebled arguments against my interpretations, only to back down from them graciously, with sanguine, pained eyes.

When his protégé came alone, we would begin more easily, more passionately seek the thug Alberto together. An easy rhythm had been established between us.

However, despite our affinity for Alberto, our desire to share in Alberto's perversions, the feeling was short-lived. Each time we came together Alberto seemed more difficult to reach, as if we were trying to contact the dead through the medium of the living script. But Alberto was not dead. He had never been living.

Then we returned to Augustin, who would join us and try to provide the missing dimensions of the thug Alberto, though this seemed to take something out of both men that it did not take from me.

For after all, what did I have to do with the thug Alberto?

Under other circumstances, I might have thought the relationship a success. My script was coming along, and it was spare and laconic, as suiting a noir. The great danger, I realized, was that I might actually make something of this option after all.

What Augustin imagined when he allowed for the option of his novel was something very different. Dialogue that might drag out in the manner of Eugene O'Neill, only with slanted, obscure responses, spoken with mannered, lilting rhythms. A vision that was forward-reaching, while mine was mired in a deep nostalgia. In short, a vision in keeping with the films he would later go on to make, the films that would make him quite famous.

It became clear that Alberto must speak, and when he spoke, finally, that my Alberto was turgid, cryptic, elusive. Utterances were being imagined as mere grunts. In some cases, the exchanges would be so obscure, they were incomprehensible. Perhaps, I could not get my mind into the mind of a man after all, despite the conviction of my own manliness. I was scripting a farce. And I think they both suspected it.

It was hard to reconcile the idea of the character I had begun with—brazen, arrogant, coolly fluid, aquiline—with the resigned and resolved Alberto I was creating. The slightly effete mannerisms in the novel were now masked in a roughshod body, and his deference in the quiet of our hotel rooms, the fluidity of his desires, and his willingness to confess them were being assimilated. But in this reconciliation, between the two figures—the semblance of the brash matador and the vulnerable artist now unmasked—sacrifices would have to be made.

A flirtation, I assure you, was all it had been. Another type of option, but one similarly suspended. But the intensity of a shared vision, however imaginary, had forged something between the three of us.

However, I did not collaborate. I would get my way in the long run, if I persisted. But I had tired of all this company.

To whom did I owe an explanation? Only to the thug Alberto, who did not exist.

I knew that we had come to the end of things—and so I summoned, first, the protégé. We moved through one final series of staging and enactments in the apartment in Porto. As if the final motion of our goodbye had been extended, time suspended, and I learned the depths of his mouth and lips, which I realized had been the full focus of all my attention in the past weeks, well beyond the mouth and lips of the thug Alberto. In these moments together, there was no mechanism to our undressing, our lovemaking, and the sleep which followed.

I phoned Augustin and told him the studio had decided to suspend the project, that the foreign subject matter and the financial complications of the location abroad were too much for them to consider at this time. They would never consider an unknown actor, someone who, it would seem, was not even a Spaniard, which would be a political gaffe. He was suspicious, of course, but he didn't push me to go further. I said, when the option ran out, if he wanted to take this book and do with it what he liked, I would make sure that was possible: only, of course, on the condition that he cast a Spaniard. Alberto must be a Spaniard. Promise me, you will only cast a Spaniard, and in a few years you will be free to move forward.

I moved on with *Slipcase*, with David, and had almost completely forgotten the whole thing had taken place, nearly erased the thug Alberto from my mind. Nearly. Until a version of him turned up in the pear bag scene of *Walkway*.

25

DINNER AND A CONJURING

In his occupational costume, calm and collected, crisp and gleaming, Chef Anatole was sitting under the umbrella of a patio table when I arrived back at my barn still damp from the passage by canoe. Cradled to his chest was the one thing that had always been missing from his completed image: a bottle of whiskey.

I've got a bottle of good rye, he said. Is that the password?

That is a password, I told him.

Then I can come in?

No. But you can take me to your sunny hillside farm. I've been invited to a dinner tomorrow night, and I need to bag a hot bird.

It's like half an hour away. I will have to take the night off.

Yes, we'll need to drive. There's a Jag in the garage, and the keys are in the glove box.

It was right to say that I would not be present in the little sports car, on the hillside, or awaiting the executioner's act, which played out mercifully offstage on the poultry farm. Once my bird was procured, and securely packaged, we motored through the most spectacular foliage, leaves now changing and giving themselves over to turning winds. We landed in a provincial jazz club—there was not even the threat of youth or anything like youth—and watched a blousy redhead struggle through a Roberta Flack number. We drank, or I did, while Anatole chatted with the middle-aged barmaid, the oily host, in between numbers he sat with the pianist, he was as easy a social creature in the world as he was on the grounds of Jaquith House. What a pair we made, I thought, and here we are, out on the town. It was a glimpse of a possible future, a future of tedious normality, or country living: I could simply anchor and take advantage of the captive lovelies until I either transcended or sank. It was not a bad way out.

Eventually the chef and I made our way back to the barn, though to be honest, I remember little of what followed apart from a few slow slides into proximity, and an encounter that was by the book, but little beyond. The sound of my voice chatted on as he fell asleep, and as I passed only near to it.

But my night out had done the trick, I suppose, because when I arrived at the door of the Syllabary that following evening, my spirits were somewhat improved. I must have been feeling low, I thought. How had I let the doctor's dark mood infect me? All his modern methods brought on further melancholy, whereas the old ways, my old ways, and my uncle's old ways, still lifted my spirits—briefly, at least, but it was long enough to climb back into my next chic carapace, which might be the only thing holding up my frame.

So there I was, in a tuxedo of the finest black bombazine, a warp of silk and a weft of worsted, and a waistcoat in amber sateen, a crossdressed wraith. By my side, my bird in a bag had cooled considerably over night in the little refrigerator behind the bar in the recreation room at Barbarêche. Fanny appeared none too swiftly, and segmented in half, having opened only the top of a Dutch door.

I brought the chicken, I said.

Yes, I see! Did you bring your invitation?

Yes, I said, and rifled the ticket pocket on my waistcoat. Here it is, I said, as requested. I handed her my card.

Astral projection! she shouted.

I looked at the card in her hand: it was the wrong invitation. But I was quite sure that I put Fanny's invitation in my waistcoat. I had a clear memory of the outhouse rooster leering at me from the washbasin vanity as I brushed down my lapels.

You'll have to give me a minute to organize the gauze and ectoplasm—and the spirit photography! I don't know if I can manage a full astral projection, but I might be able to manage a séance. And the only digestive I have is Alka-Seltzer, so that will have to do.

I think it's a mistake, Fanny. I've mixed up the post—

Don't worry! she said, and permitted me finally through the lower half of the Dutch door. She said, I love improv! It keeps me young. Get your bird in the pot, and I'll set up the Bloomsbury table for the séance. I'm not wearing my petticoats, so it will be hard to stash the oranges and lemons for the materializations, but a rubber snake will fit into my cuff if I put on my better suit. What I wouldn't give for a couple of Hungarians—and some skeptics, and maybe a talking mongoose. Did you bring any of those?

I'm afraid not.

What about a planchette and a Ouija board?

The pockets on this blazer are mostly decorative, I sighed.

Well, you can't expect me to do everything. But at least you brought the chicken.

I've worse news still, Fanny. I don't have any idea what to do with it, so you may have to be in charge of that as well.

Don't look at me! I'm a vegetarian.

You're a what? Since when?

I've been a vegetarian for fifty-seven years. I'm not going to stop now.

Then why did you tell me to bring a chicken?

I said the pot could cook a chicken. And it can, it says it clearly in the instruction manual.

Shall we ring for Anatole?

How will he get in? He doesn't have an invitation.

Could we make an exception just this once, Fanny?

Oh, I doubt it. If I didn't keep my rules strict, before you know it, I'd have Tina in here day and night. I suppose we could give you a plus one. Do you choose Anatole as your plus one?

It seems like the only choice.

All right, I'll call him, but I've got to change and gather my materials.

Fanny disappeared into the little metal staircase rising up to the second-floor catwalk and up again into the wings of the turret, where she was quickly absorbed by an enormous wardrobe in the loft. She ferreted inside, while I settled myself into the pendulum basket chair and began a slow spin. I had made barely one rotation when a knock came on the door.

Already? I called up.

You better get that, shouted Fanny.

I opened the top half of the Dutch door. On the landing was the woodsman.

It's the woodsman, I shouted to Fanny, who appeared briefly over the edge of the catwalk.

No invitation, no admittance, she yelled.

You heard her, I said, but he seemed undaunted. He handed me the clipping of a rooster in an outhouse just as Fanny arrived in her dressing gown. She snatched the card from his hand.

This seems authentic, she said.

That's mine, I said. Or was mine. He must have stolen it!

Lonnie shrugged.

Sorry, Fanny said, I'll have to honor it. Do you have a plus one, Lonnie? He gestured to the dog Ruby, who placed her paws on the ledge of the Dutch door and shoved it open. Once inside she trotted to the little velvet settee beside Fanny's easel and made herself quite at home.

We are going to need a bigger chicken! And a bigger pot, Fanny said, making her way back up to her wardrobe. But don't mind me, I'm a vegetarian. I'll make the necessary call!

I brought a cheese, Lonnie said.

Is it Canadian? I asked.

It's goat.

I see, I said.

Where did Fanny go?

She's preparing for a séance, I said.

I see, he said.

Do you know how to make a chicken in an electric pot?

I can probably figure it out, he said, if there is only one chicken and one pot.

I showed him the chicken and the pot.

You've been to the chicken farm.

Your point being?

Nothing at all. Hand over the carcass.

It's all right, Fanny, I shouted. No need to phone the chef, Lonnie seems capable of feeding us.

Too late! She called down from her catwalk, and as quickly as that the aroma of the forest drifted in through the Dutch door.

Bave Cèdres!

I beg your pardon, Lonnie asked, as he dumped the entire pale carcass into the basin of the electric cauldron. Its wings and legs flopping akimbo, a bit beyond the capacity of the crockery. He tucked in the unruly limbs and stuffed the whole thing down with the lid. A light blinked on the surface of the pot as it emitted a hiss. We looked at each other but made no move to address the aromatic shadow that had crossed the floor of the kitchen from the Dutch door. Ruby the dog sat up, alert but unconcerned. Fanny returned to us, now dressed in a smart little black pantsuit, in a gleaming synthetic textile, covered over with embroidered horses.

Who is it? she asked us.

You know who it is, Chef Anatole announced. Fanny opened the lower half of the door to let him enter, and at that moment he was looking more like himself, in an aubergine suit and a sheer T-shirt with a deep V so that his bare, waxed chest glowed in the gloaming beneath the great sequoia.

He is hardly dressed to cook, I said. You came in short notice—I hope we didn't pull you away from the dinner service.

You caught me on my night off.

Every night seems to be your night off. What luck! And in theater clothes, no less.

What? These old rags?

Come in, Chef, said Fanny.

What is he doing here? Lonnie asked.

He's her date, said Fanny.

I see, said Lonnie.

And with that Chef Anatole wrapped his arms around my shoulders and nuzzled my throat. I'm not here to cook. I am off duty, he said.

What about hot chicken mousse?

It's too late anyway, said Lonnie. It's in the pot now.

Just then the lights flashed thrice, and the mechanical blinds began to descend around the periphery of the Syllabary.

Gather round! The séance is about to begin, Fanny said, and indeed the room had been quickly set, the lights dimmed, and an oil lantern set to a low glow in the middle of the Bloomsbury table. An aperitif was positioned in front of each chair, a dark burgundy elixir in small crystal glasses. Behind the table a cardboard cutout of the archduke Franz Ferdinand, draped in some kind of hosiery or perhaps a cheesecloth.

What is that? I asked Lonnie.

A spirit guide.

A Habsburg? In tulle?

Ectoplasm.

I see, I said. So, she intends to actually conduct a séance?

Anatole took my hand and placed it on the lobe of his chest where the V of his T-shirt opened up.

Just take things as they come, he said.

But the chicken...

I have never seen anyone so obsessed with flesh! said Fanny. How do you get anything done? I'm glad I'm a vegetarian. Sit boy-girl, please, around the table. Counting me. And hold hands.

Now the lights in the Syllabary were completely extinguished, though the oil lamp still flickered and glowed so that the archduke in his gauze cast a dull shadow across the floor behind us. We gathered tightly around the small table, the Bloomsbury table with its giant purple trumpet now lost in darkness, the thin rim seemed an insufficient border to accommodate the array of bodies surrounding it. It felt flimsy and vulnerable, especially dwarfed against the long legs of Lonnie and the longer legs of Chef Anatole. Perhaps it would float, perhaps it was precisely the purpose of such a table, to apport itself with the energy of spirits.

Fanny handed out name tags and instructed us to attach them readily to our jackets: "Lagos Pap" for Lonnie, "Nandor Fodor" for Anatole, "Eva C" for herself, and for me, "honored guest."

There, she said. There will be no mistakes about who is who.

I took up Lonnie's hand in my right and Chef Anatole's hand in my left.

This philter that I have placed before you will open up your hearts, but first we need to do the incantation to activate it, said Fanny. I hope this is a ghost-friendly crowd. Don't drop hands unless I say so. Can we agree that none of you are going to try to contact a demon? If we get a demon by accident, don't try to reason with it. I mean that! People always say they understand, and then the minute a demon turns up they try to use rational thinking on it, and that never works.

What does work? I asked.

Just let me handle it. Helena, you are the honored guest, so now is the time to make your special requests.

I have no special requests.

None? Oh, never mind, I'm already getting a sleeve tug from the beyond, so here we go. She blew out the lamp and plunged us into darkness. The hands of my companions seemed to slacken and relax in my grip, and I could hear the breathing of the chef and the woodsman clearly in the little acoustic chamber of the Syllabary. Then there was the rustling inside a duffle bag of some kind, the sound of cords and cables being let out, or reeled in, smacking against the floor in a coil or a heap, some objects or devices clapping against the top of the Bloomsbury table, and then the depression of keys on a keyboard. A deafening orchestral blast with considerable reverb shook the air and the walls of the turret, as the speakers lining its ribs let out the first notes of the incantation from *The Sorcerer*.

Good Lord. Gilbert and Sullivan, I whispered to Lonnie, but with no response. That's the second time this week, I said, but he could not hear me.

Gilbert and Sullivan, I screamed toward Anatole, but I was still easily drowned out by the accompaniment to the incantation of *The Sorcerer.* Fanny shushed me.

Sprites of earth and air! Friends of flame—

A quick popping of keys, and the sound lowered considerably but not so much that it did not still fill the chamber with sound, as the intoning of the sorcerer continued with the call to demons and other night spirits, *Noisome hags of the night—*

I always liked that part, shouted Fanny, I love a hag! but then she shushed herself.

Pallid ghosts arise!

That's enough of that! said Fanny. A click and silence. Again, I heard the breathing of the gentleman adjacent, the rustling of Fanny's rayon trousers, and again the tapping of keys. Then, a pause, a duration. A mumbled curse from Fanny, and her chair scraping back as she rustled off into the fringe of the room. A door opened, and a blinking media panel suddenly lit the far-left curve of the far-left wall, and Fanny was momentarily clearly recognizable in the blinking reds and greens of the console. Adjustments were made, the closet door reclosed, and darkness again draped us.

Drink your drink! shouted Fanny.

First the hand to my left slipped free, and then the hand to my right, and we all fumbled for our glasses, which once I found it, I quaffed in a single gulp. The taste was herbal, bitter, and aromatic, a Campari perhaps. Or Cynar.

Resume the circle, she said. We need the amplifier of our linked bodies to really project the spirit energy...

Once again we took up hands, and as we waited for the building or merging of spirits, I took the liberty to fondle the very fingers of my partners, their knuckles, the slight downy hair on the fingers of one hand, the dry, nearly papery skin of the other. I touched the nails of each hand with my thumbs, and perhaps I felt the rising buzz of the energy of spirits, or perhaps the warming of the herbal liqueur had begun to spread, for I felt a dizzying effect of the proximity of these luxurious bodies to my left and to my right, and I felt the central gravity of the very compact Fanny across the table, as I waited for the first contact from the beyond. It would be vague, I was sure. It would be, no doubt, undecipherable, for this is what the spirit realm demands, I thought. Do not, I thought, do not under any circumstances ask the spirit how he or she left this world. I remembered that was one rule that must not be broken.

Then the clicking began, the clattering of a projector or the wheels of a tape, and then wind, wind. And what else? The sound of something against a window pane. That much I was sure, the sound of something—rain, or falling ice, on the casement, followed by the softening of that sound, a moving inward, toward the ambient interior rumblings of a large but nonetheless contained space, a room where people were walking, footsteps of an exaggerated kind, the sound of footsteps on stone, and then his voice piercing through:

Duty is your Watchword!

The voice was Corey, the tone venomous.

It both was and wasn't Corey—it was certainly Corey, but it was Corey from beyond a barrier. There was a crumpling of paper: he was reading out the text, cynical, distanced, mocking. Even I had forgotten what it was, this paper: a letter, a document, a handbook, an officers' field guide.

...attacked, and our neighbors invaded...

It was the first scene from my war picture.

Such fragments of speech come to me in the night... And so it begins in our bewitching prison. As officers, they hold us in the servants' quarters of a commandeered château. We stand, as often as not, hunched before the casement looking out on an unforgiving terrain.

Ah, I said aloud, the casement monologue! So many words, I never intended to write.

My lieutenant has need of my cane. My injury is not fresh; I've grown accustomed to my stick.

How beautifully you affected a limp!

Since our arrival at the château, a doctor has kindly set the lieutenant's leg. Our mission had been innocuous enough: a mapping expedition, of sorts. Reconnaissance.

And how he pronounces it.

How did we get here, how did I get here, where was I before?

Can I see him? I asked Fanny.

Spirits are only voices, she reminded me. They aren't material. Disembodied only!

(No matter, of course, I could see it all, below the acousmatic voice, as the camera surveyed the snow-covered yard of the château, the stones at the base of the tower, the stones of the sheer tower wall, rising up the wall, the weather striking on the pane of the casement, his face in close-up behind this blur of rain and ice on the glass pane, then the image moving as if by magic through the glass, the shot resolves on the other side of the pane, Corey in close-up, the others ambulating on the stones behind Corey, out of focus, the marshal, the lieutenant, the handful of stock prisoners...)

We have not been here long, I will say that. We might have been drowned but were not.

A click and the sound stopped, the voice, the ambient room sounds, silence. I was suddenly aware of the hands in each of my hands, whose palms I had nearly been crushing, and the way in which our arms seemed to have levitated, even if the table remained constant. As it turned out, I was the most buoyant surface.

Technical difficulties! said Fanny.

What do you mean?

What I said. Technical difficulties.

Can't you bring him back?

That's all of that, said Fanny. We can't sit here all night listening to a tape of a dead man.

But he'd barely begun—there is the recounting of injuries yet to come, the damage to the body he sees in those around him, and then when he speaks about sleep, and describes the costumes, and there will be dialogue as well, and soon he will go into the courtyard and talk to the others and meet the spy Dun—

Go and watch the film then, said Fanny.

Now, that is actually a good scene, muttered Anatole, who, it seemed, had shrunk, or slumped very low in his seat, his posture being reconfigured. Lonnie responded back to him, across me, muted, and in French: Tes premières lignes étaient superbes, he said. The diminished Anatole snorted: Comme d'habitude! But the French had the gross exaggeration of a British accent!

I caught a flashing in the darkness across my lap. Was Lonnie now wearing a gold bracelet? And where was the lingering scent of cedars?

What's going on here? I asked.

Hush! said Fanny. Everyone is spoiling it! One final conjuring and then my job is done!

She brought up the lights. I looked at the hands I was holding. To my left was David Trevor, who wore the name tag "Lagos Pap." To my right, Emile Laval wore the name tag of "Nandor Fodor." There they were: laughing!

David, in a blue checked suit, in a tie with green spots, his auburn hair swept back from his temples, a cultivated stubble, the lines of his face overwhelmed him as he laughed and squinted, his face dissolved into his lines, his crevices, his always-wry glare. His hair was shorter, his jacket tighter, his cheeks slimmer and in keeping with a modern dandified trend, and as he laughed he kept up his mannerism of moving his hand from his hair, to his chin, to his eyes, to his hair again. And Emile, in a suit of chocolate velveteen like the skin of an animal that seemed almost to be buttoned inside out, a chocolate scarf billowing up and around his throat, and back and down, stuffed inside his jacket, escaping the bottom, at the line of the waist of his trousers. Sleek and bald, the veins along the temples of his polished skull like a river system, they crossed down into his cheeks, into his throat, where his flesh met the silk of his scarf. What mirth these two possessed in the presence of the voice of a ghost.

Presto! said Fanny. You probably saw that one coming!

Both were laughing, laughing uncontrollably, and so beautiful. All my pastimes, together again.

Minus one.

Because this is something that you don't know if you haven't experienced it firsthand: these creatures we see on the screen are so perfect in their beauty, we imagine that some hoax has been employed to extract their perfection. Some trick of lights and shadows, the manipulation of cameras and lenses, reflective screens, makeup, costuming, grand illusions to show them to their greatest advantage, so that whatever we might count as beauty before us in a film, finally, is a fraud! However, *this* is what you do not know if you have not experienced it firsthand: the screen flattens everything, and that which is beautiful on the screen is already diminished in its beauty by half, and to behold these men in life was to behold beauty that was beyond that which was natural, organic, or authentic. It was diabolical, and in this immediate moment, as they laughed away, I felt that old feeling of possession, a diabolical possession, and with it, the desires that accompanied it, to possess and to wield this beauty, lest it overtake me. And so I once had possessed it, and wielded it! And also been overtaken by it.

Demons, I cried. I will not reason with demons!

What did I tell you? said David to Emile.

Enough of that! said Fanny. I'm going to leave you three to it, and as quickly as that, the lady vanished.

The others were gone, as well, even the dog. The pot was gone, and so was the chicken. Only the cheese remained on the Bloomsbury table, where I sat with my first and second actor in the haze of the now absent voice of my third. My first, the actor who fled, my second, who clung to me, my third, disembodied and hovering, who I cling to yet: my minus one.

Where to begin? I began, but it seemed I had no idea what came next.

26

ANTAGONISTS, REGAINED

C'est drôle de truc, Emile said, again, his hand against his temple, j'attends, attends, et bien—

I'll let you two have some time, David said to me. He still held my hand. We can run our scene later, he said. First as tragedy, then as farce, I think.

David, I said, and I meant it, because his name to me had always been a curse.

Take care, my brother, he said to Emile, though his eyes were on me as he kissed the top of his gleaming head.

À tout à l'heure, Emile said, and held David's hand for a moment before he let it drop.

A cabal indeed! There was no such thing as power over men, I thought. They will always crawl back together, always take their own sides. Did they feel an apology was in order, that it was overdue? We were surely beyond the statute of limitations. What difference would it serve coming a decade after the fact, in any case?

But it didn't matter, because Emile had already begun his barrage in French, softly, nearly incoherent, his lips seemed to swallow his words, or his bottom lip seemed to lag behind and jut left, a bit

numbed or paralyzed... Et maintenant, je fait le clochard, suis un comédien de la théâtre, pas de la cinéma—
You aren't a comedian, Emile.
So you listen after all! Then listen—c'est décidé un peu, meti de donc, c'est un question que me pose de fois, est-ce que, est-ce que d'étage pour moi—
English, Emile.
I never speak English. Why would I speak English?
You can and you do.
And you want me to—and so I don't want to.
I drive everyone back to the stage? That's it, is it? My great crime in this world is driving you and David back to the stage.
No, you don't listen. And at the same time, you don't understand. I am trying to tell you that—yes, I was angry, but, also, in this anger, I found—un figure plus fort, un personage—a character, many things.
Yes, I hear this from David also. The stage values you. Film is fakery. Film is fraud!
I made your film. I was your first!
Emile, I appreciate this sentiment, but *Mechanism* was written before I even met you.
You do not believe this.
But I do.
OK, now I am angry.
Why did you come here today really?
Because I wanted to help you, and as a favor to David.
A favor to David?
And because I was so young, and because you also were so young.
I wasn't that young.
You were younger than I was—
You lied about that as well.
About a number of things. Because of course, this was all obvious.

I didn't come to say, yes, I loved you, and yes, I was very angry, but to say that I found something in the character you wrote for me. But you do not listen, you cannot hear anything, not even that there is *this voice* still inside my head. A part of my body.

You always lead with your body. But it was my film. And the next film I made would also be my film, because ultimately, Emile, my films are always mine, for better or worse, till death, et cetera.

I came to say that I hear the angry child's voice, still, but I use it, I possess it now, for myself. I did not think of you always or say your name, because what is it? Your name is made up, and you are made up, more so than me. To me, that part is play. For you, it is different.

You haven't even spoken to me in ten years. You have no idea what is play and what isn't.

No. Perhaps you have changed, and I came here to see if it were true. But no, I don't think you have changed. You are still a counterfeit. Your jealousy, I did not understand it then, and I don't understand it now. What you are jealous for, why you are so jealous—do you know? Do you even know what you envy so much?

My jealousy? I don't know what you mean. You think that I haven't changed. I thought you had changed, but I see you are also the same Emile: pig-headed, belligerent, a poseur still!

Jealous, possessive. To have your things. To keep your things for yourself. But I came here to say to you that, still, I am grateful to you for something you gave me, or something I took. But there is no point to saying it. Tell David I am going back to my hotel.

You tell David, I said, and upset the table to get out of the Syllabary and into the darkness. So swift and overacted was my exit that I walked directly into the tree itself, the giant sequoia, which it seemed, at that moment, was the only thing holding Jaquith House up, the only thing holding me up as well. And nonetheless, a barrier, a blockade that simply did not yield, even as I beat my head against it.

27

CUT-AWAY

I fled across the western lawn, and across the grass already covered in dew, for by then it must have been midnight, or later. It felt not that hours had been lost but that hours had been regained through this conjuring, for what was it to stand in front of Emile except to feel as though the past was as close to the present as it had ever been or ever could be. I stamped through the sodden field, my movements lit only by a waxing moon. I had the feeling of having passed through a time machine. As if empirical evidence revealed that walking across the lawn could reorganize all of history.

I had reached the lake by the time David caught me.

Slow down, he said, and took my arm.

David, I don't need a second feature, thanks. Let's not and say we did.

Poor sweet Emile. He's gone back to his hotel in absolute despair. I think he must have flubbed his speech. It must feel magnificent that you can still work your magic on him.

He used to pretend to hate hotels.

I don't think he's pretending. He is used to having a great deal of isolation, a great deal of focus.

You seem to know him like the back of your hand.

We share similar wounds, I suppose.

Oh, no, not from you. I won't accept depth of feeling from you. Save that for Chekhov.

Helena, like it or not, we have you in common. It tends to bring the boys together. It makes us sentimental.

How long has this been going on?

We met again in Paris. It was an accident.

I didn't know you had met at all. Ever.

Once before, then again in Paris. He was in a production of *Endgame*. A tiny black box, in Pigalle. Very avant-garde, very acrobatic interpretation. Clov.

He must make a spectacular Clov.

I confess he did. It's not my type of performance, but it was fairly perfect for what it was. So you see, despite your cruelty, things have worked out for him in the end.

Yes, he was trying to tell me that.

Clearly that went well.

I suppose if he had just demanded an apology, I might have given it.

I don't think you would have given it.

I might have given something like it. But—no, I don't know, the timing is wrong. The person is wrong.

How so?

Because whatever I subjected Emile to was nothing compared to what I subjected Corey to.

Helena, Corey wouldn't have lasted long in any case.

Why do you say that?

Well, he burned the candle at both ends, didn't he?

Did he?

Helena, you never looked. Or you never saw.

I was preoccupied with the filming.

Surely, there were times when you weren't preoccupied, while you were together?

I have always been preoccupied with the film—even when there is no film, there is always a film. A film somewhere is failing.

You are more dramatic than my parents. And more self-absorbed, and they were actors, you know.

Yes, I know.

Do you? I'm shocked you took in any personal histories that weren't considered character background for method performance.

Just say what you want to say, David. Get it all out. Obviously, that's what the doctor wants.

Since you ask. I have often wanted to say, at some point, you might have cared about the rest of us. I wanted to say it, but there's not much point to saying it anymore.

I care about Corey.

Well, that's typical isn't it? But not very useful, as he no longer exists.

I work as I work, David. Your bringing Emile here to chastise me, your attempt to make me feel remorse for my negligence, Corey's accident, when you hated him, when you were bitterly jealous—it's just petty retribution.

I'm not trying to make you feel guilty, Helena, although I like the idea of it. I'm trying to let you off the hook. And so was Emile. But you don't want to be let off, do you? Because then what would you do with yourself?

David, you're a bad script.

A good actor can always improve a bad script. It's all in the delivery. Trite bullshit in the mouth of a master suddenly seems to express something powerful, and timeless. Not always, but often. You believe that. I know it. Otherwise, why not just start again with trees, or a glacier?

David, I have no desire to make you my confessor, but there are things with Corey that I regret that you can't understand. It's not just going to dissipate.

You mean that you had him on a hook from the start? It was the same for us all.

It goes beyond that.

Because you met before you met, didn't you? You met before those auditions.

I don't know what you mean.

I think you do. I saw an old friend of ours not so long ago. Augustin.

Augustin?

Are you going to pretend not to know Augustin as well?

It's just been such a long time. How is he?

Very rich. Very drunk. Very not long for this world.

Very sad, I suppose.

No. Not particularly. Very tired, I think. Tired of capitulating. He tells me he is writing only poetry. He also told me an old story about an adaptation of one of his projects that involved Corey.

Told you what exactly?

Very little. But enough for me to make a guess.

There's no story, really. Corey wanted to adapt his book, a drama of the Spanish underworld, so I optioned it for him. I tried, but it didn't work out—we scrapped it.

You scrapped it? You mean you killed it.

You would say so, I'm sure, but it was more complicated. You always have a way of reducing my life to the most banal soap opera.

It's your soap opera, Helena, not mine. Does it sound less banal and less soap opera to say that this complication came about while Corey was also involved with Augustin? You must have pulled quite a fast one.

PORTHOLE

It captures some of the picture, certainly, though not all of it. And you know Corey would have slept with anyone to get a part, it didn't matter much who.

Yes, well, obviously that wasn't enough. He needed a ménage à trois to get this one. Or thought he did, clearly. But you were always a step ahead of the boys.

Augustin is no hardship, for anyone, believe me.

No, certainly not. I would have slept with him, if he had asked, and as you know I'm at least eighty-five percent heterosexual.

I would have slept with him to take you off my hands.

Well, I take that as proof of true love.

I'm sure you'll take it however you like, you always have.

Poor Corey. It might have given him choices. And Augustin would have been good for you both.

That's probably all true, but it didn't happen that way. In any case, it was only ever meant to be an option. All the preliminaries muddied the waters.

Your preliminaries often do.

It was a bad script. The time wasn't right. I saved them both from a bad project.

All your scripts begin as bad scripts, when has that stopped you?

David, I never remember it being said you had any talent for writing.

No, certainly not. And I never saw the script, of course. I know Augustin's story, and I know you, and I know Corey—it is hard to imagine how such a project would not have been at least interesting. But then your projects are always doomed, so perhaps you are right. What was the title?

Madrid Plays.

A truly awful title.

Yes. It was the first of several truly awful aspects.

You want to tell me—so tell me. Get your dirty crime off your chest. I promise I won't tell anyone—though a promise from me means very little. And anyway, the person I would be most likely to tell is dead, so it doesn't matter.

How would I tell that story? I thought as the sky over the lake grew pale enough to show us the predawn fog surrounding us. It was a long story, and each part of it had its key scenes. And why would I tell David, who had already made up his mind?

What difference did all this make? The order of things could be rearranged infinitely, but the ending remains the same.

But I told him, nonetheless, sitting on the dock on the lake as the sun came up, and the fog slowly dissipated.

That was the last of it, I said, the last I thought I would see of him. It never occurred to me he would turn up again.

I don't believe it.

Believe what you like. I've told you, I saved them both from a bad project.

But, Helena, why? Why did you care? If you could tell he was good? You could work with Augustin, what difference would it make? Was it for me, darling? I might have understood.

You would have sued me.

It's true, but I sued you anyway.

That wasn't the reason. My whole life, David, I have made my own way. My work is my own. I don't collaborate. It's a central rule. And an even better rule: never let the lovelies meet.

I wonder if it would have made a difference. A different start: the correct start—sidestepping the bit scenes, the rom-coms, the light work. It might have given him a different confidence? Or you could have let it run out, let Augustin make the film himself. But you kept the option all these years! We talked about Corey, you see, after he died. A lot of us talked. Augustin never lost his interest, and they stayed in touch, he wanted to make the film. He still would, if the muse were still among us.

But he isn't.

But it was something he wanted. And it seems, something you wanted—though you can't admit that, I'm sure. Oh, Helena.

These things are not so obvious in the moment, David. Corey and I could have finished *Sanguine*, and who knows what would have come next? But I can't let an actor dictate my work. Augustin at the time was grateful. There was simply too much of him in it. He was, after all, so happy to be relieved of the awkwardness of seeing his novel mutilated before his eyes by me. Corey was not ready. He had to invent himself before he could play himself.

He would have done well, on any timeline.

I thought you considered him a hack, a doll, a—

No, not at all. I said that, of course. I always thought he had the potential for something, especially if he could get away from you and begin to trust himself. But even with you, I thought he might have become something. Why else would I have wanted to involve myself in your fiasco war film? I thought, She left me for him because he is a better actor. I needed to know. And I found out.

In the end, it wasn't right for him.

You wrote it for me.

Definitely not.

But you wrote that first one for him, and I'm sure he knew it. Keep up your screens and masks. Once I was on my own, Helena, once I had some distance, I could see through your every move. But I admit, I deserved it. I was an insufferable brat, you improved me. I resisted, and you contained me. It was lively, it was lovely, honestly. And I am grateful for the time I had, and I understand why you cut me loose. But Corey, how loyal he was to you always, and how much more loyal he would have been if you had given him some of the control he so desperately craved.

Probably.

But you scuttled it. So that's the whole story then.

For the most part. The studio held on to the option for *Madrid Plays*. They still do, as a matter of fact, though not for much longer. I had a letter about that yesterday.

Why not just pass it along to some other director?

No one wants it. Corey was the only one who wanted it. It's a minefield.

Perhaps that, too, was personal. If they were lovers.

I never cared about that.

No, you never cared about that sort of thing, did you? If you owned us as actors, little difference it makes to own us as lovers. But, professionally, you never liked to share. No one dared test your jealousy. Did you really not see it?

I made it a point to focus only on the other side of my lens. Everything else was out of frame, and so must remain there.

But don't get me wrong: I, for one, enjoyed all the extra curriculars. We, your actors, Helena, from the bottom of our hearts, thank you for your clarity and vision, and your hands-on approach.

How is Augustin?

Bulldance made him a fortune and set him up to write what he wants, to work with any studio, to make demands. But he's drinking himself to death in a prefab condo. Hel, you might have made that film together. Or you might have made something together, all three of you. Augustin was precisely what you needed. Some sort of balance to your perspective. And the three of you could have fucked your way across several continents, and now—

Corey is gone, David. He was my last hostage.

Take a new hostage. A new boy! Or a girl? You never seemed to mind the flavor. Actors are always replaceable, you've said it time and again.

David, if I believe that now, after Corey, then I really am lost. I confessed to you not because I think I particularly owe you anything, but because I might owe it to him.

Trust me, there are worse than you out there—that you think of yourself as the destroyer of actors, or the destroyer of men, that is just your residual ego rising up.

Moral philosophy from the orchestra pit.

You need other voices in the mix.

What are you pitching, David? Do you think you are the person to bring me into balance?

Honestly, Helena, I think I am getting too old to be in films where hard bodies reign supreme. I told you when last we met that the stage values me, that it is probably where I belong, as long as it holds out, which it might just across my lifetime. Though not much longer. Of course, I would do it, if you wanted, because I am vain and I am greedy, and because we have fun together. My looks are going, and you know that is a kind of bottom line.

It isn't. And they aren't.

I don't trust this newfound honesty of yours.

It's water under the bridge.

Oh, if only we had met when the water was over the bridge. So, we could have drowned together!

We didn't. And I don't think we can re-meet. I might suddenly start to care that you were fucking starlets and hat-check girls.

Oh, I doubt that. But if you did, I might do it less, who knows. I already do it less. Fatigue really. And eventually the plumbing will go. But if that is all you are worried about, I will look forward to getting your next script in the mail for the part of, what will it be—a brigand, maybe? A highwayman menacing travelers along a deserted stretch of forest road, tramping the moors in the howling wind—

A highwayman doesn't tramp. A footpad tramps, a highwayman travels by horseback.

Or what was the one you had in your little notebook when we were on Elba—a military school?

A military school.

Everything in decline, sort of ruined buildings and the like. There had been a disappearance of some kind? And some intrigue with a commander.

An illicit affair.

Yes, he'd taken up with some woman, and everyone was beside themselves, because there was a code among men. Isn't that it? That's what makes it interesting to you isn't it—all this sexy male-on-male violence, but with a woman off screen pulling all the strings?

Something like that.

Aging but still handsome, haggard naval commander—

Naval?

Naval is always best, surely? Aging but handsome commander, intrigue with a woman and some young boys, suppression, seduction, perversion, madness—I'll let you sheer my hair off. Surely, there's a story there, Helena.

There's always a story. It's the pictures that I can't manage, David. And why would you even want to?

To be honest, I don't know. Apart from just wanting to irritate your bloody-mindedness? Maybe, I want you to admit that there might be other ways of doing things.

Admitting it doesn't mean I could do it, or would.

Certainly, it does not.

Or that if I could I would ever be more than a parody of myself.

You've always been a parody of yourself, Hel. It's part of your charm—your unyielding devotion to your métier.

My métier! It's so rigid, David. Film yields only when it resists itself.

Is that a metaphor?

Yes, but also just simple science. Celluloid is incredibly flammable. It's why it works in a projector and why it is so, literally, volatile. And I find that exhausting, David. Trying to generate explosions, ruptures. You actors want to blow a hole in something—interrupt the continuity—but that was never what I was. I was best at lingering in tedium.

You've always hated being labeled experimental, haven't you?

Failed experiments shouldn't count. My forms didn't reform after their ruptures. Or rather, I was the form that didn't reform.

I always liked your form. A very compact package.

So did I, that is the problem, isn't it?

This is too much for me, Helena. You could talk yourself into and out of anything as long as your voice holds out. Yes, it's disappointing, it will disappoint. I'm disappointing to you, and I will disappoint you. So, have it out with your doctor, sort yourself out, and get on with your highwaymen or your sea captains. Only I do know that your doctor is much in need of a patron, so maybe you'll have a bill to finally pay, and that will make you accountable.

The arts as a patron to the sciences?

Sciences in quotes. I'm not convinced your doctor is following any playbook. In any case, you know where to find me if you want me, or if you don't want me, or if you want to not want me in front of me, which, of course, has always been your favorite pastime. And mine, sadly.

And with that, he left me on my dock. I watched David Trevor walk away in exactly the way I had watched him walk away through the camera lens a dozen times, in the end sequence of a film. There was little hope that either of us would ever be anything other than the clichés of our genre. But once again David Trevor was gone, and there I was still, on the dock with myself, and the credits did not roll.

I don't know how long I sat on the dock, chilled and damp, the sun never quite coming through a steel autumn sky. I had taken Jaquith House and the doctor's simplicity at face value. But it stood in as code: blitheness or naiveté, or an untried dullness, a misconception. A simple erasure?

I had begun to regret the whole undertaking. Lured by skillful advertising, I had hoped Jaquith House could put back time—it sounded possible, but what did it really come to in the end? To buy back time ends up in time secondhand, already threadbare and out of fashion. Moth-eaten. Leaking like a sieve.

I could say with confidence that I was feeling low. I was feeling low and felt confident that I would feel lower still, and now I was stuck with it.

But what I also noticed were the sounds around me, the quiet stillness of the black lake, the slight breeze, the birds awakening. Perhaps I had finally talked myself out?

Perhaps if I sat there, on the dock, someone would come and look for me, and with no effort of my own, I would be suddenly thrust into the company of others and would benefit from this company. How long would it take? I wondered. But of course, David had already found me on the dock, and now David was elsewhere, and the pattern suggested that no matter how many people stumbled upon me, they would also ultimately stride away with purpose, because the nature of a dock is not a resting point, but a way point. And then there was the nature of Helena. So, the addition of any of these hypothetical others would end in subtraction.

It was, of course, Dr. Duvaux who found me on the dock, for who else but the person you pay to look after you will find you on a dock? He was back in his camping sweater with his binoculars around his neck.

Good morning, Helena! he said. I heard you had quite an evening with our local medium.

She is very good at conjuring ghosts.

And did you have a good chat with yours?

The best that could be expected.

And what was the upshot of your visitations?

Well, Doctor, to be honest, it amounted to a comeuppance. Gently delivered, but resounding all the same.

Hmm. I suppose that was unavoidable to a certain extent, but they did come from very far away to see you. And what a treat for our little community to glimpse stars of the silver screen up close.

They are very beautiful.

I hope they were able to pierce the veil.

It felt like a final piece, certainly.

And what will you do with your final piece?

Doctor, I can't yet say. I feel shattered.

Was their judgment so cruel?

No, quite the contrary. It is more just knowing how transparent all my disguises were.

Oh, I don't think that's entirely true. But those who were close to you played along, and kept the ruse going. But that knowledge is an excellent starting point for some.

For some.

Yes, it's risky. I deal in risky practices, and it doesn't always work. I think you can see some of my charges are still struggling.

Occupational hazards.

And they are not even the worst of my failures. I have had some darker failures, which you will discover if you haven't already. Resistance to the methodology of the most final kind. Sometimes, we simply miscalculate, and someone is lost, forever. That sort of slipping away is the worst. However, explosions such as the one you experienced last night tend to have a formative effect. The shape of the self is remolded from such energetic bursts, and it doesn't necessarily mean that the original model is disowned or forgotten. We have more in common than you think, Helena. Our jobs come with so much responsibility. You can't deny that a lot of goodwill is needed to believe in our lines of work, depending on the indulgence of others, the traumas of others, and then forming some narrative out of it. What's clear to me is that such an existence can only be sustained by the communal averting of the eyes from our obvious and shocking shortcomings. The solidarity of those around us to preserve this half-life we live, for however short a moment, within the tissue of worse horrors.

It seems a tall order. You can see why I want to flee.

For myself, I am fortunate in my aides-de-camp. Everyone has a part to play, and everyone plays it beautifully, so I am very lucky. And you are lucky with your aides as well. And to cast them off would be the worst imaginable folly.

You mean David.

Helena, do you trust me to point you in a solid direction?

I would hope so, Doctor.

Wouldn't it make sense to listen to someone who actually cares for you?

You don't really need to worry. I know how to find David. And he knows how to find me. It's inevitable, I suppose, our continued collisions, but it will always be disastrous. And I don't want any more casualties.

But someone around here has to earn a living, if we want to keep a chicken in the pot.

I doubt I'm your salvation, Doctor.

You doubt it? But you haven't ruled out hope?

We'll have to see if time is on either of our sides.

Oh, there is no rush. You have several things to think about, so I'll leave you to it.

Is this a punctuation, Doctor?

Well, to be honest, I've promised to take Tina into town to pick up her Leica from the repair shop. Poor Tina. She's a disaster with her Leica, and she so wants to take pictures. I hope if you stay on with us a bit longer you will help her to—shall we say—find focus?

I won't enjoy it, Doctor, but I might try for your sake. Though I am not quite ready to return to base camp just now. Actually, would it be all right if I took out the canoe?

Of course! But be careful of wind. If the wind gets up it can be quite difficult to manage without a well-studied J-stroke. Though it seems very still at the moment. Here: take my binoculars. There are loons nesting on Gilbert. And Helena, if you must go aground, please look for a sandy spot?

28

DISSOLVE

It was still, everything around me was still, and quiet, finally quiet, as I glided through the dark lake in the little green canvas canoe still in my tuxedo from the conjuring, the bombazine sodden and stained, the starch of the lapels collapsed, and I smelled like the lake. I was moving and my eyes were moving, but everything else was motionless, and the effect was such that it appeared as though everything in my vision was moving except for me, the moment of feeling that I was the still thing, and that all the rest of the world was rushing backward. An optical illusion, but nonetheless disorienting, and so I pulled up the paddle and put it across the gunwale to rest as the little vessel slowed and drifted. The pair of islands, the dark lake, the trees cutting out from them at angles—I was no longer coming closer or going further away. The canoe was becalmed. I did not often find such a still moment. My way of seeing was always through movement. That cinematic mechanism in order to think, we think in moving.

Gilbert and Sullivan were now just differentiated in my line of vision. To be honest, I have no interest in birds—loons, however, make a romantic sound. I took up the doctor's binoculars. They were a small set, no bigger than a pair of opera glasses, their two telescopes mounted and aligned to point in the same direction—however, the nose bridge seemed petrified, so there was no hope of lining up my eyes to their lenses. I'm used to that—I have quite a narrow head. It is easier to squint and just focus with one eye, which, of course, defeats the purpose. I slid my head left and right to take in a flash from one eye, a flash from the other, that is another way of going about things. The eye conveys the fragments into something singular in the brain, but it isn't ideal.

The moving image must first begin in something fixed and still, something immobile. A starting point. The frame, the coordinates, a dramatic geometry. Staging. A wall of objects. In life, advance or retreat—in film, there is intimacy in close-up or distance in a ranging remote shot. An intimate close-up triggers the impulse to approach, to engage.

I haven't lived strictly according to my needs, no, not strictly. But I admit I built on this ground. I don't know what it would mean to yield.

So, what is the work? I wondered as I squinted and peered through the single telescope of the binocular. A form of abstraction? My own form of abstraction? The islands popped forward in my monocle, but their context was cropped.

From shadows to images in the light, and then, inside the eye. The eye is the mechanism and the mechanism is the eye, and then the approach follows and soon, the encounter. The work was in going forward to meet the object, I thought. A slow march, trudging to find one or two images that might, in some way, open up? In this way, movement was psychic. From immobility to movement, from movement to transit, the water, a boat, the boat gliding. Then what? Encounter. Out of sheer motion of vision: Confrontation. Adventures. Rendezvous. The lens opened up worlds of encounter and reflection. Toward what? A final gesture, a gesture of cancelation, an eclipse? Of course, such phenomena are best observed through a pinhole,

PORTHOLE

projected on a white page. I closed one eye, I opened wide the other, the islands approached, or I approached the island. The boat glided, the wind picked up, I reached for the grip of the throat and made a cut in the surface with the blade of the paddle. Dizzying speed. Moving swiftly from point to point, and yet, present at the porthole, the focusing lens, through a glass, darkly, watching for the next encounter, the next collision of forces.

ACKNOWLEDGMENTS

This book would not exist without my editor Rita Bullwinkel, who should get all the credit or none of the blame for whatever happens next. I am enormously grateful to Amanda Uhle for supporting my work and trusting my vision, and for the rest of the McSweeney's team for making amazing and beautiful books. Thank you, McSweeney's, for continuing to see the possibility and potential in writing that is fleeting, contingent, and striving to exist in the foggy terrain of art and language.

This book was slow to form. Many thanks to my agent, Allison Devereux, for tireless efforts through multiple drafts to help it find a final vision.

Deep thanks to those who read this book at early stages and offered much needed encouragement: Rita Bullwinkel, Patrick Cottrell, Laird Hunt, and Jesse Ball. Final stage readers, who shaped the book more than they may know or care to take credit for: Renee Gladman, brilliant and honest, as always, and Brad Kessler, last to the party, but oh, what an entrance!

I am incredibly lucky to know two women filmmakers: heartfelt thanks to Laura Colella for reading and taking Helena seriously, and for offering insights into both the enticements and entanglements of filmmaking. Bec Evans Cayley, my gratitude for conversations, fine details, and more than a little ethical counterargument to my romantic blind spots. (And for that day on the dock in Muskoka when you announced, "Everyone needs to leave Joanna alone right now: she is writing her novel!")

Thanks to those who contributed unwittingly to key pieces: Daniel Howe, Dayo Farm is where Jaquith House and Helena's barn began. Thank you for allowing me to visit this strange and magical compound! Dona Ann McAdams, the true woman behind the lens of a Leica, thank you for seeing the world through the porthole of the camera. Jill Pearlman, for help with all things French New Wave and noir, and for directing me to Jean-Claude Izzo. Caren Beilin for a vital conversation at a crucial point about Agnès Varda, Claire Denis, and Chantal Akerman.

Amanda Mosley, whose incomparable taste and vision in architecture and design helped me to imagine the grandiose structures and interiors of Jaquith House, and to her partner in crime the "right on!"-orable Robert Mosley for talking Tarkovsky and Losey with a quiet passion, and for showing me the picture book *Film: Encounter*, which wrote my ending for me: to you both I am so grateful for the houses you build, the art you make, the spaces you design and fill with your handiwork, and your boundless generosity in sharing all of it with those around you.

Finally, for those closest to me on the daily who let me ramble, lecture, obsess, and rant about movies, books, the abyss, and the Great American Post-Novel: John Cayley, Thangam Ravindranathan, Timothy Bewes, Danielle Vogel, Renee Gladman, and Joanna Ruocco, politburo member and external ego.

John Cayley: you are so nice, I'll mention you twice.

ABOUT THE AUTHOR

JOANNA HOWARD is a writer and translator from Miami, Oklahoma. She is the author of the memoir *Rerun Era* (McSweeney's, 2019), the novel *Foreign Correspondent*, and the story collections *On the Winding Stair* and *In the Colorless Round*, the latter of which was illustrated by Rikki Ducornet. She also cowrote *Field Glass*, a speculative novel, with Joanna Ruocco. Her work has appeared in *Conjunctions, The Paris Review, Verse, Bomb, Flaunt, Chicago Review, The Brooklyn Rail*, and parts elsewhere. She is a Professor of Creative Writing at Denver University.